The Cowboy Earns a Bride

By Cora Seton

To my aunt, who read some of the first stories I ever wrote and praised them all.

The Cowboy Earns a Bride is Volume 8 of the
Cowboys of Chance Creek series, set in the fictional
town of Chance Creek, Montana.

Sign up for my newsletter HERE.

www.coraseton.com/sign-up-for-my-newsletter

Chapter One

"T HAT'S CLOSE ENOUGH."

Mia Start lifted the shotgun and sighted down its length, her fingers trembling not from fear, but from the bitter cold of the early morning air. In the field of brightness created by her truck's headlights, her form-fitting, quilted, pink winter coat was the only splash of color in a quarter mile. Beyond her, the snow-covered fields and forests that lined the icy, back-country road were as black as a Montana midnight, even though it was half-past five in the morning.

"For God's sake, Mia—put down the gun." Ellis Scranton wore a formal gray wool coat over his customary suit and lifted a hand to screen his face from the truck's high beams. His Mercedes' lights were on, too, but weren't nearly as bright.

He didn't look armed.

She still didn't trust him.

"Why'd you want to meet me?" She'd been more than a little surprised to get his text late the night before and barely slept in the intervening hours. Today was Valentine's Day—hardly the time to meet with your ex.

In her fantasies she'd imagined spending the day in bed with Luke Matheson, the cowboy whose spare room she currently rented.

The cowboy she'd never get to be with—because of Ellis.

She and Ellis had broken off their relationship nearly four months ago when she announced her pregnancy and he announced he'd been lying all along; he didn't love her, didn't intend to divorce his wife and didn't intend to help raise their child, either.

"We need to talk." Ellis took a step closer. Mia raised the gun half an inch.

No, they didn't. She'd moved on. It hadn't taken her long to realize she'd been nothing more than a mid-life crisis to the forty-two-year-old man. The difference in their ages had once excited her. Now it disgusted her. She didn't want him in her life—or in her baby's either.

She was struggling with the consequences of their affair. She'd moved out of her parents' home before they could learn their twenty-one-year-old daughter was dating a middle-aged man—a middle-aged *married* man. The room she rented from Luke in his cabin on the Double-Bar-K ate most of her earnings from her job at the local hardware store. Soon she'd work for her friends Fila and Camila at their brand-new restaurant, but that wouldn't involve a wage increase. She knew she should force Ellis to pay child support, but that meant keeping him involved in her baby's life. She didn't want that. She just didn't know how else she could possibly raise this child.

The worst part of the whole mess, though, was the

ache of knowing she'd caused pain to another woman—another mother. She'd been so swept away by the older man's attentions, she hadn't thought about his wife's feelings at all. Ellis had told her he and Elaine were practically separated—that they didn't talk, didn't share a bed, certainly didn't make love. He'd told her he'd divorce Elaine as soon as he could. All lies. And she'd been stupid enough to believe them.

"Say what you have to say."

He lifted his hands. "Are you going to shoot me?"

She took in his tired, lined face, his thinning hair and felt a wave of revulsion, but not over his looks. It was his deception that killed her—the fact he'd even pretended to love her. If only he'd been honest, she wouldn't be in this fix.

If only she'd met Luke first.

"You're the one who asked me to meet you on a deserted road at the crack of dawn. Maybe you're the one planning to shoot me."

"Fair enough. I deserve that."

Mia narrowed her eyes. This was new. Ellis never admitted he was to blame for anything.

"I'm here to say good-bye, Mia."

She lowered the shotgun an inch. "Where are you going?"

"Wyoming. Elaine has family there." He took a deep breath. "She and I, we're going to try to make a go of it. We'll start over somewhere new, somewhere no one knows about the way I screwed up. I owe it to her. I owe it to my children. None of them can hold their heads up in this town."

"You think I can?" She couldn't keep her resentment out of her voice. She was over him. Long over him. Yet it hurt to be the one used and discarded.

"No one knows that's my baby."

"It won't be hard for them to put two and two together. Everyone's gossiping about us seeing each other."

"All the more reason I've got to go. But that doesn't mean you can't change the story once I'm gone. Tell them what you want—you had a one-night stand with a stranger. Someone from out of town. Just don't bring me into it. I'll deny it all the way." He took a deep breath. "Look, I'm sorry, Mia. I've been an ass from start to finish. You're right to hate me. When I think about how I came in and ruined your life, I just want to… Well, I think my leaving is the best thing I can do."

A chill ran through her that had nothing to do with the weather. "Just like that? You'll leave me pregnant? Alone? I have no money, Ellis! What about the cost of the birth?"

"This should help." He held out a small white envelope.

"A couple of fifties won't get it done!" She didn't recognize her own voice. She sounded desperate, as if she wasn't over him at all. It wasn't Ellis's desire to leave that had her tied up in knots, however. It was fear. Of being destitute. Of having to give up her child. Of failing…

"It's not a couple fifties. I wouldn't do that to you, no matter how big an ass you think I am." For one moment the old Ellis was back. The confident man who'd swept her off her feet. "Just don't go and blow it all on pretty clothes and a vacation to Hawaii. Go to Matt Underwood, the accountant—you know him, right? Ask him for help when you make your decisions. It takes a lot of cash to raise a kid right. More than you know."

Anger surged through her. He was speaking to her as if she was some dumb child herself. "And this is it? I'll never see you again?"

He studied her, as if trying to decide whether she was happy or sad about that. "That's right. Never again. But you won't be alone for long. That Luke Matheson will have you married in no time and you can bank on that family. You've lived with him since December, right? With a little luck you can pass that baby off as his."

"I would never do that. I'm not a liar, like—" She stopped mid-sentence. What was the use? Ellis was leaving. She let the shotgun drop. He stepped toward her.

"You're going to be okay, Mia. Let me be okay, too."

"Fine." She tucked the firearm under her arm, strode forward and ripped the envelope from his hand. "But you keep out of my life. Don't ever come back—don't ever come looking for this child. You've given up the right to have anything to do with him."

Ellis nodded, turned his back and walked quickly to his car. The Mercedes pulled away before Mia even made it back to her truck. Sitting in the cold cab, she tore the envelope open, expecting another of Ellis's tricks. It was too thin for its contents to amount to much. A few hundred. Maybe a thousand. There was no way—

Mia stared at the cashier's check she pulled from the

envelope.

Two hundred thousand dollars. Ellis had given her *two hundred thousand dollars*. A wave of dizziness crashed over her as she realized what this meant.

Ellis was out of her life. Forever. But he'd given her the means to do what she'd known for months she'd have to do.

Raise this baby alone.

It was several long minutes before she could start the truck and pull back onto the road. As she drove down through the dark, silent country highway toward the Double-Bar-K, Mia decided she needed a cup of decaf coffee before she could face her day. She wished she could get the caffeinated kind, but she'd have to wait a few more months for that. She bypassed the ranch and headed into town.

She couldn't sort through her emotions. She was relieved Ellis was gone. She'd lived in fear of being called out for their affair for months, and she knew the minute friends and acquaintances spotted her pregnancy, they'd have a lot to say. With Ellis—and his wife and children—out of the way, the speculation would be easier to bear. Mia would carry her shame for hurting Elaine the rest of her life; she didn't need everyone in town pointing their fingers at her. She felt hopeful, too. The money he'd given her would go a long way toward raising her baby in comfort. The money brought its own problems, however. Ellis might think Luke would step in and marry her, but she knew better. No man as proud as Luke Matheson would want a pregnant bride. By giving her enough cash to move out from Luke's spare room, Ellis had unwittingly ended her brief stint in paradise.

Living with Luke had been a dream, the kind you never wanted to awake from, but she'd never slept with the cowboy—only kissed him once. It had been enough for her to be close to him. To get to see him first thing in the morning and last thing before going to bed at night. To fall asleep knowing only a bedroom wall separated them. That proximity had kept her hopes alive.

Now it was time to leave all that behind, and with Ellis's money, she didn't even have the excuse anymore that she was too poor to move.

Two hundred thousand dollars.

She wasn't poor anymore.

She parked on the street near Linda's Diner, which opened early to suit the hours of the hardworking ranchers who lived in these parts. She found a booth where she could escape notice and smiled gratefully when the waitress, Tracey Richards, poured her a cup of decaf without even being asked.

"Anything else?"

"No." Mia thanked her and took a sip of the scalding liquid. She should have known she wasn't meant for happiness. Men always caused her trouble. Ellis Scranton was only the latest example. She shook her head at the memory of a worse offender—Fred Warner—pushing down the ache of pain it caused. Warner had ruined her beauty pageant career—no great loss except that it had dashed her mother's hopes of having a beauty queen for a daughter, and ended the closeness between them long before Mia's indiscretions with Ellis did. Ellis was the root of all her current distress, though. If only she'd never met him!

No.

Mia placed a protective hand over her belly.

No, she'd never wish their relationship away. Not really. If she'd never met Ellis, she wouldn't have this baby—this baby who already meant the world to her. Yes, in a perfect world, she'd get to have Luke, too, but this wasn't a perfect world.

"Coffee and a bagel with cream cheese, please."

Mia looked up at the familiar voice and saw Inez Winter take a seat at one of the tables in the center of the diner. Inez caught her eye and quickly turned away, color staining her pale skin.

Mia looked away just as quickly. She didn't speak to Inez these days, although they'd once been good friends. Inez had been on the beauty pageant circuit, too. She'd been a contestant in Mia's last pageant, back when they were both fifteen, but she hadn't defended Mia when rumors started flying about her and Fred Warner, who was a pageant judge. Inez hadn't said a word, even though Mia had seen her slip into a supply closet with the man during one of the practice sessions—the same closet he'd tried to lure Mia into before she'd told her mother about him.

Mia bit her lip, swallowing the pain that never quite went away. Inez hadn't spoken up. None of the other girls had. It had been Mia's word against Warner's and Warner won out.

No one believed her when she told them he'd tried to kiss her—tried to touch her. Mia swallowed. The truth—the truth she'd told no one, not even her mother—was that he *had* touched her. She'd figured out pretty quickly that no one wanted to hear that. Just speaking up about Warner and saying he'd lured her into a closet was enough to start a firestorm that turned all the other contestants against her. At first, her mother thought she'd lied, too. Mia had realized that if she told the whole truth—that his hands had gone all kinds of places on her body before she fought him off—everyone would hate her even more.

So she hadn't said a word.

Mia took a deep cleansing breath and sipped her coffee. All that was years ago. She wasn't a vulnerable little girl anymore. She was a woman—almost a mother. And now she had enough money to get her own place and begin a new life. She'd be strong for her son or daughter, and she'd always believe them when they told her things. She'd always protect them.

"Mia?"

Mia jerked and her coffee spilled over the side of her cup.

"Sorry. I didn't mean to startle you."

Mia looked up into Inez's serious face. "That's okay." Was Inez really talking to her? After six years of silence?

Inez took a shaky breath. "Look, there's something I should have said to you a long time ago. I want to say it now. Can I sit down?"

Mia nodded, bracing herself for more recriminations. She didn't know what she'd do if Inez dragged up the past and called her a liar again.

"Fred Warner raped me."

Mia clapped a hand to her mouth and her eyes brimmed with tears. That was the last thing she'd expected Inez to say. "Oh my God, Inez. Are you okay?"

"I'm fine." Inez blinked rapidly. "Well, actually, no—I'm not really fine, but I'm seeing a counselor and she urged me to talk to you when I told her what happened. I'm so sorry, Mia. I should've spoken up back then, but I was too scared. I didn't want anyone to know what happened."

Mia took her hand. "It's okay. I'm okay. He didn't hurt me like that."

"But he tried, didn't he?' Inez scrubbed her eyes with the heel of her hand. "And you spoke up—you told people. I wanted to thank you for that. He would've come after me again if you hadn't, I know it."

"I'm so sorry he hurt you. If I'd known—"

"You couldn't have known. And I wouldn't have brought it up now, but I can't stand the fact that you hate me—"

"I never hated you," Mia cried. "I just… missed you."

"I missed you, too."

Mia stood up, moved around the table and hugged Inez. "You don't have to miss me anymore. Thank you for being brave enough to tell me. I swear I won't breathe a word to anyone else."

Inez lifted her eyes to hers. "That's just the thing. I want you to speak up. Fred Warner—he's still judging beauty pageants."

"DID YOU GET a nice gift for that lady friend of yours,

Luke?"

"I sure did, Mrs. Stone." Luke Matheson smiled at the old woman who leaned on her cane on the front porch of her small house. Bundled up in her white winter coat, hat and gloves, she looked like a grandmotherly snowman. "Got her a real pretty bracelet to go with the flowers and candy I bought her."

"That's one lucky girl. 'Course any woman would be lucky to have a man like you."

"I don't know about that." The compliment warmed him, though, as he shoveled the last bit of snow off her walkway. She'd been one of his favorite people ever since he was just a boy and she and her husband, Thomas Stone, a hired hand, lived at the Double-Bar-K. Back in those days when life on the ranch got too much for Luke, between his brothers' scrapping and bickering and his father's legendary bouts of temper, he'd escape to the little log house on the edge of the property the Stones had rented—a house that had long since been torn down. His own mother was no slouch, but Amanda Stone kept the tidiest house Luke had ever seen. Stepping into it, sitting down at her spotless table, and being served a snack on her clean, white china was a welcome change from the chaos at home.

Amanda had always understood his need for order. Luke liked things in their place. He liked knowing what was going to happen next. He liked being prepared. His father and brothers, on the other hand, seemed to enjoy flying by the seats of their pants. Ned might keep his workshop tidy and Luke's mother might have been spot on with the ranch's accounts back when she did them, but the rest of them thrived on disorder and controversy. Sometimes Luke couldn't stand it anymore. The Stones had moved off the ranch over a decade ago and bought a modest house on the west side of town. Now that Thomas had passed away, Amanda lived there alone.

"Would you like some breakfast?"

"Not today. I'll be eating with the family. It's Ned's wedding day, you know."

"Tell him congratulations from me and get on home. You shouldn't be over here messing with my walk today of all days."

"Glad to help, Mrs. Stone—and don't you hesitate about turning your thermostat up if you're chilly. There's enough cash in your account to see you through the winter." A few years back he'd come over to find her shivering and discovered she didn't have the funds to pay her heating bill. Since then he'd arranged to pay a deposit to each of the utility companies in advance so if she was a little short she wouldn't lose her services. He figured it was the least he could do. When she had car trouble six months ago, he'd taken the vehicle to the shop only to find the repair bill topped a thousand dollars. He told her it was a hundred and made up the difference because he knew how much independence meant to Amanda.

These days, however, that independence was getting pricey. He'd replaced a window in her kitchen that wouldn't open anymore, dealt with a foundation issue that let moisture into her basement and soon he was afraid he'd need to replace her roof.

"Say hi to Mia for me, Luke. She's such a sunny

thing."

"I will. See you next week!"

He checked his watch and picked up speed as he stowed away his shovel in the shed he'd built a year ago, and got into his old truck to make the trip back to the Double-Bar-K. His engine refused to turn over the first time he turned the key. He held his breath as he turned it a second time. There, that did it. Pretty soon he'd need a new truck, too. That was going to stretch his finances.

As he drove home, however, his thoughts turned to a happier topic.

Mia.

Today was the day.

Today was the day he and Mia would stop being just friends and get on to the good stuff. It was Valentine's Day—and his brother's wedding day. Surely that double-dose of romance, plus the gifts he intended to shower her with, would finally convince the pretty young woman that the man she was looking for was right under her nose.

He could never tell with Mia, though. Every time he thought he'd got the measure of her, she surprised him. Hell, she'd managed to keep him at arm's length for two long months now, and they were living in the same house.

He frowned as he turned into the long lane that led to his family's home. He pulled up in front of his parents' house and parked. If he couldn't move his relationship with Mia to a more romantic level soon, he wasn't sure what he would do. Living in close proximity to her was driving him wild. It was hard to concentrate when she was around—and it was doubly hard, pun intended, to sleep knowing she was right next door.

He exited his truck and made his way into the house where the smell of bacon led him straight to the dining room, where most of his family was already seated. Everyone who lived on the ranch had gathered to eat and then help set up for the wedding. He wasn't entirely surprised to see Mia's customary chair empty, however. He knew she wanted to look extra good for the wedding. He ducked into the kitchen to wash up and slid into his own seat just in time to snag the platter of pancakes from Ned's hands. If Mia didn't make it, he'd put together a plate of food and bring it to her after he ate.

"Paris."

Luke jumped when his mother, Lisa, slapped a glossy brochure down on the dining room table in front of his father, Holt. Everyone stopped eating and stared at her. Luke didn't blame them. This early in the morning the extent of the conversation at the Matheson table was generally limited to a few grunts and an order or two, although usually there wasn't such a crowd.

Luke slathered his pancakes in butter, then drenched them in syrup, but took a moment to study his family before his first bite. Lots had changed recently. Only last September all his brothers had been single. After today he'd be the only one who could claim that status.

To his right sat Jake, his oldest brother, and Jake's wife, Hannah. Married just before Christmas, Luke hardly saw them these days because they were both so busy with classes they'd just started at Montana State and their regular work—Hannah with Bella Mortimer, the local pet veterinarian, and Jake with Bella's husband, Evan Mortimer, a wealthy man with an interest in sustainable ranching.

Holt pushed the brochure out of his way. "Nnnh?" he growled.

"Paris, France," Lisa said, pushing it closer to Holt again. "That's what I want for our thirty-fifth wedding anniversary this fall. A trip to the City of Love." She sat down beside her husband and helped herself to some bacon and eggs.

"Paris sounds lovely," Morgan said from her seat next to Hannah.

Morgan had married Luke's youngest brother, Rob, back in September. Rob had partnered with Ethan Cruz from the ranch next door, and was also helping Morgan start a vineyard. Luke bet Morgan and Rob would love to travel to France to check out the wineries.

"Why the hell would you want to go to Paris?" Holt said.

Luke saw Ned and Fila exchange a look. They sat on his side of the table, Luke closest to Holt and Fila beside him. Ned was only a year older than Luke and he and Luke had argued a lot as kids—well, as adults too, until this year. Now they found themselves agreeing about more things. He was glad Ned had found a woman like Fila to love. She'd made him a better man. She was a beauty and funny, too, with a dry sense of humor she expressed more and more as she gained confidence. In Luke's opinion, the couple deserved a memorable wedding day. Fila had been to hell and back when she'd spent ten years as a prisoner of the Taliban, and Ned had barely survived a recent disastrous trip to the family's hunting cabin last month that left him still healing from a broken leg.

"Come on, Holt, you old goat. You'll love Paris," Camila Torres said, helping herself to orange slices. Luke marveled that his old man put up with her sass. Somehow she'd gotten into his good graces. Maybe it was her amazing Mexican cooking—so fantastic, even Holt liked it. Or perhaps it was because she was co-owner of Fila's new restaurant and now that Fila had saved one of Holt's son's lives, any friend of hers was a friend of his.

"Who wants more bacon?" Lisa asked, passing the platter around. Luke was amazed his mother had pulled off this kind of breakfast today. He'd seen the kitchen. Every spare inch was filled with items for the wedding feast.

"All there is in Paris is foreigners." Holt took the rest of the bacon and used his elbow to push the brochure farther away.

Luke ignored the back and forth. At twenty-nine he knew better than to interfere when his parents bickered. You'd think they could call a truce for Valentine's Day— for Ned's wedding—but his parents' marriage seemed to run on friction, and today evidently would be business as usual.

There were no roses at his mother's seat. No box of candy, either, but if he wasn't mistaken, those were new diamond earrings in her ears.

"There's delicious food and beautiful architecture— and the Louvre, too," Lisa said.

"A bunch of stuck-up pansies."

"And shopping and art galleries and monuments."

"I'd go to Paris in a minute if it meant I could stop dealing with that damn architect. He's sent over so many alternate plans it's making my head spin," Jake said. Luke knew what he meant. Holt had given Jake two hundred acres to do with as he pleased, and he and Hannah meant to build a house this summer.

Lisa smiled sympathetically at her oldest son. "Building is always such a bother, but you'll be happy this fall when you move into your new home."

"I told Evan if I was rich I'd buy his place—let him go build."

Hannah laughed. "Yeah, but he shot that idea down pretty quickly. Apparently he and Bella are having just as much trouble getting her clinic and pet shelter built as we're having with our house."

"It'll all be done by the time Holt and I fly off to Paris," Lisa assured her.

"I ain't going, and neither are you." Holt made eye contact across the length of the table with his wife for emphasis, then caught Luke's expression and fixed him with a scowl. "What're you snickering about over there?"

Luke straightened. "Nothing, Pops."

"I have a bone to pick with you."

Uh-oh. Classic Holt technique. When an argument with his wife got too hot, he'd pick a new one with a son. Luke braced himself.

"See all this folderol?" He waved at the wedding preparations. "Time for your share. I've gotten the rest of your brothers hitched, now it's your turn."

"*You've* gotten them hitched?" Lisa got up again and

disappeared into the kitchen for a moment. She came back with a plate stacked high with toast. "More like they got hitched in spite of your interference."

"He can interfere away, Mom. I'm all for marriage."

Lisa sat back down in her seat. "Then what's the deal with you and Mia?"

"Yeah," Ned said. "What *is* the deal with you and Mia?"

Luke glanced at the empty chair beside him. "She's getting ready for the wedding. She should be here any minute." He hoped his family would leave things at that, but of course they didn't.

"You're living with her. Your intentions better be pure," Lisa said.

"My intentions are far from pure, but our living arrangements sure are. That's the problem." Shit. He shouldn't have said that out loud. Jake guffawed and Hannah elbowed him.

"Hush, Jake." Lisa turned to Luke. "Then Mia's smarter than I gave her credit for. It doesn't do to give away the milk for free—"

"Mom!"

"Slap a ring on her finger and she'll put out soon enough," Holt declared.

Lisa dropped her fork on her plate. "Is that why you married me, you old coot? So I'd put out?"

"I thought that's why you married me," Holt countered.

Everyone laughed, and Luke knew his parents' spat was over as quickly as it had begun.

"I bet Mia's blowing you off because of your truck. What woman in her right mind wants to ride around in that old thing?" Jake said.

"It's not his truck, it's his hat," Ned said. "He's worn the same one since fourth grade."

"It's the fact he hasn't taken her out to a single restaurant," Rob said. "Luke, face it—women don't marry cheapskates."

"Yeah, you're lucky we'll still be seen with you."

Luke rolled his eyes at their teasing, but some of the barbs hit home. He had a reputation for being cheap because he was often broke. And while that was partly his own fault—he liked a night out at the Dancing Boot as well as the next guy—it was more a result of helping Amanda Stone.

If he was smart, he'd let someone else know about the old woman's problem, but he knew what would happen next. Amanda's house and possessions would be liquidated and she'd be put in one of the state-run homes for the elderly. It was a smart solution—the right solution—but Amanda Stone was terrified of old-age homes. She'd broken down and told him about her fears one day five years ago—the day he'd found her shivering in her house. It turned out her grandmother had been institutionalized with Alzheimer's and Amanda had been the one to discover the systemic neglect she'd suffered. She was terrified it would happen to her, too. She'd sworn him to secrecy and he'd promised not to tell anyone about her difficulties in maintaining her home. At first it hadn't been hard to help her keep it up and cover a few of her costs, but now he was in over his head.

His father spoke up again. "I gave your brothers deadlines to speed things along."

"Won't work with me," Luke said, coming out of his reverie. "I'm not the one holding up the proceedings. Mia is. Beside, you won't kick me off the ranch. I'm the only extra pair of hands you've got left." It was true; Jake and Rob were too busy with their own ventures to do more than help out now and then with some of the chores, and Ned was still recovering from breaking his leg last month. That left Luke and Holt to pick up the slack.

"I'll think of something."

Lisa sighed. "You know what, old man? I think you'll just mind your own business for once."

"I will, will I?"

"Yes, you will. Because I'm going to set the deadline this time. Luke, you've got six months to convince that girl to marry you, or I'll help her move along. No, don't worry—I won't be rude. There's no sense in either of you keeping the other from meeting your true love, if you aren't meant to be together. Meanwhile, your father won't say one word about marriage during that time." She held up a hand when Holt began to sputter. "Not one word, or you'll take me to France. That's the deal. Keep quiet and we'll celebrate our thirty-fifth anniversary on the ranch. Speak your mind and we'll go to Paris." She beamed. "My money's on Paris."

"My money's on me finding another place to live," Luke growled, pushing back from the table. "You can't kick Mia out of my house if I want her there. Besides, I don't see what the hurry is."

Lisa became serious. "I think you will all too soon."

Chapter Two

MIA SAT ON her bed in the room she was renting in Luke's cabin and stared at the cashier's check Ellis had given her, unable to make herself go have breakfast with everyone else at Luke's parents' house. Between the check and Inez's revelation, she couldn't form a coherent thought, let alone take part in a family gathering.

Inez wanted her to send a letter to the committee that oversaw the region's beauty pageants and tell them what Fred Warner had done to her all those years ago. Inez meant to write to them too and follow up her letter with phone calls until they were taken seriously. It might be too late to prosecute Warner—Inez was looking into that, too—but maybe they could get him barred from judging pageants.

Mia had promised Inez she would think about it, but right now she had a more pressing matter on her mind. As soon as she deposited Ellis's check, she needed to tell Luke about her condition, and before she could do that, she needed to move into her own apartment. Luke would be angry at her when he heard the news. She needed somewhere else to go.

Last November when she left her parents' home, she'd first rented a room at the Cruz ranch guesthouse, run by her close friends Autumn and Ethan Cruz. The guest ranch had opened to the public only last summer, and as winter began they'd lacked the customers they needed to keep paying their bills. Autumn had welcomed Mia and two other single women—Hannah Ashton and Fila Sahar—to rent rooms on a monthly basis. Mia had loved it there until an unexpected houseful of paying guests descended for the month of December. Autumn and Ethan needed all the rooms back then, so all three women moved out—each to one of the cabins on the Double-Bar-K. Mia had ended up with Luke, which was great. She had fallen for him hook, line and sinker.

And Luke wanted to be with her. He made that clear every day. She couldn't be with him, though. Not when she was nearly four months pregnant with another man's child.

She'd promised herself she wouldn't be the kind of single mother who dated a string of men and turned her child's life upside down each time it didn't work out. From here on in, she'd have to proceed slowly, and she wouldn't let a man into her life she didn't think could go the distance.

Mia placed Ellis's check on the bed. She'd fallen hard for Luke. It wasn't his broad shoulders, or six-pack abs, or the glint in his eye when she caught him looking at her.

It was his laugh.

Luke wasn't an outgoing man. He was your typical strong, silent cowboy, which sometimes drove Mia around the bend, but when he laughed he gave in to it, and that joyful, masculine sound twisted Mia's innards into knots of longing. She'd never thought such a simple thing could make her want to rip her clothes off, but there it was. She'd never tell him that though; the man would simply laugh her right into bed.

Mia fell back on the mattress with a thump. Sex was what got her into this mess, so she shouldn't be day-dreaming of making love to Luke—yet daydreaming about Luke's hands on her body got her through a lot of difficult hours. It could never happen in real life. She'd slipped once and she wouldn't slip again, but—oh, God—she wanted to. She wanted Luke on top of her. She wanted to wrap her legs around his waist. She wanted to kiss the underside of his chin, just where she knew it would drive him wild....

A slam of the front door told her Luke had finished his earliest chores and had stopped at home to say good-morning before heading out again. She was constantly in awe of how hard the men worked on this ranch, especial-ly Luke now that all his brothers were busy with their own concerns. The Double-Bar-K employed ranch hands that came in from town every day, but Luke still labored from before sunrise to after sunset—physical work, too. His body was hard and muscular from all that work, taut and enticing. If only she was marrying Luke today.

Mia jumped up. She had to get ready for the wed-ding. She had to stop thinking about him like that. She had to stop thinking about him at all. Soon she wouldn't be able to hide the evidence of her pregnancy anymore and she had no illusions about what Luke's reaction would be when he noticed her belly bump. Disgust pure and simple—that she'd slept with a married man, that she'd lied by omission about being pregnant, that she'd allowed him to think she was available.

Of course, she was available, but even if Luke truly cared for her, that didn't mean he'd welcome another man's child into his life. If he couldn't do that, she couldn't be with him. It was that simple.

She shoved the check into the top drawer of her dresser and examined her appearance in the mirror. Hair, eyes, cheeks, lips, clothing, posture and expression. Check, check, check, check, check, check, check. She never could see her reflection without falling back into beauty pageant mode, running through her checklist so that her exterior was perfect before she stepped outside. Some lessons you never forgot.

If only Luke knew what it cost her to keep her distance, maybe he'd have some sympathy. She smoothed her hand over her belly and turned sideways to see her profile. Her belly swelled slightly, but she was sure no one else would notice it. Not yet. If Luke only knew how much she loved the child growing within her, would he choose to love him too?

Twice in the last month she'd actually seen Luke fuss over a baby in public. Once he even consented to hold one. The sight of the little mite in Luke's big, strong hands, its sweet face nestled against Luke's wide shoulder almost brought Mia to her knees.

She wanted him to hold her baby. To love it.

To love her.

She wanted it so bad.

Her thoughts broke off when she heard Luke's steps on the stairs. She wasn't usually in her room at this time. Usually she was almost ready to head to work, but this wasn't a normal day. He hesitated outside her closed door. She heard a clink and a quiet thump, then he moved to his own room. His door shut with a click and a minute later his en suite shower started.

As soon as the coast was clear, she opened her door and discovered a cut glass vase full of a dozen pink roses. Beside it sat a generous box of Ghirardelli chocolates and a small gift-wrapped box. She scooped the presents up, put the flowers on her dresser, sat back on her unmade bed and opened the box of chocolates. Biting into the rich, satisfying sweetness of a raspberry truffle, she heaved a sigh and unwrapped the box. The pretty bracelet that lay inside brought tears to her eyes.

She brushed them away impatiently. Luke might think he wanted her to be his Valentine, but it could never be.

She tried the bracelet on, considered it, and took it off again. If she wore it now, it would be too hard to part with when she left, and she knew she had to leave. She set the box on her dresser beside the roses. When Luke found out about her baby, he'd surely want it back.

It was definitely time for her to move on. Tomorrow she'd deposit the check in the bank and start hunting for an apartment. The minute she found one she'd confess everything to Luke.

Today she wouldn't have time for any of that.

Today she needed to concentrate on Fila. Her friend

deserved her fairy tale wedding. Mia had no doubt Fila and Ned's marriage would go the distance because they'd been through so much together already.

As she finished her truffle and went to fetch her dress, Mia bit her lip. Always a bridesmaid, never a bride, wasn't that how the saying went?

Her shoulders slumped. It didn't get much more accurate than that.

LUKE HURRIED THROUGH his shower and dressed quickly. He needed to get back to his parents' house to help set up for the wedding. At least the location was convenient—no rushing around town today. The tables, chairs, and extra place settings for the dinner would be delivered any moment.

He banged his shin on his bedpost and cursed under his breath. He needed to pull himself together if he was going to be of any use to anyone—but he couldn't help it. He was distracted.

He still hadn't seen Mia so far this morning, and he was starting to second-guess the gifts he'd bought her. Flowers, chocolates and jewelry weren't very original, but he'd noticed that Mia loved flowers, and she always wore jewelry, and who didn't like chocolate? Still, it bugged him that he didn't know Mia better—well enough to know for sure what she'd like. Despite living with her for more than two months, he sometimes felt he hardly knew her at all. She had a way of shutting down conversations whenever he came close to teasing out what made her tick. He should have been put off. Instead, he was only attracted to her more.

Mia Start was every man's dream. There was something about her that caught the eye and wouldn't let go, and it wasn't just him—he'd seen everyone from teenage boys in the hardware store to men older than his father on the street follow Mia with their gaze. Every flip of her long, straight-as-nails, thick, dark ponytail drew men like flies. She was petite, but curvy, her breasts something to behold even under the old baseball T-shirt she wore when she cleaned house. Her hips widened out from her tiny waist and her ass filled a pair of jeans to perfection, begging to be touched. Her pouty red lips were made for kissing. Every time Mia was around, his body responded to her. Hell, most times she wasn't around he had to force himself to stop thinking about her. When she'd agreed to move into his place in December, he thought he'd had it made.

He'd thought wrong. One stupid comment from him early on had soured any chance he had to convince her to date him. It was one of those things you said when you weren't thinking. Jake and Hannah had been feeling their way toward marriage at the time, trying to reconcile their different visions of life. When they slipped up and faced a possible pregnancy, it made things even more complicated, and when it turned out there was no baby, Luke had thought it might be a relief—one problem off their plates, so to speak.

Which is why he'd said to his brother, "No baby, no problem, right?"

The five little words made Mia visibly flinch, and she'd kept her distance ever since.

Mia wanted kids. He was clear on that now. He was

also clear she thought he *didn't*. The truth was, he hadn't much thought of it either way. He didn't have anything against children. They just hadn't been on his radar.

Until now.

On his brothers' advice, he'd been trying to show Mia that he was indeed father material by paying attention to children when they were around. He made a point to compliment mothers on their babies. He even held them now and then, which led him to understand that kids might be nice.

He just wanted to get married first. To Mia. Hell, he wanted a honeymoon and a year or two to themselves. He wanted to make love to her every which way from Sunday, as often as work and life let them do it. He wanted to know what made her tick.

Then he'd be ready for kids.

First he had to convince her to go on a date.

He slapped cologne on his freshly shaven cheeks, pounded downstairs and found Mia ready to go. Her bridesmaid's gown was hanging in a garment bag draped over the banister. She was perched on one foot, carefully tugging on a scarlet cowboy boot, her dark hair looped around huge curlers, her sexy body squeezed into a hip-hugging skirt, a spaghetti-strapped tank top and a fluffy cardigan. If he knew anything about her, she'd done her toenails this morning and was trying not to mar them in the process of getting her boots on. Later she'd get all dolled up. For now she was prepared to pitch in and help set up for the wedding.

He stifled an urge to stride over and try to tempt her into letting him have his way with her right there.

"You'd better hurry," Mia said, straightening and turning around. The lift of her brows told him she'd seen his thoughts in his expression. He couldn't keep a grin from spreading across his face. He didn't mind if she knew what he wanted. Hell, he wanted her to know exactly what he wanted. He wanted her to want it, too.

But as usual, she turned away without giving him any encouragement. Luke sighed inwardly and followed her out the door and into the frosty morning.

By the time they arrived back at his parents' place, several more vehicles were parked in the driveway.

"Looks like everyone's here from the Cruz ranch," Luke said.

"With all these helpers, it should be easy to get set up." Mia climbed the stairs and went in the front door, Luke close behind her. They found a crowd in the entryway, including most of the inhabitants of the Cruz ranch. Jamie and Claire Lassiter were standing in the doorway between the front hall and the dining room, Claire's rounded belly announcing she was well along in her pregnancy. Cab Johnson and Rose Bellingham were still shedding their coats. Ethan Cruz was just hanging his up in the capacious hall closet. His wife, Autumn—also pregnant and just days from giving birth—was nowhere to be seen, however.

Apparently, Evan and Bella Mortimer had arrived just moments before Luke and Mia did, because they were struggling out of their winter gear just inside the doorway. Evan waved a manila envelope at Jake.

"I'd have thought you were too busy for jokes," he called out over the din.

Jake looked confused. "What do you mean?"

Evan tossed the envelope at him. "All those photographs and everything. How'd you get them?"

"I don't know what you're talking about."

Luke shrugged out of his own jacket, craning his neck to see what Jake was pulling out of the envelope. Some kind of paperwork and several photographs. Hannah looked over Jake's shoulder. "Wow—look at that place. It's a palace."

"Come on, Hannah," Evan said. "You must have been in on it too. Jake couldn't pull that off all by himself."

"What is it?" Luke asked, making his way over to his brother's side. The photographs showed a beautiful mansion surrounded by green lawns that flowed down to a beach and the ocean. In the background he spotted a tennis court and possibly a putting green. He flipped the photo and read, "The Breakers, Carmel, California."

"Sweet pad. You thinking of buying it, Evan?"

"Hell, no. I've already got property in California," Evan said. "And Bella and I are settled here. This is Jake's idea of a joke."

"What's the punch line?" Luke turned to Jake.

"I don't know. It's not my joke," Jake said. "Sorry, man—you've got the wrong guy. Rob's the joker in the family."

"I didn't do anything," Rob called from the dining room.

Evan waved the idea off. "You said just yesterday you wanted to buy my house, Jake. Then today Bella spotted a guy drive up and drop this in our mailbox."

"What color was his truck?" Jake asked.

"I couldn't see. It was early—still pitch dark," Bella admitted. "But he was tall. Lean. Your size."

Jake made a face. "It wasn't me."

Luke took the paperwork from him. It was an offer to buy the Mortimers' ranch—or to do a simple swap for the property in California pictured in the photographs. *As you can see*, the handwritten note read, *the Breakers is worth far more than your property.* Luke whistled. "Well, they're right; that mansion must be worth ten times as much cash as your place. No offense."

"None taken," Evan said, though he did sound offended. "But I think my property is pretty nice."

Evan was right, Luke thought. The Mortimers' home was nothing to sneeze at. Designed and built for Carl Whitfield, a wealthy man who'd left Chance Creek after being jilted by his fiancée, it was the largest home in the district and beautifully appointed. The grounds were extensive—stretching back into the hills to the north. Only someone as wealthy as Evan Mortimer could have afforded to buy it, but it paled in comparison to the seaside estate shown in the photographs.

"I'm serious. I didn't drop that off in your mailbox," Jake said.

"Yeah, yeah, Matheson. I believe you." Evan turned away.

"Time to get to work," Camila said, bustling in from the kitchen. "Men—set up the seats in the solarium. Women—follow me. We'll work on the table settings."

Two hours later, the house was nearly ready. Ethan, Cab and Jake were busy repairing the bent metal support to one of the rental tables, so when Ethan's phone warbled, he pulled it out of his pocket and handed it to Luke.

"Ethan's phone," Luke said.

"It's Autumn," the voice on the other end said. "I'm ready to be picked up."

"Hi, Autumn. It's Luke. Someone will be right there." He figured she must have stayed home to rest before the wedding. Nearly nine months pregnant, the last time Luke saw her he wasn't sure how the woman kept her balance. Her belly was all out of proportion to her petite frame, and he figured she'd been smart to take it easy rather than try to help out with setting up.

"Thanks."

She hung up and Luke handed Ethan back his phone. "I can get her. I'll bring Mia along."

"You sure?" Ethan looked up from where he was unscrewing the support.

"No problem." It would give him a moment alone with Mia, something he was hard-pressed to get these days. A familiar frustration welled up within him. He knew nothing would come of it. No matter what he tried, Mia held back. How much longer could he wait for her to change her mind?

He found Mia in the kitchen and explained the errand. "Want to come along?"

"Sure." She told the others where she was headed, and followed him to the front hall. Luke handed Mia her jacket and led the way back outside where they hurried to their cabin to pick up the truck. Soon they were driving down the dirt lane that led out to the country highway.

"You feeling okay?" he asked. Mia's silence unnerved him. She'd been on the quiet side for weeks, which wasn't like her. Since he wasn't a big talker himself, he depended on her to fill in the silences.

"What? Oh! Yeah, I'm fine." She perked up. "I got the gifts. Thank you so much. I nearly forgot with all the fuss about the wedding."

"Are you wearing the bracelet?"

Guilt flashed across her face. "Not right now—I didn't want to break it while we got ready for the wedding."

"Oh... right." Didn't she like it? Did she think it was cheap? He remembered the ribbing he'd taken at the breakfast table that morning. Maybe he hadn't spent enough money. "I thought maybe tomorrow we could go out to dinner," he hastened to say. "Somewhere special. We'll celebrate Valentine's a day late."

And maybe do more than eat. Finally.

"Maybe," Mia said absently. She was gripping the armrest tightly, and Luke slowed down a notch, wondering if his driving had scared her. He wasn't going fast, though, and he knew this stretch of road like the back of his hand. She didn't react at all to the reduction in speed. No, something else was bothering Mia. He wished he knew what.

The Cruz ranch was just down the road from the Double-Bar-K, and the driveway was already coming up, so he couldn't do what he wanted to do, which was to slam on the brakes, lean over and kiss Mia until she had no choice but to give him her full attention.

Why had he been such a damned gentleman all this

time? It hadn't gotten him anywhere.

The answer was simple. Because he had the feeling Mia needed him to be a gentleman.

He just didn't know why.

Didn't she understand that she could tell him anything? Didn't she know she could depend on him to sort out any problem? He wanted to be her rock—her confidant. "What's wrong?"

That got her attention. She straightened and smiled, but her expression remained guarded. "Nothing."

"Something's bothering you." He pulled into the lane that led to the Cruz ranch and cursed the shortness of the drive between the properties. If he knew Mia, she'd use their arrival to cut this conversation short.

Sure enough, she said, "We'll talk about it after the wedding, okay?"

Luke grunted. He could only hope they would.

Chapter Three

MIA WAS SURPRISED that Autumn didn't meet them out on the small porch of the converted bunk-house where she and Ethan made their home, even though it was February and a chilly day. She'd texted just minutes ago that they were on their way and Autumn was one of the most punctual people she knew. Maybe she'd forgotten some last minute detail.

She opened her door and slid off the truck's high seat, her boots landing in an inch of newly fallen snow. She wore thick tights underneath her mini, but the cold made her skip over the driveway and up the porch steps. She heard Luke's door slam and his footsteps behind her. By the time she opened the door and stuck her head in, he had a hand at her waist to guide her inside.

She would miss that when she moved out—his touch, his presence. She ached to show him what she really wanted him to do. Knowing she'd never get that chance made her ball her hands into fists within her pockets.

"Autumn?" Mia called. The door led straight into a small, empty living room. "Autumn, are you ready?"

She heard a noise and cocked her head.

"Autumn?"

"Mia?"

At the strangled tone of her friend's voice, Mia exchanged a quick, worried glance with Luke, kicked off her boots and dashed toward the rear of the house. She found Autumn in her bathroom, clutching the tile countertop for dear life, bent over in pain. Her hugely pregnant belly looked like it would overbalance her. Her loose, drawstring pants were soaked.

Autumn was panting. "My water broke! And it hurts!" As Mia watched, Autumn gritted her teeth and swayed, her entire body bowing with the pain. Was that a contraction?

Mia called over her shoulder, "Luke, call 911! Autumn's giving birth! Autumn—we have to get you to the hospital. Come on, honey!"

"I can't!" Autumn's wail ended on an inhuman note, and Mia realized this was more than a contraction. Autumn was bearing down.

"No—wait! No, you can't do that yet!" Mia had read enough about giving birth to know that wasn't right. First the contractions were small and women walked around a lot, grimacing now and then. Then they got stronger and you took them to the hospital. Then— hours later, right?—they got really strong and the doctor—because there was always a doctor by then— told you when and how to push.

You didn't bend over your sink and bear down five minutes after your contractions began.

Unless—

"When did they start? When did your contractions start?"

"I don't know." Autumn was panting again. "A couple of hours—aaaaah!" She ground down into another push.

"Why didn't you say anything?" Mia shrieked.

"I thought they were Braxton Hicks," Autumn said when she could breathe again. "The manuals all said I would have them for days, or weeks, or aaaaaannnnggh!"

The noise she made became truly guttural, and Mia stared at her in horror as she realized what happened next was up to her. Either Autumn would have her baby standing up, fully clothed, or Mia was going to have to take charge.

"Luke. LUKE!" Mia screamed.

His footsteps pounded closer and he appeared in the doorway, phone still in his hand.

"You have to carry Autumn to the bedroom. Right now. She's having the baby."

"What? She can't!"

"She can and she's going to. Shut up and carry her!"

Luke dropped the phone, picked Autumn up as easily as if she was a sparrow and hauled her into the bedroom, depositing her on the queen-sized bed.

"I need towels—lots of them. Boil some water."

"Why?"

"I don't know!" Mia was close to losing control. Her hands shook as she tried to figure out what to do next. Autumn had flipped herself over and was crouched on all fours on the bed. Shouldn't she be lying down?

Luke left to find towels, probably terrified to find

himself with a birthing mother and a screaming idiot.

"Autumn, honey? Don't you want to lie down?" Mia touched her back and Autumn reared up.

"Don't touch me! Aaaaannnngh!" She fell back on all fours and bore down again, this time for so long that Mia thought she'd never stop. One thing was for certain— she had to get those pants off of her. But how?

She waited until Autumn stopped pushing. "Sweetie, you have to take off your pants. I'm just going to help and then I won't touch you anymore. I promise."

"Oh…kay," Autumn panted, but when Mia took hold of her waistband she writhed like a wild thing. Mia hurried to strip her before the next contraction hit. When the pants were puddled around Autumn's ankles, a knock on the door told her Luke was back.

"Hang in there, honey. It's all right." Mia hurried to the door. She blocked Luke's view as best she could in an attempt to preserve Autumn's modesty but she had a feeling her friend was beyond caring. As Autumn's voice rose again in a wordless bellow of pain, Mia met Luke's gaze.

"I called the ambulance," he said, his calm voice welcome in all the chaos. "It might be a few minutes, though. There's been an accident south of town."

"How many minutes?"

"I don't know."

Overwhelmed by the responsibility of caring for Autumn, Mia hesitated, wishing more than anything Luke would join her in the bedroom. She remembered all the times in the past two months he'd stuck close when he thought she might need help, the way he touched her lightly when he passed by, to let her know he was there. She wanted him beside her, wanted to lean on him, but this was the holiest of holy times for a woman, and Autumn needed privacy.

"I'll be right here," Luke said as if he'd read her mind, then bent down and kissed her softly on the forehead. "Right outside this door. I'm not going anywhere. Call me when you need me."

Mia nodded, blinking back tears. Right. She could do this. Autumn was depending on her.

She took the towels he handed her and layered some on the bed around and underneath Autumn. She kept the rest in a stack close by. She didn't know what else to do besides wait.

LUKE HAD SEEN many a cow give birth to a calf and many a mare give birth to a foal. Barring unforeseen complications, he figured he'd only have to stand in this hallway for ten minutes at most before Autumn's baby arrived. It unnerved him that a birthing mother made a sound as earthy and animal as any of the critters outside in his barns, but when he thought it through it made sense. What were people but a complicated type of animal?

He'd never thought much about the birthing process in women, though. When it came to cows and horses, he viewed it in as practical terms as any rancher. Even so, he wasn't too practical to have noticed that even in a barn every birth was attended by a hush—a holy quiet amidst the clamor of the mother's groans and the other sounds of the world around it. The hush was almost more tangible than audible—a sacredness of space around the entry of a newborn into this old, old world. It touched him like little else did, as did the sight of a newborn animal's first moments, and afterward he always found himself stepping more quietly, becoming more observant—more aware of the beauty and mystery of life itself. At least for a little while.

He hadn't expected to find that same hush here in Autumn and Ethan's bunkhouse, but he did. And to his surprise, standing outside Autumn's door, guarding that sacred space for the women inside made him feel more like a man than just about anything he'd ever done before. To lend his strength, his watchfulness—his protection to the miracle happening inside made him part of something far bigger than himself—something that linked him to countless generations of other men watching over other women. For an instant, his daily life fell away and he wondered what it would feel like to be a father himself—to know the baby coming was his.

He shifted his stance, a little uncomfortable with the depth of his thoughts, and moved on to more practical matters. How soon would the ambulance arrive? Before or after the birth?

What was the sex of the baby Autumn was bringing into the world? Boy or girl?

How would Ethan feel when he knew—

Luke slapped his hand to his head. In all the commotion, he hadn't thought to call Ethan—and Ethan was just up the road.

Luke scrambled for the phone he'd dropped and found it in the bathroom. He dialed Ethan's number, but no one answered and it went to voice mail.

"Ethan, it's Luke. Call me! Autumn's—"

He broke off when Mia shrieked, "Luke!"

"Autumn's having your baby. The ambulance is on its way." He dropped the phone and ran into the bedroom where Autumn was on her hands and knees straining and groaning, and Mia was crouched behind her. All thought of *guarding the miracle* forgotten, he scanned the room.

"I don't know what to do!" Mia cried.

Luke took the situation in at a glance. "You're doing great. Both of you are doing great." Autumn needed something to lean on, though. "Mia, stay there. Get ready to catch that baby. Autumn, honey, I'm going to climb up on the bed with you."

"Ahhhnnnggg!" Autumn cried as another contraction hit. Luke batted the pillows away that rested against the headboard, climbed onto the bed and sat crosslegged, his back to Autumn.

"Go ahead and brace your hands on my shoulders." A moment later Autumn grabbed hold and another moment later, her fingers gripped him hard as she bore down again. Gravity was the trick with birth, Luke knew. Stick a woman on her back and she had to work twice as hard to push out a baby. In this position Autumn could work with the forces of nature. He grit his teeth as her fingernails cut into his skin.

"The baby's crowning. She's coming," Mia cried. "Autumn, another push just like that one."

"Aaahhhng!" Autumn groaned again as she bore down and Luke braced his hands on his knees to keep from folding underneath her.

"You can do it, honey. You can do it," he chanted, hardly knowing what he said.

"The baby's head is out. Oh, my God, Autumn. One more push! One more push!"

With her last push Autumn nearly bowled Luke over, but he kept himself in place and from the sounds Mia was making all was going well. Autumn ended with a wail that was quickly echoed by one that was quieter, but no less strong. A girly wail, Luke thought, barely daring to breathe as Autumn collapsed against him.

"You did it! Autumn, you did it!" Mia cried. "It's a girl! Oh, she's beautiful!" Luke sensed Mia moving behind them. Autumn slid down to lie on her side on the bed and Mia handed her the baby. Luke carefully climbed off, checked to make sure mother and child were safe before he ran to get the phone again. When Ethan answered this time, Luke's voice was rough with emotion. "Ethan?"

"I'm on my way. How's Autumn doing?"

"She just had your baby!" He strode back to the bed-room. Mia had smoothed a blanket over Autumn. A thatch of dark hair graced the baby's head and its eyes were shut tight, but its little rosebud mouth opened and emitted another wail. Luke held out the phone.

"Did you hear that? That's your baby girl! Get on over here, Daddy! Hurry up!"

ETHAN ARRIVED JUST after the ambulance and paramedics.

"Let me in! Let me through!"

Mia turned to Autumn and saw her friend light up when she heard her husband approaching. The paramedics had clamped and cut the cord and delivered the afterbirth. They'd quickly cleaned mother and baby and helped Mia get them comfortable again.

As Ethan rushed into the room to crouch by the bedside, Mia followed the others out to the living room where Luke waited.

"We'll give them a moment before we take them to the hospital," one of the paramedics said. In her thirties, with no-nonsense mannerisms and blond hair pulled back into a severe bun, she was everything Mia would hope a paramedic to be. "It's really just a formality now. We'll give Mom and baby a quick look over before we send them back home. You did a fine job."

"I didn't do a thing. Autumn did all the work."

"That's the way of it when things go right," the paramedic said. "Still, I'm sure it helped a lot just knowing you were there."

Autumn affirmed those words when Mia got to see her for a minute before she was loaded into the ambulance. "I don't know what I would've done without you and Luke. It all happened so fast. I was totally unprepared!"

"I'm glad I was here. That was amazing, Autumn. You were amazing!"

"No, I wasn't—I yelled at you." But Autumn didn't look too concerned. She was too busy kissing her baby's head.

Mia didn't blame her. The baby was beautiful. Delicate and sweet. Perfectly formed. "What will you name her?"

"Arianna. In honor of Ethan's mother."

Mia nodded. From what she'd heard, Aria Cruz had been an interesting woman. "That's a beautiful name."

She watched the paramedics wheel Autumn through the house and lift her into the waiting ambulance. Ethan followed, saying, "Tell Ned and Fila we wish we could be there for the wedding."

"We will!" she assured him.

When they were gone, she turned to Luke. "Can you believe that? I thought I was going to faint when I found Autumn bearing down already. Thank God everything went okay. Luke? What's wrong?" The cowboy had the strangest look on his face.

"I want one," he said. "I want one, and I want it with you."

"I WANT A baby with you, Mia. I want to marry you." Luke knew this wasn't the right moment for a proposal but here he was, jumping the gun, proposing anyway. He didn't know what else to do. He'd tried to convince Mia to date him. He'd done everything he could to let her know how he felt. He'd wanted to make love to her for months. She'd been living right under his nose, tempting him with every sway of her hips as she moved about the house straightening up, every bounce of her breasts when she dashed up and down the stairs getting ready for a day's work. But he wanted more than that, too. He wanted his ring on her finger, his name on her debit card and his baby in her arms. He wanted it all—everything that Ethan had with Autumn, that Ned was about to have with Fila. He wanted it all and he wanted it right now.

"Mia? Did you hear me? I want to marry you."

She had gone as pale as the paint on the wall behind her. Her eyes were huge in her face and he wanted to kiss away the fear in them. What was she afraid of? Him?

"Say yes." He took her hand in his. Tugged her closer. "Damn it, say yes, Mia."

"I…" She couldn't seem to answer.

"Stop thinking. Just say yes." He bent down to kiss her, but she gasped and pulled back.

"I'm sorry." Tears sparkled in her eyes. "I'm sorry! I tried to tell you!"

"Tell me what?" He refused to let her go. His arms tightened around her waist until they formed a cage she couldn't break out of. Strength had its advantages. This time she wouldn't get away. "What do you have to tell me?"

"I'm pregnant already."

Chapter Four

M IA HUNCHED MISERABLY in the corner of the front seat, as far away from the furious man at the wheel as she could get. She'd never seen anyone as angry as Luke was now. She wished he would scream at her, rage at her, even throw things at her—anything but the grim silence that filled the cab like a living thing.

When they reached the Double-Bar-K, she dashed from the truck nearly before it stopped moving. She ran up the steps, barreled inside Luke's parents' house and almost knocked Hannah over.

"What's wrong?" Hannah raced up the stairs after her to the bedroom that had been allocated for the bridesmaids on the second floor. As Mia slammed the door shut behind them and threw herself on the bed, Hannah rushed to her side. "Was it Autumn? The birth? Did something go wrong after all?"

Mia shook her head, her tears making it impossible to speak. "She's… fine. The baby is… beautiful."

"Then what's wrong? Are you in shock?"

"It's…Luke. He knows." Mia's sobs stormed out again. Hannah sat down hard on the bed beside her, understanding perfectly. She was the only one besides Fila who knew about Mia's pregnancy. She'd urged Mia to tell Luke long ago.

"And he isn't happy." It wasn't a question.

Mia only cried harder. "He hates me. He couldn't even speak to me. I knew this would happen."

To her credit, Hannah didn't say she told her so. She only sighed and patted her on the back. "I'm sorry. I think you and Luke would make a great couple. Maybe you still will. Give him time—the news has to have come as a huge shock. Don't you think?"

Mia nodded, knowing Hannah was trying to help. But it was easy for Hannah. She was so beautiful with her white-blond hair and competent ways. Everyone admired her for going back to school to become a veterinarian, and her new husband, Jake, was head over heels in love with her—enough to change the whole course of his life and go back to school, too. If only Luke loved her like that.

But why should he when she was carrying another man's child?

She turned on her side, curled into a ball and placed a hand on her belly. Poor little bean. There would be no happy, celebrating crowd when she gave birth. She was just an unwed mother who'd had sex with a married man.

She could almost hear her mother's voice. *What did you expect, Mia? You reap what you sow.*

Well, she was definitely reaping. But it was Fila's day, not hers, so it was time to end her pity party and get her act together.

"It's better this way," she said to Hannah. "He knows, and I've seen how he feels. Now I can move on and start my life without him." Her voice wobbled.

"Mia."

She shook off Hannah's soothing tone. "No, it's better to accept things as they are and stop hoping for the impossible. I'm not going to end up with Luke. I'm going to raise this child alone. And that's okay." She had Ellis's money now. She could make her way.

"Whatever happens, you aren't alone," Hannah assured her. "You're surrounded by friends, Mia. And every last one of us is going to help."

LATER THAT AFTERNOON, Luke paced the tight confines of the room his mother had designated for him to change into his wedding clothes. The chairs were set in lines for the ceremony and everything else that needed to be lifted and moved was in place. All that remained was for him to change and wait for the guests to arrive so he could usher them to their seats. But he wasn't fit for company now. Not after Mia's bombshell.

Pregnant.

About four months pregnant, if his calculations were right.

By Ellis Scranton, a forty-two-year-old businessman who'd probably be bald in another couple of years. Luke ignored his own age for the moment. The idea of Ellis with twenty-one-year-old Mia was sickening.

The idea of anyone with Mia was sickening.

Now he understood why his talkative Mia had become increasingly silent as the weeks had passed. Now he understood why she held back every time he tried to take things further—even though he'd seen the desire in her eyes many times. The one time they'd kissed—way back when she'd first moved in—the sparks between them could have started a blaze. Since then she'd refused to acknowledge she was interested.

Now he knew why. Mia was being noble. She refused to tangle him up in a relationship because she'd already tangled with another man and gotten pregnant.

Other women would have done their best to steal his heart so when their pregnancy showed he'd stick around. Some women might even have tried to pass the baby off as his. Not Mia. She'd done her best to keep him free and clear. She hadn't wanted him to pay for her mistakes.

Maybe she'd been afraid he'd cast her aside. His fingers clenched into fists. He couldn't stand to think she'd been afraid of that. He wasn't the kind of man who ran from trouble. He was the type who stuck around and sorted it out. How could she not know that about him?

He stifled the urge to punch a hole in his parents' wall at the thought of how lonely and scared she must've been these past few months. For one second—one second—he'd just about punched a hole in Ethan's living room wall. He'd wanted to find Ellis and beat the living daylights out of him. Mia had seen it in his eyes and flinched away. That had stopped him mighty quick. Shame had flooded him—that he'd bring violence anywhere near a pregnant woman. Then he'd remembered which woman was pregnant and how she'd gotten that way and he'd stumbled right out of Ethan's bunkhouse.

He'd wanted to get in his truck, start driving, find the bastard and mete out a little frontier justice—but there was the damn wedding to get through, so he'd sat there like a beaten dog and driven the woman he loved—the woman Ellis had knocked up—back home and watched her flee inside like the devil himself was after her.

He figured the devil had already found her. The devil in the form of a cocky businessman who couldn't keep it in his pants. Ellis had power, authority and money. How simple it must've been for him to turn Mia's head. What had he told her—that he'd fallen hopelessly in love? That he'd leave his wife and children for her? That he'd show her the world? To a small town girl like Mia—just starting out in life—it must have been too tempting to resist.

"Forty-five minutes to show time. Here are your boots. I don't know when Mom found the time to shine them all." Ned stood in the doorway holding Luke's dress boots. Luke hadn't even heard him open the door. Ned frowned as he entered the room. His stride was still unsteady from breaking his leg the previous month, but it was healing well and shouldn't have any lasting effects. "Something's got you fired up."

Luke tried to get a hold of himself, but by the look on his brother's face he hadn't succeeded.

"What did she do?" Ned asked.

"Who?"

His brother chuckled. "Any time a man looks like that, a woman's involved."

"I'll tell you another time."

Ned cocked his head. "Sounds serious. I'm leaving

for my honeymoon tonight. Sure you don't want to tell me now?"

"Nope." Luke shoved his hands in his pockets and with an effort changed the subject. "Guess I'll get changed. What about you? You ready for this?"

"For marriage? Hell, yeah." A smile lifted the corner of Ned's mouth. "You'd better watch out—like Dad said this morning, he's got his sights on you now. You're the only one he hasn't helped marry off."

"He can't help me."

Ned misunderstood his meaning. "Don't underestimate the ability of Holt Matheson to bring about matrimony in the strangest of ways." He looked at his watch. "Guess I'd better get dressed." He headed for the door.

Luke just shrugged. If only their father could help him sort out this mess.

"Fact is, I thought you'd be halfway to marrying Mia by now." Ned's tone turned serious as he hesitated with one hand on the doorknob.

"Yeah, so did I."

"You love her, right?"

Luke blinked. He and Ned had never discussed love before. "Yeah."

"Then get on with it. Don't let anything get in your way."

Get on with it. Ned was right. He should get on with it. Nothing had really changed—except now he knew why Mia was holding back. She liked him all right, maybe even loved him, but was afraid he wouldn't want her in her current condition.

Well, he did want her, and he'd have her, too—after he paid Ellis a visit and made it damn clear the man had better stay out of their lives.

The door burst open again, slamming into Ned hard enough to knock him off balance. Luke jerked forward to steady him with a hand to his bicep before he fell to the ground. Wouldn't want the groom to break his leg for a second time—on his wedding day.

"Hey!"

"Sorry." Jake came in and shut the door behind him. His shirt was untucked and his hair stuck up every which way. "Shoes. Where the hell are my shoes?"

"They're on your feet." Ned regained his balance and pointed to Jake's beat-up cowboy boots testily.

"Not these. My dress boots. Mom would kill me if I wore these in the wedding."

"Aren't they in the hall outside your room? Mom polished them all last night."

"I saw them there earlier. Now they're just—gone!"

"Luke, help the idiot find his boots. I'm going to get dressed. Fila will clobber me if I'm late to our wedding. Or Camila will do it for her."

He left, chuckling. Jake didn't share his amusement. "Someone took them."

"Why the hell would anyone want your boots?"

"I don't know! Are they in here?" He commenced searching through the closet and under the bed. Luke helped him, promising himself he'd confront Ellis right after the wedding. When they turned up empty they split up and searched the other rooms on the second floor. Forty-five minutes later Luke was still looking when he heard a ruckus from down the hall.

"What the hell, man?"

Luke traced the sound to find Jake and Rob squared off in Rob's old room. Jake shook a pair of cowboy boots at Rob. Rob ducked.

"I didn't take them."

"They were under your bed." Jake swung at him.

Rob backed up, hands raised. "I didn't put them there. Besides, I haven't slept in that bed in a dozen years."

"Man up and admit it. You always loved to play a joke."

"I'm over that."

"You're late!" The new voice was decidedly feminine, with a trace of a Mexican accent that made it easy to place. Luke turned to find Camila behind him. She wore a beautiful red dress and her dark hair flowed around her shoulders like a shawl. Large gold hoop earrings swung as she talked. "You all need to get downstairs, now. You're keeping the bride waiting."

The men sprang into action. Jake slipped on his boots and tucked in his shirt. "I'll get you back for this," he said to Rob on his way out of the room.

"I didn't do a damn thing."

Camila shushed them both. "It's like dealing with a pack of children," she said to Luke as they walked down the stairs. Evan Mortimer stood at the bottom.

"Everything all right?" he asked. "Sounded like a barroom brawl up there."

Luke shook his head and sighed. "Just life as usual in the Matheson household."

MIA COULD HARDLY breathe as she stood up beside Hannah in front of the gathered guests and watched Fila move up the aisle created between the lines of folding chairs in the large back room and solarium of the Matheson house. Fila was radiant in a silvery white sheath with a lacy train. Ned looked proud enough to burst out of his skin as he watched his bride come down the aisle on his father's arm. Fila's parents had been killed in Afghanistan, and she had no relatives present, but everyone had come to know her during her time in Chance Creek, and she was surrounded by friends. As for Ned, since he'd grown up right here on one of the preeminent ranches in Chance Creek, he might as well be local royalty.

As the couple stood in front of Joe Halpern, the preacher, Mia willed herself not to cry. It wasn't just her sorrow that made it hard to catch her breath, nor was it the grim expression on Luke's face as he stood next to Ned. Her dress—a plain cobalt-blue sheath that echoed Fila's—had fit just a week ago when she visited Ellie's Bridals a final time. Now it stretched tight across her abdomen, making her want to fold her hands protectively in front of it.

She forced herself to keep them by her sides, and tried to keep her mind on the ceremony. This was one of the most important days of Fila's life. It made no difference that Mia had ruined her chances of ever marrying the man she loved. Fila, unlike her, deserved happiness, and Mia would do nothing to mar it.

When the ceremony was over and the chairs were being shifted to circle the tables that the men helped to set out, she slipped into a bathroom and took a few minutes to calm herself.

Where would she go tonight when the wedding was over? Normally, she'd run to Autumn's place if there was trouble, but not today—not when Autumn's baby had just been born. She couldn't stay here on the Double-Bar-K, either. She wasn't sure if Luke would even let her back into his cabin. Perhaps she could impose on Bella and Evan? Surely there was an out-of-the-way room in their mansion she could inhabit just for a day or two—until she found her own place. Or maybe she should rent a motel room for the night?

"Don't worry," she whispered to the small hard lump growing in her belly. "I'll make a life for us, I swear I will."

Knowing she couldn't disappear for too long without raising suspicions, she returned to the reception, where she bumped into her mother and father, who stood near a table full of hors d'oeuvres. Standing with them was Linette Wilcox, who was friends with both her parents and Lisa Matheson. Linette headed up several committees at the conservative church Mia's parents attended on the outskirts of town. She had never been friendly to Mia. In fact, Mia thought she was mean and selfish, but she'd done her best to always be civil, in respect for her parents' attachment to the church and to the woman herself.

"Mia Start—there you are. I was looking for you." Linette's voice cut through the murmur of the crowd like chalk on a blackboard. She took Mia's hand and tugged her closer. "See, I told you there was something different about her, Enid. Mia, you're getting fat!"

Mia's cheeks flamed as her mother turned around to look. Surely the old busybody couldn't have spotted her pregnancy. She searched for a quick retreat. "Sorry, Mrs. Wilcox. I have to go help out in the kitchen."

"Nonsense. You never could cook. See Enid? What did I tell you?" Her bony fingers wrapped more tightly around Mia's wrist. Mia saw heads all around them turn her way. Damn it—she had to get out of here.

Before she could move, Linette reached down and patted Mia's belly, giving a hard push on her abdomen. Mia sucked in a gasp of air.

"I knew it!" Linette crowed. "I know a pregnant woman when I see one! Did I or did I not say your daughter was hiding something, Enid? Mia always was sly. Shame on you, keeping a secret like that, girl. Where's the ring on your finger?"

Mia thought she would die. Now everyone had turned to look at her. This was the stuff of nightmares— the very reason she hadn't told a soul except for her closest friends. Her mother turned pale as parchment. Her father stood as still as the statues on Lisa's mantelpiece. She'd get no help there. They would be thinking of their church—their friends—the same friends who turned a cold shoulder to anyone with a wayward child.

"Mia! Say something!" her mother hissed. "Tell her she's wrong."

"I…I mean—" A chill swept over her, followed by another flush of heat. This couldn't be happening. It couldn't. Not at Ned and Fila's wedding.

"See? I was right. She won't even name the father.

You certainly won't find him in this crowd. I heard Ellis Scranton already left town. Things must've gotten too hot for him here. I bet you gave him what-for, didn't you, Bart?" Linette looked utterly victorious—she knew as well as anyone else Mia's father was not the type to confront anyone. Mia had a sudden flash of insight—this was about the Easter bazaar. Her mother had been nominated to run it this year. Linette's face had looked like she was sucking lemons for a week afterward.

"I...it's—" But what could she say to deflect Linette's words? She didn't want it known that Ellis was the father of this child. He was gone and good riddance. But she had to say something, fast. Maybe Ellis was right—she should say it was a one-night stand. Just a guy she'd met at the Dancing Boot. Someone she'd never seen again.

But when she opened her mouth to repeat the lie, she spotted Luke watching her. He stood just ten feet away and his face showed his feelings. Anger. Disgust. A sob caught in her throat. She needed to leave, now. Before she sank to the floor in a puddle of humiliation.

"Mia Start, you tell me if it's true!" Her mother's voice rang out, the finger she pointed at Mia shaking.

"It's true."

Mia jerked. She hadn't spoken.

But Luke had, and every head in the room swiveled toward them at his authoritative tone. Luke stepped to her side with all the calm confidence of a lion strolling through the savannah, and Mia bit back a cry of pain. Why had she told him about her affair with Ellis? Luke was going to expose her. She'd never live it down.

"Mia is pregnant with my baby," Luke announced to the crowd at large. "We're getting married. We planned to make the announcement tomorrow." He clamped an arm around her, which was a good thing, Mia thought.

Because she was going to faint.

LUKE CAUGHT MIA when she began to sag and ushered her into the kitchen quickly, pursued by Mia's mother. So much for finding Ellis and warning him off. So much for talking things through with Mia after the wedding. He'd started down a road from which there'd be no turning back.

"Luke? Oh, my goodness—what's happened?" Lisa bustled over to meet them, a spatula still in her hand. Luke helped Mia to a seat at the rustic kitchen table and faced her.

"Linette Wilcox just forced our hand. We had to announce our engagement."

Mia gaped at him, but he ignored her. As chaotic as this turn of events was, he felt in his element. He was a man of action, not words, and this situation called for action. He refused to let the woman he loved bear the brunt of other people's wrongdoing.

"Your...engagement?" Lisa's voice rose to an excited squeal. "You and Mia are engaged?"

"And pregnant," Enid said, bustling into the room behind them, her face still red with the shock of her recent encounter with Linette. "Don't forget pregnant, too. Enough to show!"

"Pregnant!" Lisa's face lit up even more, and it felt like a kick in the gut to Luke. What would she say when she found out the baby wasn't his? She'd better not say a damned thing.

No one had.

Then he remembered his mother's words from this morning when he'd said he didn't see any reason for rushing into matrimony. *I'm afraid you will soon.*

Had she known?

"When?" Lisa cried. Luke didn't know if she referred to the wedding or the birth. He squared his shoulders. "The wedding is the first weekend in March. Two weeks from today."

"Two weeks!" both mothers chimed.

"That doesn't give us any time to plan," Lisa said.

"You'll figure it out." He clamped a hand down on Mia's wrist and hoped she understood his message. She was his now. She needed a man and he'd be that man. He wasn't asking her—he was telling her, the way he should have months ago. And he didn't care what anybody said.

"Mia? Have you chosen a location for the wedding?" Lisa asked.

Mia's face paled even further—something Luke wouldn't have thought was possible.

"I… I'd like to have it right here," she said in a tiny voice. Luke's chin came up in satisfaction. She'd gotten the message.

She was a Matheson now.

Chapter Five

M IA WAS BEGINNING to think she might pass out if her head didn't stop spinning. All around her, friends offered their congratulations as they moved in and out of the kitchen helping Lisa and Camila with the food for the wedding guests. Even after the wedding party took their seats at the head table and the rest of the guests found their spots, Mia couldn't move. She wasn't sure what was real anymore. Had she actually delivered a baby today?

Was she getting married to Luke?

What had made him cross that room and claim her for his bride in front of everyone? He could just as easily have walked out and left her to confess her guilt. That was what she'd expected him to do. Did he actually mean to go through with it? Or was this a ruse to get them through the day? Would he tell the truth to all and sundry tomorrow after the wedding was safely over?

She jumped when he dropped down in the chair across from her in the now quiet kitchen. Even Lisa and Camila had gone into the main room to listen to the groom toast the bride.

She raised her eyes to meet Luke's steely gaze.

"I meant it," he said without preamble. "We'll get married in two weeks. We'll pick up a ring tomorrow. You'll be my wife."

She couldn't make her lips form a single word.

"And that baby will be mine. Do you understand?"

She searched his face. Did he really mean that? "People know," she protested feebly. "You can't keep a secret in a town like this."

"I know that." His tone was implacable. "I won't deny who put that baby in your belly, but I'll be its father. Understand?"

She wasn't sure she did and it must have shown. Luke's expression softened just a bit. "If I'm going to marry you, I don't want to be on the outside looking in. That baby won't call me Luke. He'll call me Daddy, understood? I'll raise him. I'll provide for him. We're not taking a dime from that man. Are we clear about that?"

Mia raised her chin. "I already have." And she meant to keep that money, too.

Luke stilled. "What do you mean?"

"Ellis gave me a check. This morning. He's clearing out of town. Never coming back. He said that's all I'll get from him and that he never wants to see the baby."

"Well, good." Luke leaned back in his chair, visibly relaxing. "Keep the check. Use it to buy something nice for the baby. But that's the last I want to hear about Ellis Scranton. He's not your husband. That's my job. Agreed?"

Was that how he saw it? As a job? Was he marrying her out of pity, for heaven's sake?

And did he mean to carry this take-charge tone into their marriage? Mia had never seen this side of him before except when he was directing chores on the ranch. And she didn't like it aimed at her. She studied the man across the table. His short blond hair. His clear gaze and strong jaw. Luke Matheson was a force to be reckoned with—a proud man. Was that what this was all about? His need to know whether she'd allow him that pride?

"Yes." The word was out of her mouth before she could stop it, because Luke wasn't normally like this. She could count off a hundred instances of his kindness— times he'd been there when she needed him, times he'd gone out of his way to give her what he thought she wanted. This new stiffness had to be a result of his hurt feelings. He'd get over that, she hoped. Meanwhile, she wanted to spend the rest of her life with him, regardless of the impossibility of this situation.

Her only question was, when the excitement of the day was over would Luke still want to stake his claim on her?

Or now that he finally had her, would he turn and walk away just as Ellis had?

LUKE LET OUT a breath he didn't know he'd been holding. She'd said yes. A smile tugged up the corner of his mouth. He hadn't expected to become Mia's fiancé today. He certainly hadn't expected to become a father to another man's child. But she'd said yes—she'd said *yes*—and that turned him on more than he could say. Mia was his. Forever. And that was all that mattered.

Mia stared at him. "Are you sure about this?"

"Yeah." He touched her hand. Gathered it into his. "Hell, yeah."

Something flashed in her eyes. Humor? Desire? "You're going to be my husband," she whispered.

He nearly laughed out loud with relief. The last few hours had slammed him with enough surprises to last a lifetime, but now they were over the worst. Now they had their whole lives ahead of them. Together.

"Mrs. Matheson," he whispered back.

Mia ducked her head, her cheeks blazing pink.

He tugged her hand. "You'd better come here, Mrs. Matheson."

She got to her feet and for the first time ever allowed him to pull her close. Let him settle her on his lap, tilt her chin up and kiss her.

It was a proper kiss, too—not like the one he'd stolen back in his kitchen in December when she'd first moved in. He took his time moving his mouth over hers, tasting her, then tucked a hand under the nape of her neck and deepened the kiss. He let all of the passion he'd been holding back flood through him and into her, hoping to set her feelings alight, too. It occurred to him that tonight when they went home they would share a bed for the first time. The idea revved him up more than he could say.

When his mother bustled back into the kitchen, they pulled apart.

"Don't mind me," she trilled. "I didn't see a thing."

Mia buried her face in Luke's neck. "You won't change your mind? You won't leave me, will you?" she whispered.

Luke pulled back. Cupped her face in his hands. "Never. This is it, princess. You and me together, forever, okay?"

She searched his face. "Okay."

HOURS LATER THEY climbed the steps to their own cabin. As soon as she took off her coat and boots, Mia collapsed on the couch with a sigh of exhaustion.

"Don't stop there," Luke said, coming in after her.

She pushed up on her elbows. "Why not?"

"You march your fine self right up those stairs, princess. Time for bed."

Princess again. Apparently she had a new nickname. His words sent a thrill of anticipation through her body, but she didn't know if they meant what she wanted them to mean. She'd always slept in the guest bedroom—her rental bedroom—while he slept in the slightly bigger one next door. Would that change tonight?

She hoped so.

"What's with the princess thing?" Maybe that would spread some light on where they stood.

He sat down at the opposite end of the couch, lifted her feet onto his lap and began to knead them. Mia let out a loud groan of pleasure. A full day in heels had left them sore.

"You've always looked like a princess to me, the way you stand so straight and proud. I can see a crown sitting on top of that pretty head of yours."

She sobered. There was a reason for her ramrod posture she didn't like to be reminded of. All those endless beauty pageants. She brushed off his reference to a crown with a joke. "You want to know why my posture's so good? I'm trying to look taller!"

His deep chuckle warmed her almost as much as his sensual touch on her feet. If his technique with the rest of her body was as good as this—she was a lucky woman indeed.

He tugged her ankle. "Come on, princess. Up to bed."

She got up slowly and followed him upstairs, pausing in front of her bedroom door. He shook his head. "Uh-uh. Get what you need, but you're sleeping with me tonight."

A smile curved her mouth and he grinned back. "Sounds good, huh?"

"Yeah," she admitted. "Sounds real good."

LUKE DIDN'T WASTE any time once they were in his room. He unbuttoned his dress shirt, slid it off and cast it over his desk chair, then undid his belt buckle and the button at the waistband of his best jeans and shucked them off, too. He hesitated a moment when he got to his boxer briefs, but only for a moment.

"Wow." Mia eyed him frankly and he wasn't ashamed of the way his body let her know he was interested in seeing what she had under all of her clothes too. "Would you help me with my zipper?"

"Sure thing." He undid the tiny clasp at her neck, then the long zipper that trailed down the back of her blue dress. Underneath she wore a pretty bra and panty set. He turned her around slowly, taking her all in, then reached behind her to unclasp her bra. She waited while he peeled it off, then looked up at him coyly through her eyelashes.

"Well?"

As if she had to ask. Her breasts were as magnificent as the rest of her. Full and round, with dark areolas that begged for him to kiss them. He couldn't wait to give them the attention they deserved, but first he wanted to see the rest of her.

He hooked a finger through the strap of her panties at each hip and slipped them down, letting out a grunt of pleasure at the sight of her neatly groomed thatch of dark hair.

"Beautiful." He led the way to his bed and drew her down beside him, the brush of her nipples against his skin enough to set every nerve ending ablaze. Mia entranced him. Always had. Probably always would.

He'd meant to be careful with her. Wanted to tease and delight her into such an ecstasy of longing that she'd beg him to give her more. But now that she was in his bed, instinct took over.

He gathered her in beneath him and surrounded her with his arms. Swooping down to kiss her senseless, he let his weight settle on top of her, wanting to feel her beneath him, wanting her to know exactly what she was going to get.

Mia sighed and kissed him back with as much ardor as he felt, and Luke's blood jumped. She wanted him like he wanted her. Completely. Utterly. He nearly came undone right then.

Luke took complete advantage of this opportunity to

get to know Mia's body better. He spent time lavishing his attention on every delicious part of her until he couldn't wait another minute to be inside her, and judging by Mia's moans, she couldn't wait for it either.

"Sweetheart, you ready for this?"

She nodded, her breath coming in pants. He nudged her thighs apart with his, positioned himself between them, and pushed into her slowly.

"Luke." That one word told him everything he needed to know. Being with him felt as good to Mia as being inside her felt to him. She sighed with pleasure as he began to move within her, and the sound was so sensual Luke groaned.

He gave up all thought of controlling the remainder of the encounter. He gave up thought altogether. He let his body take control—let his body possess hers in the most primal way possible.

And Mia opened to that possession with utter abandon, the sensuality of her movements and body setting him aflame all over again. When she cried out her release, his guttural groans joined hers and they crashed over the top together.

Afterward, still joined, still breathing heavily, Luke kissed her again. "I've wanted to do that for a long time."

"Me, too."

"I want to do it again."

"Yeah." She nodded.

"I didn't hurt you, did I? I didn't…" He looked down at her rounded belly. Reached out a hand as if to touch it. Pulled back.

Mia reached out her own hand, took his and pressed it against her stomach. "Of course not."

He held his hand there, feeling the tautness, trying to sense the baby inside.

"I'll do my best to be a good…" He hesitated, afraid to say the word. Afraid she'd deny him the role he wished to take on.

Sudden tears shone in Mia's eyes. "You'll be a great father, Luke."

As she threaded her arms around his neck and kissed him again, Luke knew everything would be all right.

Chapter Six

"WAKE UP, SLEEPY head."

Mia yawned, stretched and turned to see Luke enter the bedroom, the smell of barn and horses wafting in with him. She pushed up on her elbows and glanced at the time on the small bedside clock. After nine. Luke would have been up for hours and hours by now.

"It's late!"

"You said you weren't working today."

"No, I'm not."

"Get up, get some breakfast in you. Let's go buy your ring."

At his words, a memory of last night swept into her mind and she smiled. Luke was an amazing lover. Very masculine. Very sure of himself. With every reason to be. Twenty-four hours ago she'd never dreamed they would sleep together, let alone become engaged. It just went to show how your life could change in an instant.

He bent down and stole a searing kiss. "You keep thinking about that. I like the way you smile when you do."

Mia laughed, but as she climbed out of bed worry assailed her. Luke wanted her—he'd made that clear for months—and last night he'd taken her several times with all the ardor she'd expected from him, but would that ardor translate into enough love to make him actually marry her? She wasn't sure.

Suddenly shy, she hurried to fetch her robe and a change of clothes, but Luke intercepted her, sliding his hands down her back to smooth over her bottom. "Look at you. You are one fine woman."

She melted into him, stood on tiptoes and kissed the underside of his jaw. "And you are one fine man." Still, her insecurities chased each other around her brain, even as Luke kissed her thoroughly. He must have sensed that, because he pulled back.

"What's wrong?"

"It's nothing."

"Don't hide things from me."

Her cheeks flamed because she knew what he meant. Luke didn't trust her all the way—not after she'd kept such a huge secret from him. She'd have to get used to opening her heart to him, which was hard after the way Ellis had treated her.

"I'm afraid," she confessed.

He tugged her down to sit on the bed. "Because of what people will say?"

"No, not really. I'm afraid you'll change your mind. Settling down to marriage is hard enough under normal circumstances. We won't get a honeymoon period to adjust to each other. Before you know it we'll have a baby and all the responsibilities that entails. How are you going to feel when I'm up three times a night breastfeeding and I don't want to have sex? Will you still be happy you took us on?"

He scowled. "This isn't about sex."

"Really?" She indicated her naked body.

"You think that's all that concerns me? We've lived together for months, and last night is the first time I got laid. If this was about sex, it would've been over a long time ago."

"Exactly. Last night you got laid. The chase is over. Why wouldn't you lose interest?"

He pulled back. "You think I only wanted you because you were playing hard to get? You're dead wrong."

Mia shrugged. "Maybe."

"Maybe, nothing. I said I'll marry you. I said I'll raise that child as my own. That's what I plan to do." He tugged her closer. "And if you have any more complaints, Mrs. Matheson, you're going to have to take them up with management."

He lowered her back down onto the bed, shedding his shirt as he did. He climbed on top of her and kissed her neck, one hand loosening his belt and unzipping his jeans. Mia giggled in spite of herself. "What's management going to do about it?"

"Look into it very, very thoroughly," he said, trailing kisses down to her breasts as he shucked off his pants and boxers. Mia sucked in a ragged breath and twisted her fingers into the comforter. "You might even say they'll probe the situation." He settled himself between her legs and nudged against her. Mia closed her eyes and gave in to the sensation, all thoughts of future problems gone from her mind. As Luke thoroughly put to rest all of her complaints, she only knew she never wanted to leave his side again.

It was more than an hour before they left the cabin.

Luke helped her up into the seat of his truck. He started the vehicle, reached for her hand and held it the whole way into town to Thayer Jewelers.

Mia asked him to stop at the Cruz ranch on the way into town to see if Rose would come with them. Rose had worked for several years at Thayer's before quitting a few months back, and Mia valued her opinion, plus Rose was reputed to have a sixth sense about couples—whether their marriage would make it or not. Mia wanted to know what kind of hunch she got about them.

When they got to the ranch, they found Morgan and Rob with Cab and Rose. All four of them were standing outside Ethan and Autumn's bunkhouse in the snow staring at an evergreen shrub that Rob had been trimming.

"Awful cold weather for gardening," Luke called as they approached.

"I've been wanting to try topiary in case any of my customers want it in their gardens," Rob said. "I thought I could do one for Autumn as kind of a baby gift."

"What is it?" Luke asked, cocking his head.

"It's a bit of a puzzle, isn't it?" Cab said with a grin.

"It's supposed to be a horse." Rob frowned. "It'll look better in the spring when the new growth comes in. I hope."

Mia bit her lip to hold back her laughter. She hoped there would be some new growth on that bush, because the current bare spots gave it a sickly look. She wasn't sure where the horse came in, either.

"See, this is the neck and here are the four legs," Morgan pointed out helpfully.

"I see it," Rose said, but Mia saw laughter dancing in her eyes.

Another truck pulled up and Jake got out. "What the hell is that?" he said, striding up to them. He looked the bush over a minute. "A bulldog?"

"I was thinking armadillo," Cab said. "But I see what you mean about the bulldog."

Rob bristled. "It ain't a bulldog or an armadillo. It's a horse. Anyone can see that."

"Rose, any chance you could come with us to Thayer's?" Mia thought it best to ask before an argument erupted.

"Thayer's? Are you two buying a ring?" Rose looked pleased.

"Yes, I was hoping you could give us your... opinion." Mia sent her a hopeful look.

Rose nodded. "Of course."

"It's the head that's all wrong," Jake told Rob.

"It's the legs," Cab countered. "Look at them—stubby little armadillo legs."

"You know what? I need to get my ring cleaned," Morgan said. "How about you drive to Thayer's with me, Rose? We'll meet you and Luke there, Mia."

"Sounds good. Bye, Cab," Mia said, although Cab wasn't paying attention. Mia didn't blame him; the bush with its lumpy shape and bare spots did draw the eye in this winter landscape. "I hope Autumn likes her armadillo, Rob."

"It is not an armadillo. See what you started," he said to Cab.

"I can't help it if your horse is vertically challenged."

WHEN MIA AND Luke reached Thayer's, Rose and Morgan were already standing at the cash register, talking to Andrea Moore, the young woman who had taken over Rose's position.

"I'm glad Emory isn't here," Mia heard Morgan say to Rose. Emory Thayer owned the jewelry store and had been Rose's boss when she worked there.

"Emory's in less and less," Andrea told them. "He's really slowing down. I think he'll give up the store soon. Everyone will have to drive to Billings for rings."

"Someone will buy the store and keep it running, don't you think?" Rose said. "Every town needs a jewelry store."

"Maybe you should buy it," Mia said.

Rose just laughed. "I don't have the time or money. What I need is a gallery."

"Look around you!" Andrea waved a hand at the plain gray, mirror-lined walls. "There's plenty of space."

"A jewelry store and art gallery? That would be pretty weird," Rose said.

Mia didn't blame Rose for not being interested. Emory had been a strange boss at best—and he was also the father of the man she'd dated for years. When she broke up with him, things got ugly between her and Emory and she'd ended up quitting abruptly.

"Andrea, do you mind if I help Mia and Luke pick

out a ring?" Rose asked.

"Not at all." Andrea handed over her keys to Rose instantly and Mia had the feeling this wasn't the first time Rose had acted the part of sales clerk since she'd left the position. She led the way to the engagement ring display cases.

"Do you know your budget, Luke?"

Mia's heart squeezed again. They were buying a ring. She was marrying Luke.

But when Luke named a number, Mia's jaw dropped open. Where had he gotten that kind of money?

"That will give you plenty of options," Rose said, the surprise in her voice matching Mia's. She bent over the cases. "How about this one?" She pointed out a simple, delicate ring. Mia felt a rush of gratitude for her friend. The ring was beautiful and she'd love to own such a thing, but she instinctively knew it wouldn't break the bank.

"Ooh, that's pretty," Morgan said. Her thick, dark waves swung over her shoulders as she bent to look at it more closely. Mia was happy the older woman agreed with her opinion. Morgan was so competent and self-assured; if she liked the ring, it had to be a good pick.

Focusing on the ring again, Mia decided that if she'd scanned the cases for an hour she couldn't have chosen a better one herself. She slid a look at Rose, wondering if what people said was really true—that she got a feeling from the engagement ring about a couple's chances for happiness. Had Rose seen something promising in them? Is that how she'd been drawn to the right ring? When she raised a questioning eyebrow, Rose nodded at her almost imperceptibly.

Mia's heart soared. Maybe this was going to work out. Maybe she would get to have everything she wanted, after all.

Luke's voice sliced through her thoughts. "That one's too plain. I want my princess to have a real ring. How about that one?"

Mia bit her lip in consternation when he pointed to a fancy setting with multiple rows of diamonds and sapphires. She wanted to laugh out loud at the thought of how that ring would look on her hand, let alone the cost of it. She'd need a whole new wardrobe to match it, for one thing. And a cane to lean on to hold it up, for another.

Rose frowned. "I think Mia might prefer—"

"That one." Luke tapped the glass again, his tone brooking no disagreement. Rose raised an eyebrow, but pulled out the glittering ring and slid it onto Mia's finger. It was far too big. Mia had to hold it in place. Luke nodded. "That looks perfect to me. What do you think, Mia?"

Mia shook her head. It was a spectacular ring, but it didn't fit her at all. In fact, it made her feel like a fake. Like a cheap plastic rain slicker trying to pass itself off as a mink coat. "I don't think so."

"I think so. Don't be modest, Mia. It's beautiful, just like you."

Mia softened at Luke's words, but Rose still looked worried. Mia knew why; it wasn't the right ring, no matter how beautiful it was.

"I like the other one," she said softly.

Luke took her hand in his and tugged it until she looked up at him. "You're just saying that because you're worried about the price. I can afford the ring, Mia. I want you to have it. I won't let people like your mother and Linette Wilcox make you small. You deserve the best and I'm going to give it to you. We'll take this one." He smoothed his thumb over the showy ring on her finger, and Mia didn't know how to answer him. She knew that buying her this expensive ring was Luke's way of showing everyone else just how much he cared for her. He wanted them to value her too, which she appreciated in the circumstances. If only he could see it was bound to backfire—people would only talk about how unworthy she was to wear it. But she couldn't say that to him. Not now—in front of Rose and Morgan. Both women watched her expectantly.

She finally nodded. "This one," she echoed.

"Are you sure?" Rose said.

"There are lots of rings to look at," Morgan said.

"No, I'm sure," Mia said, with a glance at Luke. He took her hand and squeezed it briefly, and she knew he was pleased she'd agreed with him. But should she have? How could she be angry with a man who wanted to give her diamonds? How could she feel disappointed when the ring was so spectacular?

But she did feel disappointed. It wasn't the ring she wanted, and that didn't seem to matter to Luke as much as what everyone else thought of him.

Unfortunately, she knew it was her own bad choices that put him in a position to feel insecure.

She stood back as Luke made the arrangements to

purchase the ring. Since it needed to be sized, she slid it back off her finger gratefully and handed it over the counter to Rose. Rose held the ring a moment as if concentrating on it. When she passed it to Andrea, Mia couldn't read her expression. A thread of fear tightened in Mia's gut. Did that mean something bad?

As Andrea rang up the sale, Rose leaned in closer. "I've got news, too. Cab and I set a date for our wedding. May tenth. I'm so excited!"

"You and Mia should go wedding dress shopping together," Morgan said brightly and Mia knew she was trying to lighten the atmosphere. "Bring me along. I love that kind of thing."

Mia was all too eager to move to a more comfortable topic of conversation, too. "That's a great idea. I could go the day after tomorrow. I only have two weeks until my wedding, so I have to get right on it. You're lucky, Rose, to have more time to plan."

"Not much more. I don't know how I'll get it all done."

"I can help! We can plan together." The idea raised Mia's spirits and she made a decision that even if her engagement ring was far flashier than the one she would have chosen for herself, she'd adore it because Luke chose it for her. It was a symbol of his regard. So what if he overcompensated a little for his insecurities by spending too much money on a fancy ring? If that was the worst of her problems, she lived a charmed life.

And the thought of planning her wedding in tandem with Rose's sounded like a lot of fun. She loved to plan celebrations, though she hadn't had many in her life so far.

"I'll meet you at Ellie's Bridals the day after tomorrow then," Rose said. "I want to visit Autumn and baby Arianna in the morning, so say two o'clock?"

"I'll be there," Mia said, deciding she would visit Autumn soon as well.

"I'll be there, too. We'd better get going, Rose," Morgan said. "Congratulations on your engagement, Mia! Should we celebrate it tonight at the Double-Bar-K?"

"Sure," Mia said, a trifle hesitantly. Lisa had already voiced her approval of the match, but she had no idea how Holt felt about it. She guessed she'd find out soon enough.

SEVERAL HOURS LATER, Luke hopped out of his brand-new Ford F-250 and strode to the front door of his parents' house, disappointed no one was around to see his purchase. When he'd driven Mia to the jewelry store earlier, he'd suddenly become all too conscious of what a rattletrap his old vehicle was. His brothers were right, Mia couldn't be happy about riding in it, so he'd taken the first opportunity to fix the situation. Just as he'd thought, the Matheson name carried all kinds of weight at the dealership in town and he'd managed to finance his new truck without too much money down.

He'd have to do something soon about Amanda Stone, however. He wasn't going to be able to make the payments on this truck and Mia's ring, and keep paying her bills, too. He'd sit down and explain the situation and help her find a place she'd be comfortable living in. Maybe Reverend Halpern could help. Surely he'd had people in his congregation with similar issues.

Luke went into the office and sat at the computer to update the books. The cramped room was situated on the first floor of their parents' house, since Lisa used to do this job before she handed it over to Luke.

He pushed his hand through his hair as he waited for his accounting program to load. Lately he'd taken over more and more of the business side of the family's cattle operation, in addition to supervising the health of the herd, running the breeding program, making repairs on their outbuildings and managing the rotation of the herd through their pastures.

He was happy his mom was spending more time on her own pursuits and with her friends in town these days, and he understood why his father wasn't more help with the accounts. Holt's dyslexia was so severe he was almost illiterate. But happy or not, sometimes Luke felt like he couldn't shoulder one more thing—

A spreadsheet opened, cutting those thoughts short. He got to work.

Fifteen minutes later, the door slammed open and Jake strode in. "Nice truck, man. But first things first, you sneaky bastard. How long have you known you were going to be a father?"

Luke swore, made a correction, then looked up. "Not long."

"I can't believe you managed to keep it to yourself."

"I would've liked to keep the secret a bit longer. Didn't mean to hijack Ned and Fila's day."

"They'll be all right. Nothing could make those two unhappy right now. I've got to ask though—are you sure that kid's your own? Rumor has it Mia was seeing Ellis Scranton earlier last fall."

Luke's jaw tightened with anger, but before he could form an answer, his youngest brother Rob crowded into the office too. "Is that your new Ford outside?" He didn't wait for an answer. "I thought you said you and Mia weren't together. You said she wouldn't touch you. What was all the whining about?"

If Ned weren't on his honeymoon, Luke figured he'd be in here smothering him, as well. He stood up, squeezed past his brothers and kicked the door shut, not wanting their mother to overhear them and knowing he had to get this right or the whole family would end up in an uproar. On the one hand, he wasn't prone to lying. On the other, he didn't want Mia's fling with Ellis to overshadow their marriage for the rest of their lives.

"I'll say this one time only and after that as far as I'm concerned, the subject is closed. Mia slept with Ellis. She got pregnant. They broke up." He charged on before either of his brothers could speak. "Ellis is gone—out of the picture for good. So I'm the father of Mia's child. Got it?"

"You sure Ellis ain't coming back? Seems like something he'd do." Jake folded his hands over his chest and leaned against the windowsill.

"If he comes back I'll convince him to leave again mighty quick. And I won't have any of you treating Mia differently because of the circumstances, you hear? She's my fiancée. In two weeks she'll be my wife."

"Fine with me," Rob said with a shrug. "Morgan's already excited about being sisters-in-law with Mia, and about having their kids so close together. Did you know they're going dress shopping?"

Luke relaxed. "Yeah, I was there when they made the plan." He was glad Morgan was helping Mia pick a dress. That meant she accepted the wedding.

"What did Dad say?" Jake put in.

"Nothing at all." It had surprised Luke that Holt hadn't said a word so far, but on the other hand, why would he if he wasn't privy to the rest of the gossip? As far as Holt knew he was getting exactly what he wanted. Luke would be married in a couple of weeks, and there was another baby Matheson on the way. And as long as Holt kept his mouth shut, he'd win his bet with Lisa, too, and wouldn't have to fly to Paris.

What would he do when he discovered Mia's baby wasn't blood-related though? Luke thought Holt would have plenty to say then.

Which is why he meant to keep it a secret as long as humanly possible.

"Don't tell Dad," he cautioned his brothers.

"Don't tell me what?" Holt butted his way through the door and into the room. "What the hell's going on here? A tea party? Get back to work."

Jake and Rob headed for the door at a smart clip, but Holt still blocked it. "After you tell me what it is you ain't supposed to tell."

Luke shrugged. "Fine, we're chipping in to buy you a new teapot for your birthday. Now you've ruined the surprise." He hoped the sarcasm would work.

Of course it didn't.

"I've got all day." Holt leaned back against the door.

"Let me guess. You knocked up your bride before your wedding." He laughed at his own joke.

"Not quite," Jake said. Rob elbowed him.

Holt stopped laughing and narrowed his eyes. "So this *is* about Mia. What's the big secret? That she made the beast with two backs with Ellis Scranton? Can't blame you for being displeased with that bit of gossip."

"I don't want to hear about *that* bit of gossip," Luke growled.

"Well, you will hear about it in this town—and more than that, too. Like maybe that baby of hers wasn't sired by you."

You could have cut the sudden silence with a knife. Holt frowned. "That's what's bothering you? The gossip?"

Luke heaved a sigh. No sense in even trying to keep it secret. Holt was like a terrier that had caught a rat. "Not the gossip, Dad. The truth. The baby is Scranton's."

Holt straightened, his face mottling with color. He opened his mouth, closed it, opened it again, shook his head and left, slamming the door behind him.

Rob whistled. "You are in some deep shit."

MIA WAS READING the manual that came with the cash register at Fila's Familia the following day when her mother pushed open the door and crossed the small restaurant with determined strides.

Mia had just reached the part about trouble-shooting problems with the machine, a part she wanted to know inside and out before the restaurant opened, and the interruption irritated her. She knew her mother would want to discuss the wedding and she was right. Enid didn't bother with greetings or small talk. She went straight for the jugular.

"You'll be married at our church. I just checked, and there's an opening on the third of March. Four o'clock in the afternoon."

Mia was shaking her head before her mother finished speaking. "I'm not getting married in church, Mom. I've already told Lisa Matheson I'd like to get married at the Double-Bar-K."

Enid's chin raised. "A wedding outside of church isn't a wedding at all. On March third at four o'clock. I won't hear another word about it."

"We've already asked Reverend Halpern to marry us at the Double-Bar-K," Mia said, although that wasn't strictly true. Lisa had checked with the minister at the end of the evening yesterday and found he was available, but they hadn't made a formal decision—they hadn't had time.

"You'll have to un-ask him. I've already spoken to Reverend Tilton. I've booked the time. It's done. You grew up in that church and you'll marry in that church. The bride's family is in charge of the wedding!"

Mia's courage slipped in the face of her mother's certainty. "At any rate we'll have the reception at the Matheson's place. It's so much prettier than any rented hall."

"I see what this is about." Enid clasped her purse so tightly her knuckles whitened. "You think the Mathesons are better than us. You want to cozy up to them. You think you can shake off your past—"

"That's the last thing I think." Mia was very clear on that. "I don't like Reverend Tilton's church. I don't like the way he lets women like Linette Wilcox boss everyone around and freeze them out. I don't like the way the congregation turns its back on anyone who isn't perfect. We're supposed to be Christians!"

"Don't you speak to me like that. Linette Wilcox might not be fancy like your Mathesons, but she's a good woman. She works on a number of charitable committees. I won't have you speaking ill of her, or of the Reverend."

"Fine, I won't speak of them at all. And I won't speak to them, either." Mia saw Camila stick her head out of the kitchen to see what the commotion was all about. "In fact, I won't need to—because I'm not getting married in that church!"

"You're trying to break my heart!" Her mother clasped her purse to her chest, her voice catching. "Getting pregnant. Lying to me. You think I don't know whose child that is, despite what Luke said?" She pointed to Mia's belly. "You've just about killed me with your wild ways. And now this. I waited all my life to see you walk up that aisle—to see you married in the same church I was—"

Mia stifled a groan. She knew exactly what her mother had hoped. Enid had whispered that dream into her ear every Sunday for years as they walked down to take their seats. *Someday you'll get married up at the altar right where Mommy and Daddy did. And you'll have a big white dress and a fancy cake—* It took Mia years to realize they wouldn't eat the cake up at the altar too, featuring as it did in her mother's description.

Enid searched her face with a pleading gaze and Mia caved in. How could she deny her mother's wish when she'd ruined so many others? She'd never won the big beauty pageant like Enid hoped she would. She'd dropped out of them before she even got to that level. She'd had an affair with a married man. She'd gotten pregnant before a ring sat on her finger. It was time to give her mother what she wanted.

"Okay."

But giving in hurt worse than she could have ever imagined.

"DO YOU REALLY think you're ready to be a father?" Rob asked. They'd met up outside their cabins, Rob heading home for a quick lunch with Morgan, Luke heading up to the main house to eat with his folks since Mia was at work.

"You're going to be a father before I am."

"And I sure as hell don't feel ready. Don't get me wrong; I can't wait. It's just…well, I don't want to end up like Dad."

Luke laughed out loud. "I don't think there's much chance of that."

"I doubt he set out to be like he is, though." Rob cocked his hat back. "Seems to me it must have just snuck up on him, all that orneriness."

"Then watch out for it. Anyway, Morgan won't let you turn into Dad."

"That's just the thing that bothers me. Why'd Mom

let him get that way? She's no shrinking violet. You'd think she'd pound some sense into him. I'm telling you; I'm worried."

Luke understood why. His brother's words were making him mighty uneasy, too. "It can't happen to us. None of us are mean like that." But as he said it out loud he remembered a time when he'd been all too mean to Rob. "Not anymore, anyway. Well, maybe Ned."

"Naw, I think Ned might be in the best shape of any of us now." They stood a moment and mulled over that surprising fact. "Anyway, we've all got tempers. We just didn't used to have wives and kids to take them out on. Now we do—or we will soon."

It was an uncomfortable thought.

"None of us are like Dad," Luke stated with far more certainty than he truly felt.

He'd regained his confidence by the time Mia walked into the cabin just before dinnertime. He'd motored through the rest of his never-ending chores and had even sat down to make the list of wedding guests Mia had requested from him. They needed to get a jump on things if this wedding was going to come off right. He knew some folks took an entire year to plan such an event, but with the spate of weddings among his family and friends lately, he figured his circle were old hands at it.

"Whose truck is that outside?" she said, taking off her coat and boots.

"Ours. What do you think?"

"Ours?" She stopped in her tracks. "You bought it?"

"Yep. Nothing but the best for my princess."

"Luke, I wish you'd stop calling me that."

"Why?" He moved toward her. Dipped his head down for a kiss. She kissed him back willingly enough that he took things a little further.

Mia retreated. "Because it makes me uncomfortable."

"All right, sweetheart. I can call you sweetheart, can't I?"

A smile tugged at her lips. "I guess so. That's a pretty fancy truck. Are you sure you can afford it?"

It was his turn to pull back. "What did I tell you earlier? Stop worrying about the money. I've got it covered."

"It's just—"

"Shh." He kissed her again. "Don't you worry your head about anything. Come on and sit down."

As he led her to the couch, Luke realized Mia seemed awfully tired. He knew she was beginning to feel the pinch of helping prepare Fila and Camila's restaurant for its grand opening in a few weeks, but he was surprised by how pale and drawn she looked when she dropped onto the cushion beside him. He reached out to gather her into his arms.

"Something wrong?" He lifted her chin with his finger, the better to gaze into her eyes.

"My mother." Her tone was sour.

He tightened his hold on her. "What did she do now?"

"She booked her church for the wedding. And she wouldn't take no for an answer. I don't want to get married there."

"Well, hang on a moment." That wasn't as bad as

he'd feared. Luke thought it through. He knew Mia's parents were far more religious than anyone in his family. Their church had a large, close-knit congregation. He could see how holding the wedding there might be important to Enid. "It might make a lot of sense, now that I think about it."

For one thing, the Anglican church was the grandest one in town. Its large structure boasted a vaulted ceiling and fine stain-glassed windows—a far cry from the simplicity of the church his parents attended.

A fitting venue for a fairy tale wedding for his bride.

"*How* does it make sense?" Mia stared at him.

"A wedding should take place at the bride's church, don't you think? Besides, it obviously means a lot to your mother, and we want her to be happy, too. We want our families to get along together."

"What about my happiness?"

"Why wouldn't you be happy?" He could imagine the two of them standing in front of the minister. Him in his suit. Mia in white gown with a flowing train. Picture perfect. Every girl's dream, right? "I made my guest list, by the way."

Mia had been about to answer, but the sheaf of papers he handed her seemed to make her forget what she wanted to say. She riffled through the pages.

"This must be everyone in town."

"Just the important people."

"We can't fit all of these people in your parents' house."

"Then we'll find a bigger venue—maybe Bella and Evan's place."

"The Mortimers? What about your mother? She's already making plans." Mia flipped through the list again and Luke felt a pang. She was right—his mother wasn't going to be particularly pleased, but she'd understand when she learned the number of guests they planned to invite. "Luke, this is crazy. These people don't mean anything to us."

"They're our neighbors, aren't they?" He meant for this to be a grand event—one that would silence wagging tongues forever. He wanted no one to have a doubt that he was proud of his wife and coming family.

"If you count the entire county as our neighbors, sure." She set the list on the table. "What is this all about?"

A muscle in his jaw pulsed. "It's about me showing the world I care about you. It's about putting to rest any misunderstandings about who your husband is."

She didn't look satisfied. "No one else but us cares."

"I care. Let's put an end to all the rumors once and for all. Let's have a big church wedding and a big reception."

"It bothers you, doesn't it?"

"What?"

"That people are talking about us?"

He pulled her into the circle of his arms again, ignoring the protest of muscles that ached from his day's work. Those aches and pains were his constant companions now that he was running the bulk of the ranch himself. "Look, princess. Pretty soon there'll be nothing to talk about except us Mathesons. You, me and our baby." And he kissed away the rest of her words.

Chapter Seven

"**Y**OU'RE SO TINY," Rose sighed. "Like a fairy princess, even at four months pregnant."

"You're pretty tiny yourself," Mia said, but she surveyed her reflection in the floor-length mirror at Ellie's Bridals with satisfaction. Rose was right; she did look like a princess in this gown with its antique off-white corset top and elaborately bustled skirt. Add in a tiara and she could be the royalty Luke seemed to want her to be. The thought of what his expression would be when he saw her in it for the first time made her smile.

Her smile slipped a little bit as she thought about the ring, the truck and the way Luke seemed determined to buy her happiness. Ellis had thrown around his money like that. Fred Warner had played up his cash, too—telling her no one would take her word over a wealthy businessman's. Was she wrong about Luke's character? She hoped not.

Thinking about Warner made her think of Inez's request. She still hadn't decided what to do. What if she did as Inez asked—wrote a letter to the council—and things blew up from there? What if it got into the paper?

She wasn't sure she could handle that.

She lifted her skirts and hopped down from the pedestal in the center of the room. "Your turn. That dress is… nice."

Ellie Donaldson, the proprietress of Ellie's Bridals, clucked her tongue when Rose stepped up. "I thought that would look lovely, but it's not quite right, is it, dear?" The older woman bustled off to pull more dresses. Mia scanned the nearest racks herself.

"I swear I saw one earlier that would look terrific on you. Here it is." She held it up for Rose to see. "You'll knock Cab off his feet in this one. Try it on."

"Oh, I like that one," Morgan said from one of the plush chairs that ringed the fitting area.

Five minutes later, Rose stood on the pedestal in the new gown and Ellie circled around her, one hand up to her mouth. "It's perfect, and you know what? I would have never thought to have you try it on. Mia, you're a genius!"

"That's a high compliment coming from another genius," Rose said, twisting this way and that to see the gown from all angles. Like Mia's, the gown had a corset top, but instead of the yards of bustled fabric of Mia's skirt, hers clung close to her legs in asymmetrical folds, emphasizing Rose's hourglass figure.

"I love it," Morgan agreed.

"And here are the perfect shoes." Mia fetched a pair so Rose could try them on.

"How'd you know my size?" Rose laughed.

"Just a guess. Here, try this." She handed Rose a veil, too.

"You're stealing my thunder today," Ellie cried. Mia knew what she meant; Ellie had a reputation as having exquisite taste when it came to bridal gowns and accessories. She made sure her customers left with the perfect dresses and normally she could pick out *just the thing* on her first try.

"I'd never do that," Mia assured her. "I just love helping people dress up and throw parties."

"Then you should be a wedding planner," Ellie said, taking a seat next to Morgan. "Lord knows this town needs one. People are always asking me to help them find a venue for their reception and a caterer for their food, but dresses are what I do best. What do I know about event planning?"

"A lot, I'm sure. And Mia's already got two jobs," Morgan pointed out. "I'm not sure she can handle wedding planning on top of working the till at the hardware store and Fila's Familia."

"I'm quitting the hardware store any day now," Mia said slowly, as the idea took hold of her. Wedding planning sounded like a terrific career. It had never crossed her mind before that she could do something like that, but why not? You didn't have to have a college degree to plan a wedding. "I'm sure I could figure out how to balance it with working at the restaurant. That's a great idea, Ellie!"

Ellie blinked. "Oh, I was only joking, honey. Starting a business is hard work."

"And it takes a lot of money," Morgan added.

Mia looked from one to the other, and frowned as she realized neither one of them thought she should seriously consider the idea. "You don't think I can do it?"

"It's just you're so young," Ellie said.

"And you're about to be a mother." Morgan bent forward to touch her arm softly.

Mia couldn't believe it. "You're not that much older than me and you're about to have a baby yourself. You're starting a business. Why can't I?"

"I think you'd be great at it," Rose spoke up, "but they're right. What about the money for startup costs?"

"I've got plenty of money," Mia said. The others looked surprised. She rushed on before they could ask where she'd gotten it. "What I need is references. Rose, would you let me plan your wedding for free? If you like how it turns out maybe you'd tell people about my new service?"

"Of course," Rose said staunchly. "I'd love to have you plan my wedding. Plus you're planning your own wedding, don't forget. You can make a portfolio of photos from both of the weddings to show people."

"That's a great idea." Mia flung herself into Rose's arms as Rose stepped off the pedestal, their wedding gowns billowing around them. But she noticed Ellie and Morgan exchange a worried glance over their heads and had to swallow down a surge of irritation. They really didn't think she could do this, did they?

She'd just have to show them they were wrong.

"YOUR FATHER WILL get over it. He always does sooner or later," Lisa said to Luke.

"Generally later," Luke's sister-in-law Hannah

chimed in.

"A lot later," Claire said. She and Hannah had come to help Lisa clean up the aftermath of the wedding. Claire lived on the Cruz ranch with her husband, Jamie Lassiter, and visited the women of Double-Bar-K frequently. Now they were taking a coffee break around the kitchen table. Luke joined them, dropping down into a chair with a sigh. He was always tired these days, especially when he thought about his father's reaction to his news about Mia's baby.

"He didn't say a word. Just looked like he was about to have a coronary."

"Oh, dear. I hope he doesn't end up in the hospital again," Lisa said.

"He will if he says a word to Mia."

"Luke," Lisa chided. "That's no way to speak about your father—and he won't say anything. Remember? If he does, he has to take me to Paris."

"In other words, you'll egg him on."

Lisa smiled and patted his hand. "I wouldn't do that, now would I?"

"I don't know. You seem to want that trip awful bad."

She chuckled. "I do want that trip, but your father sure doesn't. Besides, Holt likes Mia. He'll growl a bit about her situation, then calm right down when the time comes. Mark my word."

Luke didn't believe her. "More like he'll drive her away before the wedding. You know Dad." He checked his watch. "She ought to be home by now. I'm going to find her before he does." He needed to warn her that

Holt was on the warpath. The thought of his father giving Mia hell made his chest tighten.

"Wait—did you show Luke the topiary?" Hannah asked Claire.

"The one Rob made?" Luke spoke up, glad for the change in topic. "I saw it yesterday. Didn't turn out quite like he wanted it to, did it?"

"If you saw it yesterday then you didn't really see it. Someone decided to improve upon his effort." Claire dug in her pocket and pulled out a smartphone. She pulled up a photo on her screen.

Luke stared at it. "Holy—" He glanced at his mother. "Holy smokes. He must be hopping mad. Is that a dog…?"

"Lifting its topiary leg and taking a topiary piss on the next bush? Yes, that's exactly what it is," Claire said. "Rob read Cab the riot act this morning."

"Cab did that?" He remembered Cab making fun of Rob, although he couldn't picture the sheriff standing outside in the freezing cold last night snipping away at a box hedge. Nor did the sheriff have an artistic bone in his body as far as he knew.

"He says he didn't," Hannah put in, "but Rob doesn't believe him."

"What did Autumn and Ethan say?"

"Oh, Ethan thinks it's a hoot, as long as it's fixed before their next batch of guests come. Autumn's too wrapped up in Arianna to care one way or the other," Claire said.

Luke shook his head and left. For a few months there'd been a hiatus on practical joking around these parts, but it looked like they were back with a vengeance. At least he wasn't mixed up in any of it. He wouldn't allow himself to get pulled into it, either—he'd keep his attention squarely where it belonged, on Mia and her baby.

Besides, he didn't have time for practical joke feuds. He didn't have time for anything anymore—not with the bulk of the Double-Bar-K's chores falling squarely on his shoulders.

His very sore shoulders.

He opened the cabin door five minutes later to find Mia humming as she prepared a simple dinner. He watched her for a moment, warmed by the knowledge that she was cooking for him. He loved having Mia close by and he would do anything—work any amount of hours—if it meant he could be the man to provide a home for her. In a way he felt like he was handing her a canvas to paint the picture of her life on. That's what he wanted to be—the bedrock that she stood on, the palisade that protected her. Luke struggled to arrange his thoughts into coherent words. He knew he wasn't the most eloquent of men, so he could only hope she understood his desire. It went so deep he could hardly comprehend it himself.

He entered the main room and sniffed appreciatively. Mia's cooking had improved during the time she'd hung around with Fila and Camila, and the meals she made relied far less on packaged food than they used to. Holt must not have found her yet—her mood would be darker if he had. He wondered where his father had spent the day. He hadn't seen him since he stumbled out of the office, struck dumb by the news that Mia's baby was Ellis's, but he knew he'd see Holt soon enough. If his father didn't want this wedding to take place, he'd do everything in his power to prevent it, no matter what bet he'd made with Lisa.

The thought of what Holt might get up to had bothered him all day. For all Luke's bluster about Holt not kicking him off the ranch, he knew his father was perfectly capable of cutting off his nose to spite his face. What if Holt did give him the boot? How would he make a living and support Mia and the baby? Ranching was all he knew.

"My dad's on the warpath," he said without preamble when he entered the kitchen.

Mia stood on tiptoe to kiss him on the cheek and for a moment he lost track of his worry, distracted by the deliciousness of her so close to him. "Dinner's in half an hour," she said. "I've got some news, too."

"Did you hear what I said?" He let go of her reluctantly and leaned back against the counter.

"I'm going to start a business." Mia whirled around and picked up a wooden spoon, then stirred the pot on the stove.

"Dad's—what? What kind of business?"

"I'm going to be a wedding planner! I'll do everything from helping brides pick out their stationary and word their invitations, to handling receptions, the setup of party rentals, to finding the best location for destination weddings...."

"Wait, hold on." He couldn't keep up. "What are you talking about?"

"Me. Becoming a wedding planner. Working for myself. At first I'll still work at the restaurant while I'm building my business, but maybe someday I'll move into it full-time. Of course I'll refer all my brides to Fila's for catering. I'm going to practice on Rose. Isn't it a great idea?"

Mia wanted to start a business? Now? Where would she get that kind of cash? It wasn't like either of them had much to spare; between the ring and the truck he'd just spent a small fortune. "Are you kidding?"

"No." Her cheeks flushed pink. "I'm not kidding. I thought you'd be happy for me."

The tension that had tightened his muscles for hours threatened to do him in. Wasn't it bad enough that the ranch chores were out of hand, Amanda Stone probably needed a new roof, and he'd just taken on enough debt to keep him walking a tightrope for years? Now she wanted to add more chaos to the mix? "You can't do that," he managed to say finally.

"I *can't*?" Mia looked furious, her hands planted on her hips. "Guess what, Luke Matheson—you don't get to tell me what I can and can't do with my money."

"Our money, you mean."

Something flickered in her eyes. "It's not *our money* yet. And even when it is you don't get to take control of it."

"When it's *our* money, we'll both need to agree on what we spend it on. And I don't agree you can blow it on a wedding planning business."

"Well, I don't agree you can spend *our* money on that outrageous ring! Or that stupid truck!"

Her words hit him like a slap to the face. He'd bought the ring and the truck for her. "I need that *stupid truck* for my work here on the ranch. And that outrageous ring is going to stop people from talking about you!"

"You mean you hope it makes people stop talking about *you*! I'm starting that business. And I notice that Jake and Ned and Rob do just fine with their old trucks."

He'd done just fine with his old truck, too. Luke leaned toward her, the ache in the back of his neck blooming into a full-blown migraine. Couldn't she see he was trying to make her happy? Couldn't she see he wanted the best for them—the best for the baby? "We've got two weeks to pull our wedding together. And a couple of months to get ready for that child. Do you know anything about being a mother? Because you sure as hell don't know anything about starting a business!"

She gaped at him. "That's not fair!"

"Nothing about this is fair. It's not my fault you slept with Ellis, but everyone's acting like I drove you to it. Next thing they'll say I can't support you, let alone keep you out of another man's bed."

Mia dropped her spoon and her eyes filled with tears. Remorse flooded Luke. He was taking out his anger on the last person who deserved it. "Mia—"

She didn't stop to listen to him. She didn't stop at all. She grabbed her purse, her jacket, her keys and stuffed her feet into her boots. A minute later she slammed the front door behind her.

"Fuck." Luke slammed his fist down on the counter. He didn't need his father to drive Mia away.

He'd done a fine job of that himself.

"IT'S OVER. I won't go back. Luke's just as bad as Ellis," Mia told Autumn, who sat curled up on her sofa looking like the Madonna cradling her newborn baby. Mia sat nearby. "I'm sorry. You're the last person I should vent to. You need peace and quiet to enjoy Arianna."

"That's all right. You can tell me about it. I might not be much help, though." Autumn traced a finger over Arianna's softly rounded cheeks and Mia melted a little. In a few more months she'd have a baby to hold, too. Autumn looked up, caught Mia watching and smiled. "I know Luke loves you, Mia. That's obvious."

"He loves my looks, you mean. That's all he's ever noticed about me. He thinks I'm too stupid to start a business." As hard as she tried to hold it back, a tear slid down her cheek. She'd thought Luke saw past all that to what was inside her, but of course he hadn't. No man did.

"Did he say that?"

"He said if I work people will say he can't support me. Then he made a crack about me visiting other men's beds." She blinked rapidly as more tears threatened. "It's so unfair. It's not like I had a parade of boyfriends, and I thought Ellis loved me." It was like the pageant all over again—everyone believing the worst about her. No one taking her side.

"Luke said that?" Now she had Autumn's complete attention. "That doesn't sound like him."

"He was mad. Holt's gone off the deep end, of course."

"What did he do?"

"I don't know," Mia wailed. "We didn't get that far. Luke was too busy being an ass!"

"Sounds like emotions were running high."

Mia huffed out a breath. That was one way to put it. Another way would be to say the Matheson men were out of their minds. "Anyway, I'm done. I knew it would never work with Luke. I should have saved myself the heartache. I rang Thayer Jewelers and told them we didn't need the ring after all, and I called Ellie's Bridals and told her I didn't want the dress." Mia's voice wavered and she wiped her eyes with the back of her arm. Got herself under control again. "Do you think Luke will let his mom know she doesn't have to plan a wedding supper? Or should I call her, too?"

"Why don't you wait a day or two? See what happens. I'm sure Luke will apologize." Arianna yawned and Autumn's face went soft. "Oh, you're just the sweetest thing!" She planted a kiss on Arianna's head.

"She really is," Mia said, calming down a little. "It doesn't matter whether Luke apologizes or not. He doesn't respect me, and I won't marry a man who doesn't. Plus he seems to think he'll get to control my money the minute we're married."

"What money?" Autumn looked up quickly. "I'm sorry—that wasn't nice. I just didn't know you made much at the hardware store."

"I don't." Mia hesitated. She didn't think it was wise to tell anyone about the two hundred grand now sitting in her bank account. "But if and when I have some, it'll be for me to manage—not my husband."

"Maybe you should tell Luke how you want to handle things and see if you can come up with a compromise."

Mia shook her head. "Forget it. From now on I'll stay single. I don't need a man."

"Well, when Arianna's ready to get married you can plan her wedding." Autumn's attention drifted again. Mia didn't blame her. The precious little girl in her arms was worthy of her mother's undivided attention.

"I hate to ask, but can I have my old room back for a while? I promise I'll help out with the baby," Mia said. "And I'll pay rent, of course."

"Sure thing. We won't have any guests for the next month. We blacked out the dates specifically to give us time to get used to being parents. It'll be great to have another pair of hands around for a few weeks. By then you and Luke will be back together."

Mia sighed. Was no one prepared to take her seriously? She shook her head. They never had, had they? So why should they start now?

As Autumn cooed to Arianna, Mia came to another important decision. It was no use speaking up about the past—what had happened with Fred Warner. No one would listen to her. Nothing would change. She'd just expose herself to more ridicule and gossip.

And she'd had enough of that.

"WHO WAS THAT?" Jake asked later that evening when Luke clicked off his phone and stuck it in his back pocket. The two of them were out in front of Jake's cabin where they were trying to un-jam the snowplow blade on Jake's truck in the glare of the cabin's flood-lights. More snow was due overnight, which meant they needed to be able to plow the driveway and lanes around the ranch. It also meant he'd have to make time to get over to Amanda Stone's house, too, in the morning to shovel her walk again. Which was the least of his problems right now. He took a deep breath.

"Thayer's."

"Is Mia's engagement ring ready?"

"No. They called to tell me she said she doesn't want it."

"Shit." Jake turned to him. "She must be pretty pissed if she's given back your ring."

"You think?"

Rob stepped out onto the front porch of the main house, spotted them and waved. A minute later he joined them. "What's up?"

"Mia dumped Luke." Jake went back to working on the mechanism holding the snowplow blade in place.

"A one-day engagement. That's got to be a record or something," Rob put in.

"Shut up." Luke's jaw tightened as he fought for control. He didn't know whether to go find Mia and talk some sense into her, or give her time to cool down. The thought of doing nothing had his shoulders bunching and the muscles in his neck tying themselves in knots.

"Calm down. You'll get her back," Jake said. "Just go find her and turn on the Matheson charm."

"I don't think that will work. Not this time." Mia had already proven herself immune to it.

"And you were worried that Dad would scare her

off. Where'd he go, anyhow?"

"I don't know. He got a phone call this morning and he's been gone all day." Luke was glad he hadn't seen Holt. If it wasn't for his father, he wouldn't have flown off the handle and yelled at Mia like that. Jake was right, he needed to talk to Mia—just as soon as she got home. He'd waited an hour in the cabin, then packed up the dinner she'd made. Jake's knock on the door to ask for his help had come as a relief. He couldn't sit still another minute. He could see now this wedding planner idea was important to Mia. He could scare up a few dollars to help her get started, maybe.

Emphasis on maybe. In truth he was a tiny bit relieved she'd cancelled the ring. He did want her to have something special enough to stop all the speculation about his commitment to their marriage, but after their blow-out he'd had to admit to himself the ring would take years to pay off. That wasn't very practical. Not to mention the damned truck payment. The fact that Mia hadn't even been impressed by it—or the ring—galled him. Why'd he let his brothers convince him he needed something so flashy to win Mia's love?

And why had he pushed Mia so hard to accept a ring she didn't even want? The ring she'd liked was far more affordable. He should have let her have her way.

"Did you see what Cab did to my topiary horse?" Rob asked them. "Sick son of a bitch."

Despite his problems, Luke chuckled.

"It's not funny. I'm going to have to take the whole damn bush out and start over," Rob said.

"Aw, come on—there's still enough left you can turn

it into a horse," Jake said.

"A quarter horse, maybe," Luke said.

"Ha, ha, very funny." Rob's eyes flashed with anger. "Those bushes aren't cheap, I'll have you know. Not ones that big."

"I'm sure you'll recover from the expense," Jake said.

Luke's laughter died away. He wasn't sure he'd recover from his own expenses any time soon. It weighed on him that his credit card had a running total, too. He'd never meant to accrue it, but life was expensive and until recently Holt had barely paid any of them for their help around the ranch. Instead he'd given them an allowance that was enough to make a payment on a beater truck, cover drinks at the Dancing Boot and that was about it. He'd used his credit card to bridge the gaps in his income. That had been a mistake.

He wouldn't be able to front Mia much money for this new business she wanted, which made him angry all over again. He wasn't sure she'd find enough clients in Chance Creek, anyway, and they couldn't afford to throw good money after bad.

Still, if it was a business she wanted he'd try to help her. Anything to make her happy—to convince her to give him a second shot. A new thought occurred to him—what if she didn't come back? He shook his head. She had to come back. He loved her. One night with her in his bed had done nothing to quench his desire for her. When they'd talked of marriage, one thought had been uppermost in his mind: that every night she'd be waiting for him to come home. He liked the thought of her eager for his company, touching him as she served the evening meal, snuggling up close when they watched television afterward, leading him by the hand to their bedroom.

It was selfish. It was old-fashioned. It was probably wrong.

But could anyone blame him?

Chapter Eight

"HERE YOU GO," Hannah said the next day, handing Mia a small suitcase. "I hope you know what you're doing. I felt like a secret agent slipping into your cabin and rummaging through your things."

"Thanks for using up your lunch hour to do it," Mia said. Between work at the Pet Clinic and school, Mia knew Hannah rarely even took lunch, so she'd felt bad about asking her to sneak enough clothing and toiletries out of Luke's cabin to see her through her exile at Autumn and Ethan's place.

"That's all right. Next time I need someone to infiltrate my house I'll know who to call. I think you might be overreacting, though. You shouldn't dump Luke over one little fight."

Not Hannah, too. Everyone seemed to take Luke's side. Even the people who didn't come right out and say so made it clear they thought she was crazy to leave him. She knew what they thought: Luke was willing to take care of her, even when her baby wasn't his, so she should let him. Everyone obviously thought she was incapable of caring for herself, so they didn't see why she'd turn him down.

"It was a pretty big fight, actually—our ideas about marriage and how we want to live are totally incompatible. He was completely against me starting a business."

"You are having a baby soon."

Mia tried not to take it personally, but it really bothered her that no one thought her wedding planner idea was worth a try. No one but Rose, that was. "Don't you think I can do both?"

Hannah shrugged. "Maybe. But Luke's going to inherit a quarter of the Double-Bar-K eventually. Think of the lifestyle he could give you and your baby."

"Jake's going to inherit, too, but that hasn't stopped you from pursuing your dreams. Why doesn't anybody think I can do this? What is it? Am I stupid? Naïve?"

"You're twenty-one. You're pregnant. You barely graduated from high school." Hannah ticked the reasons off on her fingers.

Mia reared back. "Hey! It's okay for me to say that about myself. It's not okay for you to go on about it."

"You asked me a direct question and I gave you a direct answer. I don't want to hurt your feelings, but the way you act is the way people perceive you, Mia. If you go around dressing like a teenager, people will treat you like a teenager. If you make mistakes, like it or not you'll be judged for those mistakes."

Mistakes. She'd sure made a lot of them, and she'd suffered for every one. Which was exactly why she'd called Inez and told her she wouldn't take part in her campaign to get Warner off the beauty pageant judge circuit. Inez hadn't been happy, of course. Her final words had stayed with Mia all morning, flooding her with shame. "I get it. No one stuck up for you when Warner hurt you. I guess you think you don't need to stick up for anyone else."

All she'd get for speaking up would be more judgment, though, and people were judging her enough. Just wait until her belly was as big as Autumn's had been. The whole town would be talking about her.

Mia scrambled to her feet and made a show of looking at her watch. "You'll be late getting back to work. Thanks for all your help."

Hannah sighed. "I'm not trying to be a bitch, Mia. I'm trying to help. If you want to be taken seriously, you need to be serious. Go ahead and prove everyone wrong. I'd like that more than anything. And for what it's worth, I think you do have what it takes to be a wedding planner, but only if you take it seriously. Stop trying to be such a beauty queen all the time and be a grownup instead."

Be a grownup. Wasn't that what she was trying to do? Didn't grownups provide for themselves? Didn't they stand up for themselves, too?

Don't they stand up for others? a small voice inside asked. She pushed the thought away. She couldn't take on Warner right now—she just couldn't.

Mia kept quiet as she showed Hannah to the door, then returned to her room to unpack the bag Hannah had brought. The room was small but pleasant, with a queen-sized bed, desk, dresser and its own bathroom. Its window overlooked pastures that sloped off down to Chance Creek, but at the moment even the gorgeous view couldn't lift Mia's spirits.

She thumped the suitcase down on top of the bed and unzipped it, but before she started unpacking she trailed across the room to look in the mirror above the dresser. As much as she hated to admit it, Hannah was right; she did dress young for her age. Today she looked like a teenager, and a rather sullen teenager at that. The beauty queen remark was completely unfair though. She grimaced at her reflection. Or maybe not. It was true she never left the house before she put on her makeup and pulled her waist-length sleek, black hair up into her signature high ponytail. She knew the deceptively schoolgirl look left it swishing seductively with her every movement. Knew too that ponytail fascinated men. She wore clothes that accentuated her figure. She always had. *She's not too bright, but she's a looker.* How many times had someone said that about her? Or her favorite: *Don't worry about your grades, honey; that figure will land you a good husband.*

People were right; she'd never done terribly well at school. Her pageant schedule kept her too busy to study much. By the time that ended she had other things on her mind. She was sure she could have done much better if she'd applied herself, but maybe not. She frowned at her reflection. Maybe she was as dumb as everyone thought.

No. She wasn't going to talk herself down anymore; she had plenty of other people to do that. She had a baby to care for now, which meant it was time to get her act together. Hannah was right. If she wanted people to take her seriously, she needed a new look. She could spend just a little of Ellis's money on that, couldn't she?

She met her own gaze in the mirror and nodded firmly. Yes, she could.

MIA HADN'T COME home.

Luke sat on the sofa in the dark in the cabin's small living room. Once he'd arrived home, exhausted from rushing through his chores, then going to help Amanda Stone with hers, he'd parked himself there, expecting Mia to arrive any minute and explain where she'd been. He hadn't believed it when she never came home the night before. He'd barely slept a wink, pacing the living room floor until all hours. He'd spent all day hoping she'd finally appear so they could make up, then maybe go out to dinner like he'd planned, or skip all that and go straight to bed. He'd meant to carefully explain his reservations about her wedding planner idea, but tell her he was prepared to be supportive.

He never got the chance. Mia was through with him.

His phone rang at nine and he jumped to answer it, only to find Ethan on the line.

"She's here," he said simply. "Thought you'd want to know. She's packed enough to stay a while."

Luke couldn't believe he hadn't thought to check Mia's room. Had she snuck back in while he was doing his chores to pack her things? He'd been so sure this was a temporary setback. If he was honest, he'd admit he didn't think she'd have the guts to leave him for good—not in her situation. In his mind he'd built a whole daydream in which she was the helpless maiden and he was the savior on a big, white horse. Turned out Mia didn't want saving.

At least not yet.

She'd change her mind, though. She had to. How would she manage once she'd had her baby if he wasn't there to support her? How would she pay for childcare when her job at the restaurant paid minimum wage? Even if she didn't love him, she'd see what he had to offer her. A good home. A secure job.

Hell.

Luke surged up off the sofa and paced the room. He didn't want her to need him—he wanted her to want him. To love him back as much as he loved her. What if she'd thought it over and decided she didn't? Fifteen minutes later, his mind no clearer, he entered the kitchen and opened the fridge. He hadn't eaten dinner—hadn't had time. When he spotted the neatly stacked storage containers of leftovers from the last meal Mia cooked, his heart sunk. What if she never came back?

He reached for one to reheat in the microwave, then spotted a fresh six-pack and grabbed a can instead. Maybe he'd just drink his dinner. At least that way he'd sleep tonight.

He was such a fool. He'd been a lousy fiancé. He'd undercut her the first time she'd shared her dreams with him—bullied her about what she should do with her life.

No wonder she left him high and dry.

Eight hours later, pounding on his door woke him up. Stiff and sore after a night on the couch, he sat up slowly, groaning when he took in the crumpled cans on the sofa, coffee table and floor. His head ached and his tongue was thick in his mouth. Another rough day of work. Another night without Mia. What was the point of going on? A glance out his window told him the predict-ed snow had fallen and he groaned. He'd have to clear Amanda's walkway again.

The pounding started up again. "Luke? You in there?"

Jake. For God's sake, couldn't his family leave him alone for two minutes? He lurched across the floor, the polished wood smooth and cold beneath his bare feet.

"What?" He opened the door a crack. Jake pushed his way in.

"Jesus, it stinks like a bar in here. What the hell, Luke?"

"Leave me alone." He turned away, ready to collapse back on the couch.

"It's five-thirty. You're late. Dad called me to roust you out of bed."

Double hell. Late for chores wasn't a good choice to make on the Double-Bar-K. "Why'd he call you? Why not do it himself?"

"He said he couldn't talk to you."

That sobered Luke up in a hurry. Holt unable to talk? That was a first. "You think he's still mad?"

"I'd say that's an understatement. Get your shit to-gether and get to the barn. I'm supposed to be helping Evan today. And I've got class in a few hours, too."

"Give me five minutes." Luke rubbed a hand over his face. Felt the stubble on his jaw. He needed a shower and a shave, but that would have to wait. The critters came first.

Ten minutes later the cold February air cleared the last of the cobwebs from his brain as he hurried through the snow to the barn. Mia hadn't come home. And she'd given back the engagement ring. Those were drastic steps for her to take. She was serious in her determination to leave him.

And what had he done? Sat on the couch? Gotten drunk? Hell of a way to get her back.

Jake met him halfway. "It's all yours, buddy. I'm off."

"What the hell do I do?" He hated the desperation that rang in his voice.

"Feed the damn cows, what do you think…oh, you mean about Mia?" Jake shoved his hands in his jacket pockets. "Find out what she wants and give it to her. That's the easiest way, I've found." He shook his head. "We might be bigger and stronger than them, but we don't seem to win many arguments. Good luck with that, and by the way—Dad's taking this not talking thing pretty seriously. Guess he really doesn't want to go to Paris."

Luke nodded. "Guess so." No wonder Holt had bolted yesterday. No wonder he hadn't stopped by last night to chew him out.

Luke headed back to his cabin several hours later, hoping to find Mia there, but he could tell from fifty feet away she still hadn't returned. No lights were on inside and the driveway in front was empty of any vehicles except his own. His trip out to Amanda's place had been for nothing. Her walkway had been clean as a whistle when he reached her house. She'd stepped out to tell him a friend had stopped by and done the work.

Now he stopped in front of the stairs leading up to

the cabin, unwilling to encounter the silence inside. The beep of a car's horn made him jump and he turned to see a Chevy Malibu pull up beside him. He was surprised to find Camila Torres behind the wheel. She rolled down the passenger side window. "I saw you walking and thought I'd come say hi before I stopped by your parents' house. Is your dad around?"

"Should be," Luke said. "What do you want him for?"

"Oh, I just thought I'd drop off a couple of enchiladas for your parents' lunch. You know Holt loves enchiladas."

Luke scowled. Holt had acquired a taste for Mexican food in recent weeks, an unusual turn of events for a meat and potatoes kind of man. He still wouldn't admit that any fare at Fila's Familia was fit to eat, but Luke had seen him consume both Fila's Afghan food and Camila's Mexican dishes at the restaurant's test run with the same relish with which he demolished a steak.

"You drove all the way out here to drop off lunch?"

She smiled sweetly. "Anything to make a potential customer happy. See you around, Luke. Oh, by the way... Mia will be in at the restaurant later today. Our opening is coming right up."

"I appreciate the information." He straightened up and watched Camila turn the car around and drive back toward the main house. He'd find a reason to head into town and pop in at the restaurant. He and Mia had some talking to do.

"DON'T YOU DARE!" Rose called out as she burst into

Marjorie's Manes and dashed across the beauty parlor to yank the scissors from Marjorie Douglas's hand.

Marjorie shrieked and tugged Mia's thick ponytail hard, wrenching Mia's head back against the plastic-covered seat.

"Ouch! Rose, what are you doing?" Mia cried.

"I saw you through the window. You can't cut your hair! Are you crazy? Most women would kill to have this." She batted Marjorie's hands away again and fluffed Mia's thick, straight locks.

Mia shrugged her off. "I want a change. All this hair makes me look about ten years old." It was also one of the features that drew men's attention her way, and Mia had decided after thinking long and hard that drawing men's attention was what had gotten her in trouble every time. A short, short haircut would change all that.

Rose eased between Marjorie and Mia, keeping the hairdresser at bay. "Your hair makes you look utterly beautiful, Mia."

"Being beautiful hasn't done me much good, has it?" She failed to keep the pain out of her voice.

Rose softened. "Being beautiful is part of who you are, though. You don't have to cover that up if it's respect you're after. And you don't have to cut it if you want a more sophisticated style, either; you just need to change it up. Marjorie, show her some updos, would you?"

"Sure thing. Let's start with a chignon." Marjorie looked relieved and Mia stifled a groan. It had taken her ten minutes to talk the stylist into giving her a short haircut. Now that Rose had interfered, she'd never manage it again.

"I wanted a big change. Something that people will notice."

"They'll notice this," Marjorie insisted. She manipulated Mia's hair with deft fingers and in no time flat she'd sleeked it back into the sophisticated style. "What do you think?"

Mia tilted her head to examine herself from different angles. She did look different. Older. More worldly. "Not bad," she admitted. "But I'm not sure I can do it myself." Was the change drastic enough? She wasn't sure. She'd wanted to draw a line in the sand between the old, pushover Mia and the new, confident, competent one.

"Sure you can. It just takes practice," Rose said. "Marjorie will show you, then you can try. This style makes you look really mature."

That's what she was shooting for. Mia relaxed back into the chair and let Marjorie have at it. The hairdresser demonstrated the style step by step, then took it out and let Mia try. After Mia had practiced it several times, Marjorie demonstrated a French braid, several kinds of buns from severe to sexy, and several beautiful twists.

"What about makeup?" Rose asked when they were running out of styles.

Mia wrinkled her nose. "What about it?" She had plenty of makeup. She wore it every day.

"Let's go buy some new stuff when you're done here."

New stuff? "What's wrong with what I've got on?" She caught the look that passed between Marjorie and

Rose. "What?"

"Honey, you're beautiful," Rose said. "And you put on your makeup like a pro. It's just you always apply it like you're about to take to the stage. You said you wanted to change your look. Let's try lightening it up a little. I bet you'll like the results. We'll go look at some clothes, too. Some sophisticated clothes."

Several hours later, Rose and Mia stumbled out of the freezing wind that had kicked up into the living room of the Cruz guesthouse, laden down with shopping bags, to find Rob, Cab, Jamie and Ethan sitting at the table eating a mid-afternoon snack.

"What's going on? Where's Autumn?" Rose said, unwinding her scarf from around her neck. Mia peeled off her coat and stepped out of her boots, still shivering from the cold.

"Sleeping," Ethan said. "All those two do is sleep. I'll take her something in a minute."

"But first we have to settle this once and for all," Rob said. "It's cowboys."

"Man, you're full of shit. It's sheriffs," Cab said, and took a bite of his sandwich. Rose trailed over and kissed him on the head.

"Whatever it is, it's definitely sheriffs," she said.

"What's the question?" Mia asked. "Which one's sexier? Cowboys, hands down." She bit her lip. She wasn't supposed to be interested in her cowboy anymore.

Cab turned around. "The question was who's more badass, cowboys or sheriffs, but I'll have you know sheriffs are a helluva lot more sexy than any cowboy."

Rob snorted. "You wouldn't know sexy if it bit you

on the ass."

"Cab's the epitome of sexy," Rose said, dropping down into the seat beside him. "As for badass, there isn't a cowboy in the world as badass as you, baby."

"Ugh," Rob said. "That's downright embarrassing. Jamie, tell Cab he's not sexy and he's not badass."

"Hell, I can't do that," Jamie drawled. "Cab's the sexiest, most bad-assed sheriff I know." He blew a kiss at Cab. Cab pelted him with a piece of his sandwich.

"I'm going to take this stuff upstairs before my IQ level drops to that of the present company," Mia said.

"I'll join you in a minute," Rose said. "I'm pretty smart, so I can lose a few points while I grab a glass of water."

Mia trailed up the stairs to her room, dropped her bags on the floor and flopped onto her bed. She wondered if people would have taken her more seriously all along if she'd changed her look before now. Maybe Ellis wouldn't have played with her the way he did. Maybe Luke would think she was capable of running her own business. Rose found her a few minutes later. "Who knew this transformation stuff could be so exhausting," she said, stretching out beside Mia.

"I'm the one doing the transforming," Mia pointed out.

"Thank goodness. It's tiring enough just watching you. I can't wait to see what people think about the new you, though."

"I've got to get to the restaurant now. I'm supposed to help out. I don't know if I can even stand up, though. We hit every store in town."

"Just be grateful we don't live in a big city. We

wouldn't have made it home for a week. Come on, let's pick out an outfit for the brand-new Mia Start."

"What, right now?"

"No time like the present."

Mia got up slowly. Rose was right. Mia the beauty queen was dead. Time to unleash Mia the businesswoman on the world.

LUKE IGNORED THE hand-lettered sign announcing that Fila's Familia would open in March and barged through the door, letting a swoosh of icy wind blow into the restaurant with him. He was ready to confront Mia and demand she come home. At first he'd taken Jake's advice to give her whatever she wanted to heart. He'd prepared to come and discuss her business notion and see what he could do to help. But as the day progressed, he grew angry that she found it so easy to turn her back on their engagement. One little hiccup and she was out of there. He figured it was time they both put their cards on the table. He wanted to be with her. He wanted to know if she wanted to be with him. If she did, then to hell with the rest of it—they had to stick together through thick and thin. He'd tell her she couldn't walk away from him again. If they fought, they'd argue through an issue until they reached a resolution.

The restaurant was empty, however—except for a woman behind the counter with her back turned to him. Small and slight, like Mia, her dark hair was pulled up in a severe chignon—a style Mia never wore. The woman rummaged through some supplies stacked on shelving that ran the length of the back wall. Luke cleared his throat.

The woman straightened. Turned slowly.

Luke gaped.

It was Mia. But a Mia as unlike herself as a moth to a butterfly. Her new hairstyle made her look ten years older. Her bright, dramatic makeup was gone—no, not gone, just drastically lightened. What little she did wear made her softer somehow. More mature.

Even her clothes were different. On a day like today when her work might consist of heavy-duty scrubbing, he'd expect to find her in ratty, torn jeans and a tight T-shirt that showed all her blessed curves. Instead she was downright matronly in classically cut slacks and a fresh blue blouse.

Where was his Mia? His fun-loving, sassy, sexy Mia? Who was this…woman? The tirade he meant to unleash fell away.

"I'm right here," Mia said, as if in answer to his question, and she even sounded different. Stiff. Mature. Like a school teacher. "What do you need?"

Need? He needed the woman he loved. The original one, not this frumpy, new version. Not that she looked all that frumpy, he admitted to himself. Not really. A little more mature, maybe, but still beautiful; nothing she wore could ever hide the truth of Mia's body. Still, these clothes and that hairstyle didn't stir up his libido like her normal style did. Mia used to be sex on a stick. Now she was…he didn't know how to put it.

Respectable.

"Luke?"

"I… uh…" Hell, he was stuttering like a child. "I need to talk to you." There. That was direct.

"What about?"

"What about?" He braced his hands on the counter. "About us, that's what. About you walking out on me."

"I don't want to talk about it."

"You're gonna talk about it." He stared at Mia. A stranger stared back at him. He expected her to give in, or at least look away first. This Mia met his gaze as bold as brass.

"No, Luke, I'm not. Not while I'm at work, anyway. If you have something to say to me you can meet me tonight at Ethan and Autumn's place. Where I live now. We can make arrangements then for me to pick up the rest of my things."

"Damn it, Mia!" He leaned farther over the counter. "You said you would marry me."

"And you said I didn't know a thing about business!" The cool, collected new Mia suddenly lost her control. "You said you couldn't keep me out of other men's beds." Two bright spots of color highlighted her barely-rouged cheeks. "I don't need anyone to say things like that about me. Certainly not my fiancé. Go on, get out of here. Go back to your cattle. That's what you really want, isn't it? Not a wife—just another cow to herd."

She slammed through the swinging doors that led to the kitchen and they shut behind her, leaving Luke alone again. A cow to herd? That wasn't what he wanted at all.

He wanted a wife. He wanted Mia. And damn it, he was going to get her back. Before he could follow her into the kitchen, however, his cell phone rang. He answered it when he saw the call was from his mother.

"Luke? You'd better get back here quick. We've got a problem."

Chapter Nine

"SOMEONE LEFT A letter for you today," Ethan said when Mia arrived back at the Cruz ranch later that afternoon.

"A letter? Like a bill?"

"No—a real letter. Don't see many of those these days." He handed her the thin envelope and Mia frowned at the shaky block letters that made up the address. She didn't recognize the handwriting. In fact, she was amazed the post office had been able to make out the directions, the printing was so uncertain. She slipped a finger under the flap and forced the envelope open to find a single small square of paper inside.

Mary him.

There was no signature. Nothing except those two words. Mia shook her head at the misspelling. Who could have written it? Was this some kind of a joke?

"What is it?" Ethan said, looking up from his own bills long enough to notice her confusion. She handed the slip of paper over to him. His eyebrows shot up as he read the words. "Marry him? Huh, that's pretty direct.

Who's it from?"

"I don't know. I've never seen anything like this handwriting. It looks like a child's."

Ethan was quiet a moment. "The postmark says Chance Creek. Do any kids in town know about your situation?"

"I don't think so. It's not like I have any nieces or nephews."

"A mystery, then." He smiled. "Maybe you should marry Luke."

"Not you, too."

"Come on. Give the guy a break. He's crazy about you. Has been for ages."

"He's crazy about getting laid." She would have laughed at Ethan's shocked expression if the topic didn't anger her so much. "He's not crazy about what's up here." She tapped her forehead, remembering the way he'd stared at her in the restaurant this afternoon—like she'd suddenly grown horns. He obviously didn't like her new look at all.

"Well, he is a man."

"Don't give me that. I've lived with you and Autumn, remember? I know what a real marriage is supposed to be like. Until I can find a man ready to give me that, I'll stay on my own, thank you very much."

"He'll get there," Ethan said. "Just give him a little time." Mia wanted to hug the tall cowboy for his sentiment, but she held back, both out of a sense of propriety and because she wasn't at all sure he was right.

"I hope so."

BY THE TIME Luke walked through his front door that evening he felt like he'd been flattened by a freight train. The icy wind that had whipped through Chance Creek all day had pushed the snow in the pastures into drifts, and his mother had called because it packed so hard in one place that a dozen head of cattle had wandered right up and over a fence. He'd spent all afternoon searching for them, luring them back into their pasture and fixing the fence. Now his muscles ached, he was dog-tired and hungry as anything, too. He'd taken another run out to Amanda's place and been relieved to find that all was well. Maybe some old geezer had taken a fancy to her because she referenced her *friend* again, and her walkway was clear of snow.

The envelope lying on the floor of his cabin stopped Luke in his tracks. Was it from Mia? His heart rate kicked up a notch as he bent down to retrieve it. It was odd Mia would write a letter rather than text him. She was rarely without her phone. His stomach dropped as he took in the address, written in uneven block letters, as if done by a kid—or a psychopath. What kind of letter was this?

He made short work of opening it. Two words were written on a scrap of paper in the same block handwriting he'd seen on the envelope.

Buety Pagint.

What the hell did that mean?

Luke squinted at the paper. Cocked his head. Beauty pageant? Some squirt of a kid didn't even know how to spell the words? What kind of a stupid joke was this?

He stumbled toward the couch, sat down heavily and

leaned back against the cushions. Beauty pageant. The words meant nothing to him, although…didn't Mia used to be in those pageants when she was young? He wondered which of her friends would know the answer to that. He couldn't ask Mia directly, not after their last confrontation. If he did, she'd say he didn't listen to her, and that wasn't true—it was just sometimes when she was talking he made the mistake of looking at her and then he lost his concentration.

Beauty pageants. Who knew about beauty pageants?

He let the letter fall from his hand.

Rose Bellingham. He'd bet anything she had the skinny on them. She was close to Mia's age, too.

He'd call Rose tomorrow and ask a few questions. Better yet, he'd head over to the Cruz ranch to talk with her face-to-face. He let his head fall back against the cushions and shut his eyes, just for a moment. Tonight he needed to head to the Cruz ranch to talk to Mia. Maybe she'd have calmed down by now. She couldn't stay mad at him forever.

He hoped.

A second later, he was asleep.

MARRY HIM. THE note she'd received was still on Mia's mind when she returned from work late the following afternoon. Why should she marry him? Luke hadn't even bothered to stop by and talk last night like she'd suggested when he came to the restaurant yesterday afternoon. Apparently, sorting out their differences wasn't all that important to him.

She shook her head as she made her way up to her

room. Alone in the big house, she was all too aware of the many empty rooms around hers. Ethan and Autumn still made their home in the converted bunkhouse on the property. They hoped to build a family suite on the first floor of the guesthouse, but hadn't earned enough from running it yet to justify the cost.

She was about to descend to the main floor and make use of the wide screen television there when she saw movement outside and went to the window to see who it was.

It was Luke. But instead of coming to the guesthouse, he was walking toward another cabin on the property—the one where Cab and Rose lived. As partners in the ranch, they'd moved onto the property a few months ago. Mia felt a pang of jealousy that they'd invited Luke for dinner and not her. No one in their right mind would invite both of them when they were fighting, but if the couple was going to choose one of them to cheer up, shouldn't it be her? She was good friends with Rose.

Luke wasn't that close with Cab, was he?

She stood on her tiptoes and watched Luke disappear among the trees that separated Cab and Rose's cabin from the guesthouse. Through the branches, the small house blazed with light and looked cozy as could be in the dark, snowy landscape. That's how Luke's cabin would look if she still lived there with him. For the first time her anger diminished enough for her to wonder if she'd been wrong to leave.

No. She wasn't wrong. He'd said horrible things to her.

She turned away from the window, wishing more than anything for someone's company. When her phone rang a few minutes later, she grabbed it and held it to her ear.

"Hello?"

"Have you lost your mind?"

She stifled a groan. Her mother.

"It isn't bad enough you're pregnant with a married man's baby? Now you've thrown over Luke, too? Are you going to sleep with the entire town?"

"Only the male half." Shoot, had she actually said that out loud? Yes, she had. And her mother was not amused.

"You get over there and beg him to take you back. He was willing to make an honest woman of you, something that Scranton man certainly wasn't. You won't get another chance like this, believe me. You're used goods, Mia Start. No man's going to want you now."

Mia clicked the phone off, the first time she'd ever hung up on her mother. Used goods. What was this, the nineteenth century?

She paced the living room in the Cruz guesthouse, too agitated to watch television now. It all came down to gossip, didn't it? Her mother didn't want to be shunned at her church. Luke didn't want to be talked about by his friends. Now she was supposed to be too embarrassed to show her face.

And she was too embarrassed to speak up about the incident with Warner. Too embarrassed to speak up and maybe stop it from happening to someone else. She sat down on the couch as painful memories from the past swirled through her mind. She remembered the way the other girls at the pageant had looked at her, the way they'd repeated the rumors that she'd tried to trade sexual favors in order to win. The way everyone had retreated from her when she walked into a room—as if she carried a fatal disease that they might catch.

She stood up and strode to the kitchen. Maybe cooking her dinner would dispel both the memories and the pain. She wasn't ready to speak up about Warner and expose herself to that kind of treatment all over again.

She just couldn't. Not now.

"THANKS FOR DINNER," Luke said as he pushed back from the table. Fried chicken, mashed potatoes, gravy, and green beans. What more could a man ask from a meal? Except to have it served by his fiancée, not his friend.

"No problem." Rose smiled at him. She and Cab had welcomed him into their house and invited him to dinner as soon as he showed up at their door. Normally he considered Cab more Rob's friend than his own, but the sheriff was a good host and had enough stories to tell to make any social occasion an interesting one.

"How's Mia doing?" Cab asked, finishing his own meal.

Luke shrugged. "That's what I came to talk about. Is there something I should know about her past? About the time when she was doing those pageants?"

Rose looked surprised. "Pageants? That was a long time ago. She stopped doing them when she was about fifteen, right?"

"I don't know. Can't say I was paying attention back then." He grinned, relaxed by the good meal and good company. "Would have been pretty creepy if I had been, seeing as how I was about twenty-three." Luke went on to describe the weird note he received and didn't miss the look that passed between Cab and Rose. "What?"

Rose shrugged and looked uncomfortable. "Well, I wasn't friends with Mia either, back then—there are a couple of years between us—but I knew her, and those pageants were icky if you ask me."

"What do you mean?"

Rose took a moment to answer. "I guess a lot of the girls wanted to be there, but there were others who competed because their mothers wanted them to, you know? And I think Mia was one of them."

Luke didn't know Enid Start all that well. She was short, like Mia, and decidedly middle-aged. In her conservative clothes and understated makeup, she kind of faded into the background, so it hadn't occurred to him that she would be the motivation behind Mia doing pageants.

"Mia didn't want to do them?"

"I'm not sure I'm explaining this right," Rose said, offering him a basket of biscuits. "Little kids don't sign themselves up for pageants, right? Someone has to do that for them. Mia started really young. And I get why a parent would do it, you know? You get to dress your kid up and show them off, but by the time they're preteens, it's a little dicey. You have to ask yourself why a mother would want her daughter to stand in front of a crowd in a fancy dress—and then a bikini—to be judged on how her body looks."

"Lots of girls do beauty pageants. It doesn't hurt them." Luke had grown up seeing articles in the local newspaper about them. He knew plenty of girls who had participated.

"No, you're right. It's probably fine for most girls, but I don't think it's good for all of them. For some it's too much pressure. I mean, what kind of a message does it send?

"The kind of message that gets women killed," Cab put in darkly.

Rose shot him a look. "That's going too far. Beauty pageants don't lead to murder—but they can lead to bad body images."

"When you train a woman to need approval or to determine her self-worth that way, you train her to be vulnerable." Cab was adamant.

"I'm not disputing that," Rose said. "But back to your question, Luke. Mia's mom put far more emphasis on those pageants than she did school. She made it pretty clear: Mia's job was to look good enough for a man to want to support her."

"Well, it worked," Luke joked. "She looks great and I do want to support her. Nothing but the best for my Mia."

Rose shook her head. "You're missing the point. It's Enid who thinks she should trade looks for security. Not Mia."

"I don't want to trade anything," Luke said. "I just want to marry her."

"Then maybe you better start by figuring out why Mia quit those pageants—because she did, all of a sudden. There were some rumors, too—nasty ones." Rose stabbed a piece of chicken so hard her fork scraped across the plate.

"What kind of rumors?"

"I hate to even repeat them, since they've finally died down over the years." Rose took in his expression and sighed. "There were rumors Mia offered to trade favors for the crown of one of the more important pageants."

Luke pushed back from the table. "No way. Not Mia."

"No. Of course not. But something happened, and whoever sent you that message wants you to know what it was. If I were you, I'd look into it."

A wave of defeat overtook Luke. Of course he'd look into it, but when would he have time? And what had happened to Mia when she was fifteen?

His fists clenched under the table. He was damn sure going to find out.

Chapter Ten

"**A**RE YOU SURE you still want to help me plan my wedding?" Rose asked the next day when Mia joined her at Linda's Diner for a breakfast meeting. Mia had opted to hold the meeting away from both Rose's cabin and the Cruz guesthouse, needing a change of scenery after spending the previous night wondering what Luke's visit had entailed.

"Of course." But the truth was, she wanted to grill Rose about what Luke had said the night before far more than she wanted to talk about invitations.

"Listen." Rose cupped her mug of coffee with both hands, huddling over it as if hoping it would warm her entire body. "Luke stopped by last night. He ended up staying for dinner. I hope you don't mind."

"I don't mind. He's your friend."

"Sort of," Rose said. "Anyway, he asked about you."

"Oh?" She tried to be nonchalant. Probably failed.

"About your pageant days."

Mia stilled. "Why did he want to know about that?"

"I don't know." Rose took a sip of her strong, black coffee. "I might have spoken out of turn."

Mia's unease deepened. Why did the pageants keep coming up suddenly? She'd put all of that behind her years ago. "What did you say?"

"I told him your mom pushed you to do them. That maybe you would have preferred to do something else."

Mia wrinkled her nose. "Damn straight. I wanted to get a job so I could save up for a car. Plus…" She trailed off, not eager to talk about the rest of it.

"Plus what?"

"There was an… incident. A judge who got a little handsy. You know."

Rose pushed her cup away. "I might have mentioned that, too," she said in a small voice.

Mia's heart sunk.

"I'm sorry," Rose rushed on. "It just came out. I didn't think until later that maybe you hoped he didn't know."

"Well, he knows now," Mia said. She felt like a noose was tightening around her neck. She wanted to get away from the past, but it kept creeping up on her and drawing her in again.

"What happened?"

Mia considered refusing to talk about it, but decided to open up instead. She could use a friend's opinion about what to do, and Rose had proved herself a true friend these last few days.

"I was fifteen and competing in my first big pageant. I was so nervous. I wanted to win so badly. It was the one place my mom and I really connected, you know? I knew she'd be proud of me if I won, and besides—who doesn't want to be crowned queen?"

She took a sip of her orange juice. "Fred Warner was one of the judges. I met him in one of the practice sessions, where they tell you how the pageant will go—where to stand, and so on. He seemed ancient to me, but was probably only middle-aged. He was kind. Asked me if it was my first big pageant. Gave me some tips. He told jokes, too, and made me relax. I thought he was like any other adult I might meet—like one of my parents' friends, or someone from church." She swallowed hard. "But during the second practice session, he took me aside. He led me to a storeroom in the convention center where the pageant was being held. I'd seen one of the other girls come out of that room with him, so I believed him when he said he was just giving some of the better contestants some special tips." She lowered her gaze. "You can imagine what happened next."

"Oh, Mia."

Mia pushed on. "It wasn't as bad as it could have been. He got me in a tight clinch. His hands were everywhere—I hadn't experienced that before; Mom kept me on a pretty tight leash up until that point. The worst was that I couldn't get away—that he was stronger than me. I thought—I thought he'd…" She choked back a sob. "Finally, I bit him—hard. He was surprised and loosened his grip for a second. I got out of there. I ran to the washroom and cried and cried. One of the other girls found me and I made her go get my mom. I was so hysterical she had to take me home."

Rose didn't say a word, just waited for the rest of it. Mia was grateful for that. If she stopped now, she didn't think she could go on. "She didn't believe me. She thought I was exaggerating, or... I don't know. She didn't want to believe—I realize that now. She didn't want to think she'd put me in danger. She made me go back the following day."

"No!" Rose's shocked exclamation made heads turn their way.

Mia lowered her voice. "She said I had to carry through with what I'd started. She said I had an obligation."

"That's insane."

"No." Mia shook her head tiredly. "That's denial. It makes us do stupid things. I've forgiven my mom for it. She didn't know what to do, so she pretended nothing happened at all. And I went back. I was shaking in my boots, but I did it. Mom walked with me to the dressing room where everyone was preparing for the pageant. When I went in you could have heard a pin drop. Then the other girls started whispering."

Her hands were shaking as she lifted the juice to her lips again.

"Mom got me out of there, fast—I'll give her that much. We drove home and I never entered another pageant again. We never spoke about it again, either."

Rose was blinking back tears, but Mia found her own eyes strangely dry. She felt calm, too. Saying it out loud wasn't as hard as she'd thought it would be.

"I'm so sorry, Mia. I know it was bad, but I'm so glad it wasn't worse."

"That's the thing," Mia said and her voice broke. "It was worse for someone else." She lowered her voice to a whisper. "Warner raped one of the other girls. And he's still on the circuit. I don't know what to do."

Rose's eyes went wide. "You have to tell someone."

Pain clogged Mia's throat. There it was again—the need to haul herself before a crowd and expose her shame and humiliation. "I'm not sure I can."

"I know you can," Rose said. "Mia, you are one of the bravest women I know. You can do this."

"Maybe."

"If you need someone by your side, you know I'll be there, right?"

"Yeah, I know that." Rose had already stood by her when others hadn't. "I'll think about it, okay?"

"Okay." Rose gave her hand a squeeze. "Now how about those invitations you told me about?"

"Take a look at this." Mia pulled out her phone gratefully and showed Rose the website for a local printing company. "Here are a ton of stationary samples. If you go through and favorite some of them I'll take a trip to the store and get real samples you can hold in your hand. I'll drop them by later tonight."

"Wow—that's great service."

"That's the whole point of me being your wedding planner. I do the hard work. You get to relax and enjoy yourself." She felt calmer now that they were on safer ground.

"You're going to be a genius at this." Rose settled down to choosing her stationary.

Mia let out a long breath. She could figure out what to do about Inez and Fred Warner another time. Right now it was her job to concentrate on Rose, and she turned to the task willingly.

"Is this seat taken?" Cab dropped onto the bench seat next to Rose without waiting for an answer.

"Are you going to help me pick out stationary?" Rose asked.

"Just here for some coffee, although I wouldn't mind a couple shots of Jack Daniel's while I'm at it."

"Jack Daniel's?" Rose checked her watch. "It's barely eleven-thirty in the morning. Why would you want to get wasted?"

"Because I've been getting honked at, whistled at and laughed at everywhere I go today. And to top it off, Marge Ransom patted my ass."

"Marge Ransom?" Rose cocked her head. "Isn't she about eighty years old?"

"Maybe she thought it was your head," Mia said.

Cab glared at her. "She read the sign."

"What sign?"

"The one some jackass taped to the back of my cruiser."

"Uh-oh," Rose said. "What did it say?"

"*Honk if you think I'm sexy.* And it was duct-taped to my car. You try getting that off."

"Honk if you think… Oh my God, was it Jamie?"

"Had to be. I'm telling you, he doesn't take my god-like physique seriously."

"Well, I take it seriously." Rose pecked him on the cheek. "I take it very, very seriously."

"You take it any way you can get it," Cab growled, kissing her back, then seemed to remember they had company. "Sorry, Mia."

"That's okay. At least someone's getting along."

Cab focused on her. "Still on the outs with Luke? He cares for you a lot, you know."

"So everyone tells me," Mia said, gathering her things. "Too bad he doesn't act like it when I'm around."

As THE DAYS passed, Luke's mood dipped further. He could no longer pretend he would marry Mia the first week in March. Instead of making up with him, she threw herself into preparing for the opening of Fila's Familia, and helping Rose put together her wedding to Cab.

That stung more than anything else. Whenever he ran into the sheriff, it was clear Cab was overjoyed to be with Rose, and anyone could see Rose adored him back. The couple obviously had a healthy sex life, too, if all their kissing and caressing was anything to go by. The sheriff was no ladies' man and here he was getting lucky every night by the looks of things while Luke was stuck home alone. He was frustrated, irritable and downright mad at the way things had turned out. How was he supposed to fix things with Mia when she would never spend any time with him?

At least he knew where she was—at the restaurant with Camila and Fila most of the time now that Fila was back from her honeymoon and opening day was looming large. Luke made it a point to drop by every few days on one pretext or another, but while Mia was perfectly polite she always kept the counter between them. Luke was beginning to think he'd never get to touch her again, and he ached to touch her. One night with Mia was definitely not enough.

It had become clear to him, however, that his attraction to Mia had clouded his judgment. He'd been too busy missing her sexy, come-hither attire to stop and wonder why she'd changed her image and pulled away from him. After talking to Cab and Rose her intentions were more clear. While he liked Mia dressed up sexy, she probably attracted a lot of attention that wasn't positive—like the unwanted attention she'd received at the beauty contest years ago, and Ellis Scranton's, too.

She'd changed her look because she wanted a different kind of regard. She wanted respect. He could understand that. Too bad instead of showing her any he'd tried to undercut her self-confidence and belittled her dreams. He hadn't been swift to correct his mistake either. Somehow the restaurant felt too public to have a heart to heart, and the Cruz ranch guesthouse tended to be full of Ethan and Autumn's friends in the evenings. Mia wouldn't invite him upstairs these days. His pride had kept him from making amends in front of an audience and with each passing day it became harder to admit he was wrong.

Today he meant to make amends for that. He touched the small package in his coat pocket as he drove the tractor he'd used to haul feed out to the cattle back to its shed. It contained two jeweled hairpins he'd bought for Mia. He hoped she'd use them for those new hairstyles of hers and understand he thought her new look was beautiful. He hoped she'd understand he wanted another chance. Without him having to say as much in words.

He parked the tractor, shut it off and hopped down.

"There you are."

Luke nearly jumped out of his skin when his father moved into the shed. Now he was in for it. Holt had never kept his opinions bottled up this long. Luke could only imagine what he wanted to say.

"Let's talk about your bank account."

Bank account? Luke frowned. "What about it?"

"I see a fancy truck in your driveway. I hear that you purchased a ring that cost more than my house."

"It didn't cost more than your house, and Mia gave it back anyway."

"Smart girl. But I have a feeling those aren't your only outstanding expenses. I've heard about the way you're throwing your money around."

That damned truck salesman. Luke should have known better than to trade on his name to secure financing when he didn't have the money in the bank for a real down payment. The man probably hinted about it to Holt down at Rafters—a watering hole favored by older cowboys who didn't care for the loud music and crowds at the Dancing Boot. Holt wouldn't have liked that.

"Well?"

"It's under control." Luke tried to push past Holt, but Holt grabbed his arm.

"Don't get into debt. It ain't worth it."

Too late, Luke thought. "I said it's under control."

Holt stopped him again. "You've chosen a hard road, son. Don't make it harder."

"What's that supposed to mean?"

His father hesitated, then shook his head. "No, I

ain't having that conversation. You know damned well what I mean. I will say this. That girl of yours is a fighter. Don't underestimate her."

Luke stilled. A fighter. What did Holt know about Mia? Something told Luke he wasn't referencing Ellis, or the fact that she was about to be a single mother. He was talking about something else. "What do you know about beauty pageants?" he blurted out.

Holt turned away. "Pageants? What about them?"

"Something shady was going on—about seven years ago. Did you hear about that? About one of the judges?"

Luke thought his father wasn't going to answer, he hesitated so long. "I did hear something about that. Something I didn't like at all."

"What did you hear?"

"Fred Warner. Biggest ass I ever met. Hung out at Rafters for a time, until the rest of us let him know he wasn't welcome anymore."

"Why? What did he do?"

"Ran off his mouth a lot when he'd had a few too many—which was all the time. Most of it was bullshit. Bragging. That kind of thing. This was different."

Dread crept into Luke's gut. He'd been tamping down a thought that kept creeping up—an idea of what might have happened to Mia. He didn't think he could bear to hear it out loud. "Spill it."

"Let's just say he made it clear he sometimes used his status as a judge to get special treatment from the contestants. That's how he put it—special treatment." Holt's expression was hard. "Said they were all too willing to give it to him, most of the time. Said when they weren't he knew how to persuade them. That's what got to me. He knew how to *persuade them*."

He shook his head. "I didn't understand it all at first. Thought it was ugly but didn't realize how ugly. I didn't have daughters—I didn't know the first thing about pageants. I figured those girls he was talking about were twenty, twenty-one. Old enough to know better." Luke heard the regret in his father's voice. "Should have shot that man, that's what we should have done." He turned to Luke. Held his gaze. "Few weeks later a friend of mine was bragging about his girl—how she won a pageant. I was surprised. 'But Inez is just a little thing,' I said. My pal nodded." Holt swallowed. "'That's right,' he says. 'Just turned fifteen and won regionals.' I thought my ticker would give out right then and there when I put it together. Regionals. The pageant Warner was judging. Well." He nodded. "I had a word with Warner. Should have had more than a word. Regret now that's all I did."

"What did Warner do?" Luke's hands were icy cold and not just from the weather.

"Left town not long after. Moved west, I think." He slid another look Luke's way. "Your girl was in those pageants. Mia."

"Yeah. Yeah, she was."

"I JUST STOPPED by to make sure you hadn't changed your mind," Inez said, leaning on the counter.

Mia wiped an imaginary spot with a rag, and couldn't meet her eye. "I don't think so. I'm sorry, Inez," she rushed on when the other woman began to speak. "I know it's the right thing to do. I know I should do it, but

I don't think I can. I'm not brave like you."

"Sure you are." Inez chuckled grimly. "It was your bravery in speaking out in the first place that's stuck with me all these years. It's what made me brave enough to finally speak up."

Mia turned aside. "What if they don't listen to us?"

"I think they will. If they don't, at least we tried."

"I don't want to see him again." She finally put her worst fear into words.

"I know." Inez touched her arm. "The thing is, I think we might have to."

Mia closed her eyes. She thought Inez would keep trying to convince her, but instead the other woman waited patiently. Mia thought again of all the girls who were in the pageants Warner was judging. She thought about him leading them into small rooms, backing them into corners, pawing them. Forcing himself on them.

Damn it, couldn't she ever get away from the past?

No. Not until she faced it down.

"Okay," she said reluctantly. "I'll do it. I don't want to, but I will."

Inez let out a breath. "Thank you, Mia. We can stop him. I know it."

The door opened behind them and Tracey Richards walked into the restaurant. "Hi, Mia. Hi, Inez."

Mia straightened her shoulders and smiled. "Hi, Tracey. We're not open for a few more days. Is there something I can help you with?"

"Yes," Tracey said, rushing forward and holding out her left hand. "You can help plan my wedding. I just got engaged!"

WHEN LUKE WALKED into the restaurant an hour later, he hoped to find Mia alone. He didn't know yet what he'd say to her. He wasn't sure how she'd react when she found out he'd pried into her past. He wasn't sure if he should ask about Warner, either. Would she want to talk about it if the man had—

Luke couldn't even finish the thought. Every time he thought about what Warner had done, how he'd taken advantage of young girls, how Luke still didn't even know the extent of it, he had to choke back the bile that rose in his throat. If that animal hurt Mia—

He forced himself to take a deep breath. First things first. He needed to show Mia he was on her side—that he supported her desire to be respected. He spotted Tracey Richards deep in conversation with Mia in one of the booths, talking quietly but excitedly. When she saw him, Mia exclaimed, "Look, Luke. Tracey's engaged! And I'm going to plan her wedding!"

A lock of Mia's hair had slipped from the loose, artful bun she wore at the nape of her neck. Luke longed to slip the errant strand behind her ear and to draw her into a deep kiss, but he suspected that wouldn't go down too well, so he only said, "Congratulations, Tracey. Who's the lucky guy?"

"Bart Herkimer, from Butte. We've been dating for months and decided to make it official. Look at my ring!"

It was a pretty, graceful ring, not unlike the one Mia had preferred to the flashy piece he'd forced upon her finger. A stab of regret pierced Luke and he wondered if things would have been different if he'd simply gone along with Mia's choice that day at Thayer's.

But no—it wasn't the ring that caused the problems between them. It was the way he'd told her she didn't have a head for business. The truth was he had no idea if she did or not. He was afraid of the consequences of finding out, too. He was afraid they'd dig themselves deeper into debt. That wasn't his call, though. Not his alone, at least. He was here to support Mia. If she wanted to be a businesswoman, he'd do all he could to help.

"That's real nice, Tracey. I hope you two will be very happy," he made himself say.

"I've got to run. See you Friday for our first consultation," Tracey said to Mia. "Bye!"

"Bye." Mia turned to Luke. "That's two weddings in May! And Lila White asked me to help with her family reunion, too. Three events in one month—two of them paid!"

Luke blinked. She'd already racked up three events? Maybe she would make a go of it after all. Except…

"That's a lot going on in one month. You'll still work at the restaurant full-time, too, right? When's Tracey's wedding?" Mia was going to be as exhausted as he was these days if she took all of that on.

A worry line creased Mia's forehead. "I forgot to ask. But I know she knows about Rose's wedding, so there's no way it's on the same day."

"When's the reunion?"

Mia looked away. "It's the day after Rose's wedding, which isn't perfect timing, but I'm sure I can handle it."

"The day after? Won't the wedding go until late?"

Mia shrugged.

"Sounds to me like you've bitten off more than you can chew. You should carry a calendar around so you don't double-book yourself like that."

She pulled back. "Like you know anything about it."

"I know that much." He tried to take her hand. She yanked it away. "Come on, Mia. That's just good business."

"If it's such good business, why don't you get yourself a calendar? Maybe then you'd remember to come over when you say you're going to!"

Luke bristled. "The only time I've ever stood you up was because there was an emergency on the ranch. If you haven't noticed, I'm the one running it these days. Everyone else is too busy. But it's still all getting done."

"I pity those cows," Mia said.

"Well, I pity those brides. You're going to be so tired from running around trying to handle all those events you won't get anything right. By May you'll be as big as a house, too."

Mia pulled back, hurt written all over her face. Luke swore. He'd screwed up again—he hadn't meant to hurt her, just to make her see sense. "Mia, that's not what I meant to say. I just want…"

"Go home, Luke." Mia pushed out of the booth and brushed past him. He caught her arm. Swung her around.

"I don't want to go home because you're not there." He bent down and stole a kiss, knowing he wouldn't get one any other way. When Mia didn't pull away, he stole another one, and another. She stayed rigid in his arms, but she let him kiss her. When he pulled away, she leaned toward him, as if she couldn't bear to part, either. He knew she wanted him as much as he wanted her and he pressed his point home. "You're driving me crazy. I just want to be with you; that's all I ever wanted. Look, I brought you something." He pulled the small, wrapped box out of his pocket.

"I won't be with someone who doesn't know the first thing about me. Who doesn't care about what I care about." She tried to break free from his embrace, but he moved with her, placing the box in her hand, and wrapping her fingers around it.

"I know something about you. I know you're the most stubborn, determined, hard-headed woman I ever met."

"That's not good enough. You need to know something real." She got free of him this time and headed toward the back of the restaurant where she slapped the small box down on the counter. Luke knew he had to work fast or he'd find that damn counter between them again.

"Like about the beauty pageants?"

Mia stopped in her tracks. "What about them?"

Luke thought fast. How could he put it without scaring her off again? "You spent all those years looking for approval—from older men, mostly. That left you vulnerable." He bit back Warner's name. He wasn't ready to talk about that yet. Wasn't sure she was, either. "That's a good setup for falling for Ellis's tricks."

"And yours," Mia said evenly. "You're almost a decade older than me."

"Is that why you don't trust me?" Luke moved closer to her. "You know I'd never hurt you. Not like those other men."

Mia stared at him. "Maybe not deliberately, but that doesn't mean you wouldn't stumble into it." Her frank statement stopped him.

"Like I said, I just want to be with you."

"And *like I said*, I want you to know me before you say that again. I want you to know what I want. What I need. What's most important to me. Until then, I want you to go, Luke. I have a career to build."

In an instant, the counter was between them once more. Luke knew better than to try to follow Mia to the other side. Without another word, he turned on his heel and left the restaurant.

He knew damn well what was important to Mia, but he wouldn't tell her. He'd show her instead.

Chapter Eleven

THREE EVENTS IN a row. She'd booked three events
in a row.

How stupid could she be? Mia sat at her desk in her
rented room at the Cruz guesthouse, her newly acquired
day planner laid out in front of her, the beautiful hairclips Luke had given her still in their box, and dropped
her head into her hands.

Luke was right. She'd end up making short shrift of
all of them, having taken on too much. But what could
she do? She'd given everyone her word and she didn't
want to start off her business by disappointing a customer.

When she'd called Tracey and found out that the
young woman had planned her wedding for the Friday
night before Rose's Saturday affair she hadn't known
what to say.

"You're going to skip Rose's wedding?" she'd asked,
scrambling for her calendar.

"No, we'll be there. We're not taking our honeymoon until next spring. We're spending the night at a
hotel in Billings but we'll be back by late afternoon when

Rose's wedding starts."

"But—" Didn't Tracey realize how rude it was to plan her wedding that Friday night when many of her guests would have already penciled in Rose's wedding the following day? Both women were well-liked in town, and they hung out with much the same crowd. What was Tracey thinking?

Mia couldn't think of a way to convey that without hurting Tracey's feelings though, so she'd hung up, still booked for both weddings. She fingered the hairclips, loving that Luke had chosen them for her—that he'd obviously noticed her change of hairstyle and supported her attempt to update her image—but hating the fact that he'd been right about the three events in close succession being more than she could handle. Why, why, why did he have to be right?

She heard voices downstairs and jumped up, hoping that someone had arrived who might help. When she went downstairs she found Autumn, Claire and Morgan in the living room.

"Thank God," Mia said. "I need some advice."

"What is it?" As usual, Autumn carried Arianna, who yawned sweetly and snuggled against her mother's shoulder.

"Tracey Richards scheduled her wedding for the Friday night before Rose's. Can you believe that? I can't figure out how to tell her to change it."

"That is… strange." Morgan regarded her with a smile. "She's invited to Rose's wedding, right?"

"Yes, and she's coming, too. She acted like it was the most normal thing in the world."

"I'll go to Linda's Diner tomorrow and see what I can figure out," Morgan said to Mia's relief. "I'm sure Rose will understand either way. You don't have to worry about it."

"It's just I'm Tracey's wedding planner, too," Mia explained. "I didn't know her date when I accepted. I figured there was no chance she'd pick the same weekend as Rose."

"And you took the job?" Claire said. "That's not very responsible, Mia. You'd better back out."

Mia was used to Claire's habit of speaking frankly, but it still rankled. "I can't. She'll tell people and I'll get a reputation for unreliability."

"If you don't back out you'll get a reputation for letting down your customers. What about Rose's rehearsal? And the rehearsal dinner? Won't those be the same night as Tracey's wedding?"

"No. They're on Thursday, thank goodness."

"What about Tracey's rehearsal and dinner?" Claire said. "Won't they be on Thursday, too?"

"I'll tell her she can't do that."

"You'll tell the bride what she can and can't do?" Claire's tone was caustic. "That's not very businesslike."

"What am I supposed to do? She's the one who booked her wedding on that ridiculous day," Mia cried.

"It's *your* business. You're in charge. Get on the phone and sort it out. Apologize and tell Tracey there's a scheduling conflict, and that she has two choices: change the date of the wedding or find another planner."

"I've been friends with Tracey for a long time."

"That does seem harsh," Autumn put in.

"It's practical," Claire said, her black bob swinging with her vehemence. "Businesspeople make tough decisions all the time, Mia. If you can't do that, you shouldn't be one."

"Mia is still learning." Autumn adjusted her blouse to nurse Arianna. "It takes time. Everyone makes a few mistakes. Mia, find out where Tracey intends to hold her wedding and reception as soon as possible. Get as many details as you can. Maybe there are things on her list and Rose's that overlap and you can dovetail the planning you'll need to do. A busy New York City wedding planner has back-to-back events all the time. If they can do it, you can, too."

"Thanks, Autumn," Mia said, a wave of gratitude washing over her. She avoided meeting Claire's eye as she stood up and crossed the room back toward the stairs. "I'll go call Tracey right now."

"She'll never pull this off. She's so young," Mia heard Claire say as she went upstairs. Mia increased her pace, not wanting to hear any more, but Autumn's answer floated up toward her.

"Don't underestimate her, Claire. I think she's more on the ball than any of us give her credit for."

"WHERE ARE WE putting this thing again?" Jamie called out as he and Cab struggled to get the queen-sized mattress out of the guest room door and down the staircase of Luke's cabin.

"The basement over at Mom and Dad's." Luke took hold of one end of the box spring while Ethan grabbed the other. They tipped it vertically to fit through the bedroom door.

Luke hadn't remembered how hard it was to get a bed in and out of these rooms until they were too far into the job to call it quits. He directed the operation as best he could, hoping against hope neither of the other men would take a tumble down the stairs before they were done. He'd grabbed Jamie, Cab and Ethan from Linda's Diner, where he'd gone to lunch after another run out to Amanda Stone's, and asked them to help him real quick before they got back to their workdays. His own brothers were all busy today and there was no way he'd ask Holt to wrestle a mattress down a flight of stairs, not with the stiffness in the old man's hip. Besides, his dad was nowhere to be seen these days. His mother said he had a new project brewing that he hadn't even told her about.

"You sure it's a smart idea to build a nursery for Mia before you two even sort things out?" Ethan asked him.

"The whole point is to show her why we should sort things out. I need her to know I'm the kind of man who puts her and the baby first."

"Where are you going to get all the baby stuff?"

"I'll buy it." On credit, unfortunately. His next truck payment was going to eat up a big swath of his monthly income. Luke backed out into the hallway until Ethan's end was free of the door. Then they changed directions and Ethan backed slowly down the stairs. Cab and Jamie were nearly at the bottom when Cab stumbled, yanked the mattress forward and pulled Jamie off his feet. Fortunately the mattress broke his fall, but he landed on top of it in an ungainly heap.

"Where's my camera?" Ethan said. "There's a pinup pose if I ever saw one."

"Ha, ha." Jamie scrambled up and set his hat back on his head. "Cab, you okay?"

"I'm fine. Just got tangled up in my own feet."

"Well, untangle them, pick up your end of the mattress and get to it."

"Why don't you both get to it," Ethan called down.

They managed to make it the rest of the way to Luke's parents' house without incident where they stored the set in the basement. Back at his cabin, Luke thanked everyone for their help.

"Just remember sets," Ethan told him. "Everything has to match—the crib, the changing table, the dresser. And the baby blankets have to match the curtains. And then pretty soon you'll find Mia trying to match the toys to the wallpaper. It's like an illness."

"Match everything. I can do that."

"What's her favorite color?"

"The baby's?" Luke frowned.

"Mia's, idiot. Does she know if she's having a boy or girl?"

"Not yet. I don't think."

Ethan rolled his eyes at him. "Find out. In fact, you'd better go to that appointment; it's an important one. And don't buy anything or paint anything until you know. But then don't use pink or blue—those are out. Choose yellow or green, but make it masculine or feminine depending on what the baby is. You know."

Luke was glad to see he wasn't the only one staring at Ethan. "I don't think I do know."

"You will," Ethan said darkly. "Trust me."

"IT'S THE ONLY weekend Tracey's sister can make it," Autumn reported back to Mia several days later. "Nora is a Marine on active duty. If Tracey doesn't hold her wedding on that Friday, her sister can't come."

Mia sighed. "Well, at least that explains things. I didn't think Tracey was that insensitive. Did you tell Rose?"

Autumn nodded.

"Good. Well, that's that. I'll just have to be super-organized. The whole weekend will be like one big party."

"Let me know if I can help."

"I will." Mia was already making lists in her head as she trailed up the stairs to her own room. She was due to meet with Tracey tomorrow morning, Lila White tomorrow evening, and Rose the day after. She decided she'd put together a big checklist for each event and start calling venues and suppliers. By the time she met with each of her clients she'd have everything under control.

Her phone buzzed and she picked it up.

"Mia?" It was Inez. Mia's gut tightened with anxiety.

"Yes."

"I drafted my letter. Can I e-mail it to you to take a look at? How is yours coming?"

"Great." Actually, it wasn't coming at all. She'd tried once or twice to sit down and put the events of six years ago into writing, but no words had come.

"I know it's hard."

"I'll do it." Mia overrode Inez's comforting words.

"It is hard, but I will do it."

"Thank you. I'll send my letter over right now."

"Maybe it will help me to read it."

Mia found herself reluctant to open Inez's email when it came, however, and while she found its contents frank and well written, when she heard a commotion in the living room fifteen minutes later, she was grateful for the interruption. She ran lightly to the head of the stairs and found Jamie squared off with Autumn down below.

"I'm going to kill him. I can't believe Ethan did this!" He looked fit to be tied, waving his hat for emphasis.

"What did Ethan do?" Autumn stared at him, protectively cradling her baby.

"Entered me in a calendar pinup contest." He read from the screen of his phone as Mia slipped downstairs and joined Autumn. "'Dear Mr. Lassiter, we're pleased to inform you that you have made it to the finals in our Cowboy of the Month Calendar contest. Your photos and description have been posted on our website for the final voting phase. We will announce the twelve winners on May first. If chosen, you will be notified and a time and date set for your calendar photo shoot.' Can you believe that?"

"You think Ethan entered you in that contest? Why would he do that?" Mia asked.

"Hell if I know! But he told me I looked like a pinup just the other day."

Autumn looked at him askance. "Ethan said that?"

Jamie colored. "We were moving a mattress—" His gaze darted to Mia. "I mean, we were just fooling around—oh, to hell with it. Just tell Ethan he'll get his."

He stormed out of the room. Autumn shook her head. "I don't understand men," she said to Arianna.

Before Mia could answer, the doorbell rang. She got up to get it and was surprised to see Luke.

"Can I come in?" he said, and she fought the urge to hurl herself into his arms. As angry as she'd been with him, she'd missed him like crazy since she'd moved out and it was torture to keep her distance. She longed for the little things like sharing a meal with him, or chatting with him after she came home from work, but she missed the big things, too. Making love to Luke had been everything she'd ever dreamed sex could be, so to only have one night to enjoy it seemed much too cruel.

Something of her thoughts must have shown in her eyes because the cowboy smiled. He came inside, shut the door behind him and leaned against it, one arm behind his back. "You have an appointment coming up, don't you?"

It was the last thing she expected him to say and it took her a minute to gather her thoughts. "What appointment?"

"Your doctor visit. It's an important one, right? To find out if you're having a boy or a girl?"

"Oh—yes. Next Tuesday." How did Luke know about that?

"Can I drive you?"

His nearness made it difficult for her to concentrate. It conjured up images of the night she'd spent in his arms. He'd made love to her so tenderly and thoroughly it made her ache now to think of it. "O-Okay."

"What time?" Luke reached out and touched her,

just a gentle caress of his hand along her arm. He bent down and brushed his lips over hers. She shivered and leaned closer. She craved his warmth, his strength. She wished he would hold her until all her worries slipped away.

"Nine-thirty. In the morning."

"I'll be here at eight forty-five. Take care of yourself until then. Don't work too hard." He tugged her a little closer. Mia held her breath. "Go to bed early." He pulled her closer still and kissed her again—a longer kiss this time—making her breathless. As his kiss went on and on, Mia forgot everything else but the handsome cowboy holding her. The cowboy she wanted more than anything else. When he let her go and straightened up, he had to hold her steady until she regained her balance. He handed her the single pink rose he'd held behind his back and opened the door. "And think about me, because I'll be thinking about you."

After he was gone, Mia clutched her flower and walked unsteadily back to the living room, where Autumn waited, her eyes dancing with mischief. She laughed when she saw Mia's face. "Uh-oh, I know that look. That's a girl who's come under a cowboy's spell."

"Just when I think I've figured him out, he does something like this."

"They're crafty, those cowboys. Luke's set his sights on you and he won't give up easily."

Mia flopped down on the sofa again. She hoped he didn't give up. She wanted them to work out a way to be together. She wouldn't give in on what she wanted, though.

If only Luke would be the man she knew he could be.

ON TUESDAY, LUKE jingled his keys in his hand until Mia shot him a look that told him to stop. He noticed that her foot was tapping up a storm, though, so he wasn't the only one nervous about the appointment ahead. He had never felt as out of place as he did in Dr. Fitzpatrick's waiting room. Done up in grays and browns, it was tailored, modern, and much too cold for Luke's taste.

He sat on a cushioned seat beside Mia, surrounded by other women, most of them visibly pregnant. One mother-to-be's belly stuck out so far she looked like she'd swallowed a watermelon.

Or perhaps a basketball.

He glanced surreptitiously at Mia's only slightly rounded abdomen and wondered if she'd even come close to looking like that.

A new thought occurred to him. What if she had twins? He panicked a moment as he tried to think where they'd fit another crib into the already packed spare room, then cautioned himself to take it one step at a time. No sense letting his imagination run away with him.

"Mia Start?"

Mia stood up when a nurse called her name, and Luke followed suit awkwardly. Now that he was here, he couldn't imagine they would let him in to the examining room. On the other hand, he needed to stake a claim to Mia—and this baby—right now, before it was born.

Something told him it would be too late if he waited until afterwards. He'd seen how wrapped up Autumn was in Arianna. If Ethan got a sidelong look from either of them he was lucky. No, he couldn't give Mia any more chances to push him away. He meant to be her partner in this, starting right now.

"You're coming in?" Mia asked.

"That's right." He waited for her to protest, but she didn't. Instead she mutely paced after the nurse. So far, so good.

Inside the examining room, the nurse instructed Mia to change into a paper gown and take a seat on the table. Luke sat down in one of the chairs to the side as if he belonged there and prepared to enjoy the view.

Mia picked up the gown and turned her back to him, undressing so carefully he only caught glimpses of skin as she changed—enough to alert his body that something interesting was happening, but not enough to satisfy him.

Not by a long shot.

When she sat on the table, her legs dangling over the side, Luke sighed. She looked so sweet. And delicious.

"What's wrong?" she asked.

"You know what's wrong."

"Luke."

"Don't Luke me. We belong together. You know that."

"I know that I'm not interested in being told what to do."

A knock sounded on the door before he could answer her, and Mia called, "Come in." A doctor entered and smiled at the two of them.

"Good morning, Mia. Good morning…"

"Luke. Luke Matheson. Nice to meet you." He stood up and shook the doctor's hand.

"Nice to meet you too, Luke. I'm Marion Fitzpatrick. Are you the father?"

"Yes," Luke said at the same time Mia said, "No." Dr. Fitzpatrick raised an eyebrow.

"I'm going to be." Luke stared Mia down.

"Hmm. Let me put it this way," Dr. Fitzpatrick said. "Are you going to be present for the birth?"

"Damn straight."

"No," Mia said quickly.

"Yes, I am."

If Dr. Fitzpatrick's eyebrows rose any higher, they would disappear under the fringe of her bangs, Luke thought. But he wouldn't back down. He was going to be Mia's partner in all of this, whether she wanted him to be or not.

"Well, if you two work this out, there's a birthing class starting up in a couple of weeks. I think you should attend, Mia. And if Luke here is going to be involved in your baby's life, I think he should attend, too." She handed Mia a brochure. After Mia skimmed through it, Luke took it from her and tucked it into his pocket. The corner of Dr. Fitzpatrick's mouth curved into a smile. "Let's take a look at your baby, shall we?"

Luke had seen ultrasound machines in movies, of course, and had an idea what the image would look like when the doctor squirted clear goo on Mia's belly and pressed the rounded tip of the ultrasound wand against her skin. At first the screen stayed grainy, with odd, rounded shapes appearing and disappearing as she moved the wand around. Then something came into focus and Luke's heart lurched.

"Is that the baby?"

"That's the baby," Dr. Fitzpatrick confirmed. "Can you hear its heartbeat?"

Luke realized the strange sound he was hearing was the fast-paced whomp-whomp-whomp of the baby's heartbeat.

"Is it a boy or girl?" he asked the doctor.

"Do you want to know the sex, Mia?"

"Yes." Mia's gaze was held by the shifting images on the screen. Luke realized he'd taken her hand and she was squeezing it tight—holding on for dear life. He knew exactly how she felt.

"Let's see." Dr. Fitzpatrick moved the wand around again, angling it this way and that until she froze. "There."

"There what?" Luke asked.

"See that?"

"No—I don't see anything," Mia said.

"Exactly. You're having a girl. Congratulations." Dr. Fitzpatrick beamed at both of them.

"Did you hear that, Luke? We're having a girl!"

Luke pulled her into an awkward embrace, reclined as she was on the examining table. He kissed her neck, her ear and finally her mouth. "We're having a girl," he echoed.

A moment later, Mia shifted away. "I mean...I'm having a girl."

Luke decided to let it slide. Her initial comment told him a lot. She still cared for him, for one thing. She still thought of him as partner material, whatever she said. And it made her happy to share her news with him.

Sooner or later, Mia would be his.

Chapter Twelve

"ARE YOU READY for this?" Mia asked Fila two days later. They stood behind the counter of Fila's Familia, where Mia would soon take orders and run the till. The restaurant was due to open in twenty minutes and already a line of their friends and family snaked down the block.

"I think so," Fila said, but she didn't sound too certain. "I'd better get back in the kitchen. I can't believe how many people are waiting. What if they don't like the food?"

"Are you kidding? They'll love it! Don't you remember our test run?" Mia gave her friend a tight hug then spun her around toward the kitchen. "Get back to cooking—I have a feeling we'll go through everything we have available tonight."

"Don't say that," Camila cried from the kitchen where she was busily prepping enchilada fixings. "I don't know what we'll do if we run out of food!"

"Close down, silly." Mia laughed at Camila's horrified expression and moved back to her place behind the till. Twenty minutes later, her hands were damp with sweat, though, when she unlocked the doors and ushered the first customers in. What if she messed up the till? Or couldn't keep up with orders? What if she ran out of change?

She took a deep breath, smiled at Morgan and Rob and said, "Welcome to Fila's Familia! What can I get you?"

Four hours later, she thought her feet would fall off they ached so badly. She hadn't sat down once, nor had she had a chance to take so much as a bite of food. The restaurant was still packed because some of the guests who'd eaten early and gone home had come back to celebrate the end of the first night. Starting tomorrow, the restaurant would be open from eleven in the morning to nine at night. Mia was glad they'd only started with dinner today. She didn't know how she'd last through a full shift tomorrow.

"How are you holding up?"

She hadn't noticed Luke standing in line, but then she could barely keep up with the whirlwind of orders the customers ahead of him had thrown at her. A large party of cowboys had just come through the line, back from some event somewhere. They had each ordered multiple entrees, as if they were cramming in calories before a fast.

"I'm doing okay. Tired."

"You shouldn't work so hard."

Mia laughed. "This is nothing. I've got longer days ahead of me—but that's all right. I'm strong."

"Here. I got this for you." He handed her a green striped gift bag with yellow tissue paper poking out the top.

"I don't think I'm supposed to stop working."

"It'll just take a minute. Open it up."

She did, and found a small, plush teddy bear inside. A green ribbon around its neck held a card. When she opened it, she found an invitation to a private viewing. The address listed was Luke's cabin on the Double-Bar-K.

"A private viewing?" she whispered, scandalized that Luke was propositioning her right here in line.

"It ain't what you think. Be there, tomorrow morning at nine."

"I work at eleven."

"I have to work, too. It won't take much time."

"Hmph. That's not much of an invitation." She hadn't meant to snort aloud, but she did. Cheeks burning, she darted a glance at Luke and found him grinning back at her. He put his hands on the counter and leaned forward.

"It can take as long as you want." His voice was low and intimate. "It's up to you."

"Go on, get out of here." She stuffed the teddy bear and gift bag on a shelf under the counter.

"I've got to order first."

"Well, hurry up!" But it was hard to stay angry. She was flushed with the success of Fila's Familia and the truth was she'd love to spend a good long time with him at the bunkhouse tomorrow morning. She couldn't, though. She had to stand strong—at least until Luke proved he was taking her seriously.

BY THE TIME Mia knocked on his front door at nine-fifteen the next morning, Luke was ready to jump out of his skin. He'd begun to think she'd decided to stand him up and he didn't know what he'd do if that was the case. He'd worked hard on the nursery and he wanted her to see it. Hell, he wanted her to fall in love with it. If she didn't even bother to stop by, what was the use of all his work?

But she had come at last. He pulled the door open and she tumbled in on a cold breeze.

"Take off your coat. Come on in." Luke bit back more inane sentences that sprang to his mouth. He'd lived with Mia for weeks. No need to act like she'd never been here before.

"Something smells good," Mia said. She handed her coat to Luke, kicked her snow boots off clumsily and leaned against the wall for a minute.

"Mia? You okay?"

She instantly straightened. "Yeah, I'm fine."

But she didn't look fine. Not at all. "You look tired."

"Thank you very much. Just what every girl wants to hear first thing in the morning."

"You know what I mean." He held his ground. "You're always beautiful, and you're usually full of energy, too. What happened?"

She sighed and moved into the living room. "Fila's happened. Those customers ran me ragged last night. I didn't get a break once. Then we were up late cleaning and prepping for today. I have no idea how I'll get through a full shift. Especially since I'll probably have to stay late again. Plus, there are other things going on."

Luke bit back the words he wanted to say—that she should quit her restaurant job, that she should forget about her wedding planning business. That she should let him take care of her. "Would you like some breakfast? I made French toast."

"That sounds good, actually."

Mia brightened up as she ate and she confessed she'd slept until the last minute and hadn't eaten before she left the house. Luke piled on slices of French toast, bacon and orange slices and was gratified when she cleaned her plate. He kept the conversation light, but as soon as she finished he stood up.

"Come on." He held out his hand.

She took it and let him lead her to the stairs. "If you're really going ahead with this private viewing you shouldn't have let me eat so much." She flashed him an uncertain smile that he found all too sexy.

"It's not that kind of a private viewing, although that could be arranged any time you'd like." He grinned, letting her know he'd be glad to do just that.

"Hmm," was all the answer he got. He led her upstairs and paused in front of the guest room door.

"I can change things if you don't like it."

Mia was frowning. "Luke, I'm not going to move back in. We're not—"

Luke pushed open the door and Mia's words trailed off as she stepped inside the bedroom and took in the crib, changing table, and dresser, the sunny yellow walls, white trim around the windows and doors and the colorful rag rugs on the floor.

"Oh, Luke." She bit her lip and her eyes shone with

tears. "Oh, it's beautiful."

His heart leaped. For once he'd gotten it right. "It's all for you. And for our baby girl. I want you to come back home. I want us to make this a home together." He followed her around the room as she examined the furniture. "What do you think?"

"I love it. I can't believe you did all of this."

"You know I love you." He drew her into an embrace. "You know I do, Mia."

She nodded, her gaze searching his.

"Don't you see?" He waved a hand at the room. "I can give you everything you need. Everything. You'll never need to work another day in your life."

Mia went rigid in his arms. "I'm not giving up on my wedding planning business."

"Look at you, honey. You're exhausted after one day at the restaurant. You haven't even started event planning. How will you handle that on top of everything? And once you're a mom you won't want to leave the baby, will you?" He couldn't bear to see Mia as tired as she'd been when she walked in this morning. She took too much on. She needed him to help her.

Mia backed right out of his arms. "Is staying home with the baby mandatory?"

"What do you mean?" And why was she staring at him like that, with her arms crossed over her chest? Luke stepped away, too. "Don't you want to?"

"Sure! Of course. But I want to work, too. It doesn't have to be either/or."

"You can't work two jobs and take care of a baby." Why would she want to when he was there to pick up the slack?

She spun on her heel and marched out the bedroom door. "Watch me!"

MIA DIDN'T KNOW why she was crying when she drove back to the Cruz ranch, except she was so exhausted she could hardly hold her head up. She didn't understand it. She'd managed to make it through her first trimester without anyone even noticing she'd been pregnant. Now a couple of weeks later, she looked like something the cat dragged in and felt worse. When she reached the ranch, she managed to slip upstairs in the guest house without running into Autumn or anyone else. She sank down on her bed and had a good cry.

She'd actually thought Luke finally got it—that he realized how important it was to her to succeed in her wedding planning business. Not so much for the money, as for the proof it would give everyone that she wasn't just a pretty face. It was sweet that he wanted to provide for her, and a year ago she would have accepted gladly. But now she didn't want to quit, and she wanted Luke to support her in it. It hurt her feelings that no one except Rose seemed to believe she was capable of anything other than running a cash register. Was it because of all those beauty pageants? Couldn't anyone look beyond her face? She was capable of far more—she knew it. And she wanted to show everyone else.

Luke was right—it was lousy timing to start her business now, but if she worked hard she could have things established before the baby was born. Then she could buy one of those baby slings that were all the rage, wrap up the baby and keep on working.

It wasn't only the work wearing her out, anyway. Last night she'd tried to write the letter Inez wanted, and it had dredged up so many painful memories she'd hardly been able to sleep. It was so tempting to give up and let Luke have his way. She could lie in bed and let him take care of everything. If she told him about Warner, he'd probably take care of that, too.

Mia frowned. He might take care of it in all the wrong ways. She had to admit, there'd be a certain satisfaction in knowing Warner had gotten what he had coming, but she didn't want Luke to get into trouble and she wasn't a woman who approved of violence.

No, she had to do things the right way. She had to finish the letter and do whatever else it took to get Warner banned from the pageants for life.

That decision made, she rolled over onto her side, plumped a pillow under her head and daydreamed about what it would be like to hold her baby.

A girl. She was having a girl. Would the baby look like her at all?

She hoped so.

A tiny Mia. No—the baby needed her own name, just like she'd have her own personality. A tiny...Jasmine, or Lucy, or Pamela.

She needed to make a list.

She allowed her daydream to expand and saw a two-year-old with long dark hair racing around a playground. She saw herself chasing the little girl, playing tag with her, going down a slide.

She saw Luke pick her up and put her on his shoulders, the three of them walking back to their car.

No. Darn it—no! Luke wasn't in this picture. It was just her and Lucy. Or Pamela. Just the two of them. Going home to their…apartment.

Mia sat up. Apartment? That might be okay while Pamela was small, but not when she grew older. Mia wanted a yard for her child. Room to roam.

She thought of Ellis's two hundred thousand dollars sitting in her bank account. Maybe she could buy a house. A small one.

She lifted her chin. She'd go look at real estate her next day off.

Without Luke.

·

Chapter Thirteen

"I 'M GOING TO go out of my mind if this leg doesn't heal soon," Ned said a few days later as he, Luke, Ethan and Jamie leaned against a corral on the Double-Bar-K.

Jamie had stopped by to take a look at Silver, a mare that had grown increasingly skittish the last few days. She'd taken to bucking and rearing when anyone tried to handle her—odd behavior in the normally placid animal. In a way, the mare reminded Luke of Mia, who also seemed to have changed from a sweet young thing into a woman determined to have her way. Ned, Ethan and Jamie had managed to get the horse from the stable to the corral without incident, but only just. Luke hoped Jamie would have some insight into the matter, since he was known around these parts as something of a horse whisperer.

"And *I'm* going to go out of *my* mind if I keep having to do all your work," Luke said to Ned, watching Silver dance around in the corral. After a few moments she calmed down, walked a few steps, then suddenly shied to the left in a big leap before circling the corral again in nervous, tentative steps. He didn't have time for this new problem. It was calving season, he still needed to check the rest of the fences, and he had plenty of other chores to do, too.

"You must have loads of time on your hands if you're redecorating your cabin." Ned resettled his hat on his head and leaned on the top rail of the corral.

"How'd that go?" Jamie asked. "Did Mia like it?"

Ethan turned an interested look his way.

Luke couldn't believe Jamie didn't know the answer to that already. He bet Ethan did, from his expression. "She liked the room just fine, but she didn't like what I had to say."

"Sorry to hear it." Jamie's attention was back on the horse. After a few moments of concentration, he slipped his phone out of his pocket and clicked away at it.

"Calling for backup?" Ned shifted again and Luke could tell his leg was bothering him. It was out of its cast, but he'd need physical therapy before it was truly right again.

"Of a kind."

"Autumn says Mia was pretty upset when she got home the other day." Ethan moved closer.

"She was pretty upset when she was here."

"I don't think you're seeing the forest for the trees. You need to—"

"Speaking of trees, I think that's your problem," Jamie said. "Hold up a second." He listened to the person on the other end of the phone. "Yeah—could you hold up your phone so I can hear?" He kept the phone to his ear and held out his left hand for silence. They all watched the mare step nervously around the corral. Suddenly Jamie pointed at the horse just as she bucked and bolted again. "Yep. That's it!" He turned to the others. "They're logging over at Hardy's place. The chain saws are spooking her."

"I can't hear any chainsaws," Ned said.

"Nope. But she can. I had Nancy Hardy step out of her kitchen and hold up her phone. Every time the chain saws start up, your horse jumps."

"Now how the hell did you think of that?" Ethan cocked his hat back.

"I've seen it happen before, and I overheard Bill Hardy talking with his buddies about the logging last week at DelMonaco's. It was just a hunch."

"One hell of a hunch," Ethan said.

"Don't you ever get hunches?" Jamie slipped his phone back into his pocket.

"I've got a hunch you spend way too much time with horses. And listening to other people's conversations at restaurants."

"I've got a hunch you haven't gotten laid in a long time," Jamie rejoined. "You're mighty testy these days."

"Dude—the man just had a baby," Ned said, then grinned. "Probably has hemorrhoids on top of everything else." Ethan gave him a good-natured shove, which nearly unbalanced Ned, but he managed to grab the fence rail and hold on. "Jamie's right. You are testy."

"Wait 'til you have kids. I haven't slept a full night in weeks."

"Yeah, but it's worth it, right?" Jamie leaned against the corral and watched the mare kick up her heels again.

"Yeah, that's for sure. Think you and Fila will have kids?" he asked Ned.

"We're working on it."

Luke felt the other three men's satisfaction as if it was wafting off of them in waves, and suddenly his chest ached with frustration.

He should be married to Mia already. He should be preparing to be a father to her little girl.

Instead he was still alone.

IT WAS SEVERAL days before Mia got a chance to stop in at one of the real estate offices in town. The wall to the right of the entryway was covered in corkboard and held all the current listings. A receptionist sat behind a counter typing at a desktop computer. A row of faux leather chairs formed a waiting area. Only one other potential client was in the office—a lean man in his early thirties with light brown hair and gray eyes. He had the build of a serious athlete and Mia bet he spent his off hours doing extreme sports. He didn't look like a rancher, exactly. He lacked the easygoing, down-home attitude, for one thing. Instead he had a kind of intensity she couldn't entirely place.

Mia smiled and nodded at him politely, then turned to examine the wall of possibilities. She wouldn't want to spend all the money that Ellis gave her on a house. She needed savings to start her business and to tide her over until she got enough clients. She also wanted a college fund for baby Pamela. And she wanted to travel some-day—just enough to give Pam a wider sense of the world.

As she began to examine the house listings, she bit her lip, surprised at the prices. The cheapest ones were well over a hundred thousand dollars and they all had frightening words like *water damage*, *needs work* or *handyman special* in their descriptions. The houses closer to a hundred and fifty thousand dollars were somewhat better, but they weren't in the best parts of town and most of them had postage stamp lawns. She'd hoped for something more than that. Trailers were cheaper, of course, but then she'd have to pay a pad fee, and most of them barely had yards at all.

When she finally spotted a house she really liked, its list price was a hundred and seventy-five thousand dollars. Her fingers tightened into fists in the pockets of her jeans. That left just twenty-five thousand dollars from Ellis's money. What if the house needed repairs, or her truck broke down, or the baby got sick?

What if she did?

Still, a house was something special. Maybe it was worth the risk.

She hadn't realized she'd sighed until the man glanced over at her. "Find a good one?"

"It's too expensive." She pointed to the one she liked, a yellow house with white shutters on a comfortable lot on the south side of town.

"What's your limit?" He moved closer and scanned the listing.

"I'm not sure. I have—" She broke off. She shouldn't talk money with a stranger.

The man chuckled. "It's okay. I promise I won't tell anyone else. My name's Carl."

"I'm Mia. Are you looking for a house?"

It was his turn to sigh. "Yes, unfortunately. I was stupid enough to sell the one I had."

"And now you want it back?"

He shrugged. "Seller's remorse, I guess you could say. So what's your limit again? There are some nice ones around two hundred and fifty thousand."

"That's way over what I can afford. I've got two hundred—but this one is one-seventy-five."

"You have two hundred grand to spend? Or that's all you have in the world?"

"Two hundred grand is a lot of money," she said, surprised at his tone.

"I didn't mean it wasn't." His expression was kind and she relaxed.

"That's all I have in the world. So I think this one is too expensive."

He leaned against the wall and surveyed her thoughtfully. "Most people don't buy houses with cash, you know. They make a down payment—about twenty percent is good. Then they get a loan for the rest."

"I wouldn't qualify for a loan," Mia admitted. "So it's cash or nothing."

"Then this one is definitely too much. I wouldn't go over ninety-five if I were you. Get a fixer upper and learn to do as much of the work yourself as you can."

Jolene Manning appeared from the back of the office, a stack of file folders in her hand. She deposited them on the receptionist's desk and walked right over to them. "Mia Start—are you looking at real estate? You must be marrying Luke, after all. I heard conflicting reports on that."

Heat rose in Mia's cheeks. "Actually, no. We're not getting married. I'm looking to buy a place for myself."

"Oh." Jolene's surprise was clear. "Then honey you'd better look at rentals. I don't think you'll qualify for a loan, and you'll need one even for the condos."

"I don't need a loan. I want to buy a fixer-upper. With cash."

Jolene laughed, her white teeth bright against her red lipstick. "Sweetie, did you look at the prices up there? You can't buy these places with pocket change, you know." She turned to Carl. "I'll be with you in just a minute, sir." She faced Mia again. "Honey, you go home and make up with Luke and come back together. I'll be able to find just the right place for you if you don't want to live on the Double-Bar-K."

"I've got money of my own," Mia protested.

Jolene took her arm and walked her firmly toward the door. "No, you don't," she said in a quiet voice that brooked no dissent. "I'm sorry, Mia, but I know your circumstances and you can't afford a house. I work on commission. I need to talk to the customer that can afford one." She tilted her chin toward Carl. "Make an appointment if you want me to explain real estate to you. I'm busy right now."

A second later, Mia was out on the sidewalk, blinking back tears. She jammed her hands in the pockets of her winter jacket and hunched her shoulders against a biting wind that had just started up. The sky was the color of lead and the thaw that had seemed imminent this morning now seemed as distant as the moon. She couldn't believe Jolene wouldn't even listen to her. So much for her new professional look.

But then again, why would Jolene believe she had enough money for a house? No matter what she wore or how she styled her hair, she still worked a cash register for a living, and like everyone else Jolene believed that was all she'd ever do. She wasn't proving to be an ace at business either. Look at the way she'd scheduled three back-to-back events in a single weekend.

The panic she'd been fighting for days surged up again. What if she'd overextended herself? What if she couldn't do it? What if she ruined two of her friends' weddings and Lila White's reunion?

What if sending the letter to the pageant commission brought Fred Warner back into her life?

She turned and walked slowly toward her truck, trying to calm her own fears. Warner was far from Chance Creek. She didn't have to worry about him. She'd get through these first three events and she'd be careful about scheduling more in the future.

Meanwhile, there were other real estate companies in town. Mia thought about visiting one now, but she didn't have the heart to do it. She'd go home, regroup and figure out what to do next.

"Hey, Mia!"

Carl appeared on the sidewalk behind her, the door to the realtor's office swinging closed. Mia stopped walking and waited for him to catch up.

"Want to grab a cup of coffee?"

"I thought you were buying a house."

"I decided that woman wasn't the realtor for me. If

she treats you with disrespect—someone she knows—I figure she'll treat me with disrespect too someday."

"She treated me with disrespect *because* she knows me." Mia kept her eyes on the pavement. "She knows I'm poor."

"No one with two hundred grand in their bank account is poor."

"Well, I was poor until Ellis gave it to me."

"Ellis? Not Ellis Scranton?"

Mia wilted. Of course this nice man would have to know Ellis.

"Why did Ellis Scranton give you two hundred grand?" Carl peered down at her. "What did the old scumbag do to you?"

"Got me pregnant," Mia said dejectedly. Everyone else knew about it. Carl might as well too.

He snorted. "Figures. Listen, I'm still up for that coffee if you are. I'm not Ellis—I won't hit on you. I'm a businessman, though—just like him. I might be able to give you some advice."

"Or maybe you'll talk me right out of my money." Mia was done with men taking advantage of her.

"I swear I won't do that. Can I tell you a secret?"

Mia hesitated. Looked him over. "I guess."

"I've got more money of my own than I know what to do with."

"How much?" Mia didn't think she'd ever met anyone so frank about his circumstances. Carl was a little strange, but she liked him for that.

"Last I checked? About fifty million dollars."

She stopped dead. "Are you shitting me?"

Carl laughed. "No, I'm not. So I promise I won't take yours. How about that coffee?"

"Okay—but I'll buy my own." Millionaire or not, she still wouldn't trust a man fully. Not anymore. "Where do you want to go?"

LUKE MET UP with Ethan and Autumn in line at the post office that afternoon when he came in to mail in his credit card payment.

"Why don't you pay that on the computer?" Ethan asked as the line advanced toward the counter.

"Dad's paranoia has rubbed off on me. He thinks online banking is the next best thing to throwing cash on a bonfire. What're you here for?"

"Picking up a package." Ethan held out the yellow slip. "Although why they didn't just leave it at the ranch, I can't guess."

They found out when they reached the counter.

"The sender asked for the package to be held for you here. It's marked fragile all over the thing," Carrie Benton said and disappeared into the back room to fetch it.

"What did you order?" Luke placed his envelope on the counter.

"Nothing." Ethan watched the door to the back. Autumn shifted Arianna into a better position. When Carrie came back she set a tall thin package on the counter. As she'd said, it was stamped *fragile* in many places. She took Luke's envelope and the money he offered her and put on a stamp.

"It looks like a bottle of wine. Or maybe champagne.

Where'd it come from?" Autumn asked. Ethan bent to scan the label.

"Can T. Siddown. Who the heck is that?"

Luke cocked his head. Suppressed a laugh. "Can't sit down?"

Ethan read it again. "Naw." He made a face. "You don't think…"

They moved aside to let the next people in line reach the counter. Greg Hutton and his wife Eleanor held out another package slip for Carrie to fetch.

"I think I'd be careful about how I open that thing," Luke said.

"I still think it's wine. It's got to be. Look at the box." Autumn shifted Arianna again. "Open it!"

Ethan set the package down on a side counter and did just that, tearing the cardboard flaps apart. He reached in and pulled out a handful of tubes.

"What is that?" Autumn bent closer. "Preparation H? Why'd you order so much?"

Luke noticed the Huttons listening in. Eleanor nudged her husband when she spotted the tubes. "He must be as constipated as Grandma Hutton. She always had a stockpile of that around for her piles."

"I didn't order it!" Ethan's face turned a mottled red. "I'm not constipated!"

Luke laughed out loud. "It was Ned—it has to be! Remember what he said?"

"No, what did he say? What's going on?" Autumn said, looking from one to the other of them.

"Just Ned's idea of a stupid joke," Ethan said, tossing the tubes back in the box disgustedly. He closed up the flaps and tossed the whole box into the trash. "Come on. Let's get out of here."

Autumn giggled. "Why does Ned think you need Preparation H?"

"Drop it!" Ethan stalked away.

Luke held out his hands for Arianna and Autumn handed her over as they followed the angry cowboy. "Thanks," Autumn said. "Now how about explaining what's going on?"

Chapter Fourteen

"HI MIA," TRACEY said as Mia and Carl settled themselves into a booth at Linda's Diner. "What can I get for you two?"

"I'll have a cup of coffee and a slice of that apple pie I saw on the way in," Carl said. "Mia, what would you like?"

"A glass of milk and a chocolate chip muffin. Thanks." She smiled at Tracey, who cocked an eyebrow when she turned her back to Carl. Mia hoped she wasn't coming to the wrong conclusion about this meeting.

"That's funny." Carl watched Tracey head back to the kitchen. "I don't think she recognized me."

"Tracey knows you?"

"I used to come here now and then when I lived here before. Maybe she just forgot."

"Maybe you look different. Was it a long time ago?"

"Not that long, but I guess I have lost some weight. I took up mountain climbing when I left here last year. I climbed a lot of mountains." He made a face. "So tell me more about your situation. You've got money in the bank, but you won't qualify for a loan, which means your job situation must be tenuous."

"Not tenuous, exactly—I always have work—but I don't make a lot of money at it. I work behind the counter at Fila's Familia, a new restaurant in town. And I'm starting an event planning business. I have three events already." Mia wondered what had propelled him to climb all those mountains. A broken heart?

"Paid events?"

Mia dropped her searching gaze. "One is free," she admitted, "but the other two are paid."

"How much?"

"Well, I haven't gotten that far really. I mean…"

Carl tapped his fingers on the table thoughtfully. "Okay, here's the deal, Mia. You've got a businessman sitting across the table from you. A businessman with a hell of a lot of money burning a hole in his pocket, and he's taking the time to chat with you. What do you do?"

Mia blinked. "Talk to him back?"

"No. You sell him."

"On what?" She was getting the same feeling she used to have in trigonometry at school, when the teacher would write an equation on the board and ask her to come and solve it. But at least he wasn't treating her like just a pretty face.

He stopped tapping. "On your event planning business."

"Like, try to get you to hire me to plan an event for you?"

"Well, that's one way to go about it. That's the small businessman's way to go about it. Know what a businessman like me would do?"

Mia shook her head.

"I'd come up with a gimmick and try to sell someone like me on making it a franchise. That's what I'd do."

"Like McDonald's?" She frowned.

"Exactly." He stopped. Got a faraway look. Tapped his right forefinger twice. "But that's not what you should do," he said a moment later.

"Okay, now I'm confused."

He twined his fingers together. "You know what? So am I. Maybe I shouldn't be trying to help you. Maybe you should be helping me."

Tracey arrived with their drinks and pastries, and another significant look at Mia. When she was gone again, Mia said, "What do you need help with?"

"Learning how to act like a human being. Like the kind of guy who can live in a small town and not piss everyone off."

"Is that what happened before? You pissed everyone off?"

"You wouldn't believe the half of it," Carl said. "But I'm a changed man, I swear."

"You must be. You haven't pissed me off." She smiled at him.

"Give me twenty minutes and see how you feel then."

They laughed together over his remark, but Mia had a feeling he was serious. There was something wistful about Carl, especially when he looked at the occupants of other tables—people Mia knew well, and were part of the community. He must want some of that community for himself, she thought. And then added internally, *He should be careful what he wishes for.* Being known to everyone wasn't always what it was cut out to be. People tended to pigeonhole you and not let you change.

"So I won't hit you up to help me start a franchise," she said some minutes later, when they'd eaten, "but I wouldn't mind some advice. A lot of people won't take me seriously. My friends think I can't handle running a business. What do I do about that?"

He nodded thoughtfully. "That's a tricky one, but building a reputation is something every new businessman faces. You don't have to cut yourself off from your friends, or give up relationships that are meaningful to you, but you do need to surround yourself with a group of believers, or you'll struggle to get anywhere. Pick out a group of cheerleaders and spend most of your time with them. They're the ones to share new ideas and plans with. The people who drag you down can find out what you're up to after you've accomplished it. After a while the people who don't support you will fall away. You won't have anything to talk to them about. You won't want their negative energy around. Success sometimes means losing friends. Are you prepared for that?"

She wasn't sure. But one thing she did know was that her conversation with Carl had helped her more than any she'd had with anyone else except Rose. She decided that meant that Rose and Carl were now her cheerleading team. She asked for Carl's number and wondered aloud if he'd be willing to have coffee again sometime. He agreed readily. "I could use a friend in Chance Creek."

"You've got one." She took the business card he handed her, then entered his number in her phone—

under a brand-new group, *Business Contacts*—and left the diner feeling more upbeat than she had in days.

Until she realized that Luke hadn't made the cut for her cheerleading squad.

"BUDDY, I HATE to break it to you, but you've got competition."

"What do you mean?" Luke looked up from curry-combing Bullet, a roan gelding he'd had for several years. They'd taken a quick ride out to check on some pregnant cows.

Jake leaned against the side of Bullet's stall. "Hannah heard the gossip at the veterinary clinic. Marcy Sharp came in with her cat and said she'd seen Mia at Linda's Diner with a very handsome man. So I knew it couldn't be you."

"Ha, ha." Luke got back to work. "Mia doesn't know any handsome strangers."

"She does now. Jolene Manning confirmed it. She says the guy was looking at properties in her office when Mia came in. The two talked and he followed her when she left."

Luke straightened. "Followed her? What is he, a stalker?"

"A friendly stalker. They ate muffins together."

"Hell, doesn't anyone have anything better to do than to spy on people?" He paused. "What does this guy look like?"

"I don't know. Lean. Brown hair. In his thirties. That's what Marcy said."

Luke fought the urge to throw the currycomb. This

was all he needed—some other guy putting the moves on Mia. "Does he know she's pregnant?"

"I don't know. No one recorded their conversation. Come on, don't take it like that. I just wanted you to know so you can step up your game."

"Step it up how? I made her a nursery. That didn't work." He hadn't managed to talk to her about the pageants, either. He stood there, currycomb in hand, too frustrated to smooth it over Bullet's coat.

"Yeah, about that." Jake took the currycomb from Luke and got to work on the horse. Bullet looked back at him, snorted, then returned to chewing from his feed bucket. "How did you manage to screw that up?"

"Damned if I know. I told her she didn't have to work. I told her I'd do it all—take care of her and her baby. She got mad and stormed out."

Jake stopped what he was doing and rested his head against Bullet's flank. "Oh God. Not you, too."

"What?"

Bullet shifted and Jake straightened up. "That's pretty much the same mistake I made with Hannah. She says Mia wants to start her own business."

"Yeah. She's got this crazy idea she can be a wedding planner and work for Fila. And have a baby. I mean, she was white as a sheet the other morning when she came over here, and that was after only a half day at Fila's. She needs her rest."

"Here's the thing. Careers are like babies to women. Hell, they're like cubs to momma bears. You don't get between a woman and the job she wants to do—not if you want to keep your head on your shoulders. Believe me—I know."

Luke nodded. He knew Jake and Hannah had scrapped over whether she should go to school or have children. In the end they'd decided to move forward with both. "This is different. I'm telling you, Mia didn't look good at all. She shouldn't be at work. In fact, I've debated whether I should call Fila and tell her that myself."

"It's one thing if you're concerned for her health. It's another thing all together if you're trying to control her."

Luke grabbed the currycomb away from his brother. "I'm not trying to control anyone. I'm trying to help."

"Yeah, well you're helping yourself all the way to losing that girl. Smarten up."

"YOU GOT ANOTHER letter," Autumn said when Mia got home from work that night.

Mia sighed. Her feet ached again, and she hadn't managed to eat any dinner. She knew she should find something to eat now, but the truth was she didn't have an appetite. "What are you doing here so late?" Usually Autumn was home in the bunkhouse by now.

"Some guests are coming to stay next week and I'm planning a menu. Don't worry—we'll still have plenty of room for you."

Mia accepted the letter Autumn held out for her and sat down heavily on the couch. "I'll be out of your hair soon, I promise. I've been looking at real estate."

"Real estate is expensive." Autumn got up and returned a minute later with a cup of tea. "Here, I had just made a pot. Are you feeling okay?"

"I'm fine." Mia accepted the cup gratefully. "Just a little tired." She would have said more about her house search, but she remembered Carl's words—that she should surround herself with cheerleaders. She'd always thought of Autumn as a terrific friend, but Autumn hadn't been too encouraging about her business plan, and now she didn't sound enthusiastic about the idea of her buying a house, either.

"Have you talked to a bank about a loan?"

"Not yet." She decided to turn the conversation. "I bet you can't wait to start gardening again."

Autumn smiled. "You're right. I'm starting some seeds at the bunkhouse. I think this year I'll get Ethan to build me a greenhouse. If we have enough money," she added with a sigh.

"You'll have enough money," Mia said. "I bet this year you'll get a ton of guests. Your website looks great." She dug her finger under the flap of the envelope and began to open it.

"That's what I love about you, Mia. You always make me feel good about the guest ranch. You're such a great friend."

I like being a cheerleader, Mia thought. Now if only more people would encourage her about her wedding planner idea. She opened the envelope and pulled out a small slip of paper.

Don't cheet.

"Huh." Mia shoulders fell. She knew exactly what it referenced: her meeting with Carl in Linda's Diner. She bet all the gossips talked about it afterward.

"What does it say?"

She handed the note to Autumn.

"Cheat? Who would you cheat with?"

"No one." Mia grabbed it back, crumpled it up and stood. "I'm going to bed. I have an early morning." And she still had to finish the letter for Inez. She wasn't looking forward to that.

"Mia," Autumn called after her as she walked toward the stairs. "Take it easy, okay? Don't tire yourself out too much."

"I won't."

She didn't think she could get any more tired than she already was.

Be persistint.

Luke scanned the two words on the page again. He was no English professor, but he was pretty sure that wasn't spelled right.

Besides, he had been persistent. He'd spent every waking hour—at work, while eating, even when he was supposed to be asleep—trying to figure out how to get Mia back. He was insane with worry over it. His body ached more from pent up frustration than from over-work. His chores were suffering and his accounts were a mess because he couldn't concentrate. He knew he was the right man for Mia. He knew she was the right woman for him. It should have been simple, but instead she was slipping away.

Persistent. He'd told her how he felt. He'd gone to her doctor's appointment. He'd transformed his spare room into a nursery. How else could he prove that he would be a good husband and provider?

Should he try the ring thing again? He could go back and get the one she'd first chosen. Luke thought about that, decided he would purchase the ring Mia had wanted, but he wouldn't propose to her again yet. Not until they'd worked things out. The day they were supposed to get married was already long gone. March had arrived and with it a warm, wet breeze that was melting just enough of the snow to turn every stock yard and driveway into a muddy mess.

Should he buy her something else? He wracked his brain for what that might be. Flowers and chocolates hadn't moved her. The bracelet and hair clips hadn't either.

Should he go and reason with her?

Definitely not. Every time he talked he dug himself a deeper hole.

How could he win her without talking to her, though?

The answer to that question made him smile. He didn't think he could trick her into coming to his place again anytime soon though, and he needed privacy for what he had in mind. Good thing the Cruzes cleared out of the guesthouse every night. Mia was the only one staying there at present.

Which meant that right about now she was probably alone.

Chapter Fifteen

MIA WASN'T SURE what woke her an hour or so after she fell asleep. She thought she'd heard a sound that had no place in the house at this time of night. She sat up and listened over the thump of her heart in her chest. Had a door shut downstairs? Was Autumn still down there?

It was awfully late.

Instinct had her climbing out of bed and throwing on her robe. She searched in the dark until her hand closed around the heavy metal flashlight Ethan had given her when she first moved back. She remembered what he told her then. "I like this brand. It's a good light and it's heavy enough to use as a weapon if need be."

Just like a man, she'd thought at the time, but now she understood what he meant. She moved on silent feet to her door and positioned herself to the side that it opened toward. Because now she was sure there was an intruder in the house.

As she pressed her back against the wall and held her breath, straining to hear footsteps or the telltale creak of a stair tread, she longed for the cell phone she'd left downstairs in her purse.

Maybe the intruder would take that purse, steal her money, and go away. Please, she found herself whispering. *Please, please just go away.*

But when a footfall sounded right outside her door, Mia knew she wouldn't get off that easy. She clutched the flashlight in both hands, raised it above her head and waited, stifling a scream when the doorknob turned and the door opened an inch, and then another.

"Mia?" a man said softly as he entered the room, and she didn't wait another instant. She'd meant to smash the flashlight down on the intruder's head, but instead she flung it at him.

"Ow! What the fuck?" The man swung a hand out to defend himself and knocked the door wide open. It slammed into her, the doorknob bashing her hip.

"Ouch!"

"Mia? Jesus, is that you?"

"Luke?"

The man fumbled around the doorway and found the light switch. In the glare of the overhead lamp, Mia cringed back, one hand on her bruised hip. Luke stood in the doorway, a hand to his head.

"What did you hit me with?"

"What the hell are you doing in my bedroom?"

They faced each other, both of them breathing hard.

"I came... I just wanted to be with you." Luke looked at his hand. "I'm bleeding."

"It's no more than you deserve! You scared me to death! How did you even get inside the house?"

"The front door was unlocked and the lights are on

downstairs. I assumed you were still up."

"So you tiptoed through the house and barged into my room?" And why were the lights on at this hour? Had Autumn meant to come back for something and forgotten about it?

"I didn't tiptoe. I sauntered."

"Like hell!" But she moved closer and touched his hand. He *was* bleeding. "Come on into the bathroom— let's take care of that."

"I can't believe you hit me." He chuckled. "It's worth it, though, to get a look at you in that robe."

"Luke." She knew all her curves were in plain sight through the soft, silky fabric.

She led the way into the bathroom, turned on the light and tugged him toward the sink. Turning on the tap, she moved his hand under the running water. He jerked his hand back and hissed.

"You have to clean that."

"All right." He put his hand under the water again and this time let her minister to him. She cleaned the cut as gently as she could with a washcloth.

"I mean it. You look stunning." His voice was husky and when she glanced up and followed his gaze, she realized she'd given him an eyeful when she'd bent over his hand. He couldn't seem to look away from the curve of her breasts exposed by her robe. "I'm sorry I scared you, honey."

"You did scare me." She fought against her awareness of him. Tried to stay immune to his familiar, sexy scent.

"Did I hurt you?" His free hand slipped under her

robe to her hip. Mia gasped, but not from pain as he smoothed his palm over her bare skin. "You know I'd never hurt you on purpose."

She did know that. As aggravating as Luke was—as blind to her needs as he could be—the cowboy meant well. And he was so… intoxicating when he touched her like that.

But she had to be strong. She finished cleaning his cut, patted his hand dry with a towel and moved to fetch a band-aid.

"I don't need that," Luke said. "But there's something else you could help me fix up."

"What?"

He took her hand, pressed it against the front of his jeans. He was hard below the fabric. Mia's breath caught in her throat. "Luke."

"I want you," he whispered as he reached out to undo the ties of her robe. She tried to cover herself back up. "Mia, don't."

She heard the longing in his voice, and she wasn't sure if it was because she was so tired, the late hour, or the way his body always got her attention, but she found she didn't want to fight him. She let her hands fall, and he slid the robe off of her, then led her to the bed. "Climb in."

"What about you?"

He smiled. "Be there in a minute." He turned off the bedroom light, closed the door and she could hear the sound of him undressing. She knew she was crazy to let him join her—especially after the stupid move he'd just pulled, but she didn't want Luke to leave. She didn't want to be alone.

When he slid under the covers, she shivered with the cool air that followed him, but in just moments, he warmed her up again. He scooped her into his arms and pressed her body against his. Mia sighed when her breasts rubbed against his chest.

"Feels good, doesn't it?"

"Um-hmm."

"I bet I can make you feel even better."

She knew he could, so she offered no resistance to his caresses. Instead she rolled over onto her back, relaxed against the pillows and offered herself to him. Luke didn't hesitate. He commenced a sensual exploration of every part of her body that soon had her writhing beneath him in ecstasy. Gone was the exhaustion that had weighed her down all day. Under Luke's touch, she came alive.

"I want you inside me," she finally breathed and in an instant he was in position above her, letting her know with his body just how ready he was to be with her, too.

He hesitated only a moment—just long enough to see if she had any objections to the position, which she didn't. She liked that Luke had taken control and that all she had to do was lie back and let him ravish her.

He did so—pressing into her so tenderly and slowly at first, she was ready to scream with frustration and desire. Then he sped up his movements until all Mia could do was hold on for dear life. When she came, she arched up to meet him and cried out, thankful for the empty house so that she didn't need to hold back. Soon Luke was there with her, grunting in time with his thrusts.

Afterward, when he pulled out, she wanted to do it all over again. When they made love everything was perfect. They were completely aligned—completely of one mind.

Why couldn't they be like that all the time?

"Luke?" she asked when the silence stretched too long. "What is it?"

"I don't want to say anything. I don't want to mess things up and have you kick me out again."

She sighed, hearing the depth of his love for her in his voice. "Then we won't say anything. We'll just touch."

"Like this?" He stroked a finger down her arm and then shifted to circle her breast.

"Exactly like that."

LUKE STUCK TO his guns and didn't say more than a word or two the rest of the night. In the morning, he slipped out of bed, made Mia a quick breakfast—after checking his phone for messages and breathing a sigh of relief when he found none—and took it to her in her bedroom. He set the tray on her lap, kissed her good-bye and went home to do his own chores, a spring in his step that hadn't been there in a long time.

Several hours later he heard a commotion outside of the barn where he was working and went to check it out. Rarely had he seen Ethan lose his temper, but today the rancher was letting Ned have it.

"At least be man enough to admit what you did! You went to enough trouble to embarrass me!"

"I don't know what the hell you're talking about!"

The two men faced each other near the closest corral. Luke hurried over to see what was the matter.

"Hemorrhoid cream. A whole damn box of it. In front of everyone at the post office! Eleanor Hutton's been telling the whole town about my piles. Someone offered me a donut pillow at the drug store yesterday."

Ned guffawed. "Wish I'd been there, but it wasn't me. Now if you don't mind, I've got a snow blower to fix." He indicated his mechanics shed in the distance where he kept all the equipment on the ranch in working order.

"Ned ain't smart enough to pull a practical joke," Luke said, joining them. "It's gotta be someone else."

"Not the sharpest tool in your tool shed? Is that what Luke means?" Ethan said to Ned.

"I'd be sharp enough not to be fooled if someone played a practical joke on me."

"You Mathesons." Ethan made it sound like a dirty word. "I don't need your shit! I can't get a full night's sleep. I don't have enough guests booked for the month. I've got bills coming out of my ears!" Luke could sympathize with his pain. Ethan walked around in a circle. "How am I supposed to pay for college if the guest house can't even pay for its own electricity?"

"College?" Luke chuckled. "Arianna's what—three weeks old?"

"And seeing how she's yours, she won't be too bright," Ned added. He ducked when Ethan took a swipe at him.

"She'll be smarter than you."

"She'll probably read before she's thirty, at least," Luke added. Then wished he hadn't. "Shit. I didn't mean…"

"To hell with both of you," Ned said and stalked away stiffly, his face as white and pinched as it had been the first time Luke saw him after he broke his leg.

"Damn it." One night with Mia and he was so giddy he'd forgotten to watch his mouth. He shouldn't have said that. Ned was chancy to joke with at any time, but if you brought up his dyslexia to his face he was sure to get ornery.

"I'll leave you to mend your fences." Ethan turned to go. "But you can tell him I don't consider ours mended yet."

"I GOT THE strangest note in the mail the other day," Carl said when Mia met him for coffee again at Linda's Diner one day in the middle of March. He fished a folded envelope out of his pocket and laid it on the table.

"Hi, Mia!" Tracey appeared to take their order. "What'll it be today? And I loved the ideas you emailed me about the flower arrangements. They're perfect!"

"Glad you liked them. I'll have some peach cobbler and a glass of milk." She was getting sick of milk, but everything she read told her she needed to watch her calcium intake. Her baby had a lot of growing to do.

"Coffee—black—and a slice of cherry pie." Carl handed the menu to Tracey and waited until she walked away.

Mia picked up the envelope and her heart sank when she recognized the writing. Not Carl, too. She pulled out the slip of paper inside it.

Leeve her alon.

"I assume you're the one I'm supposed to leave alone?" Carl said.

"Probably. I've been getting notes like this, too."

"Is it your fiancé?"

"I don't think so. Luke would just come out and say it if he was angry about something. I can't think who is sending them."

"Someone who saw us together, I guess."

"It doesn't have to be someone who actually saw us. People gossip."

"Maybe we shouldn't meet anymore."

Mia looked him in the eye. "I want to meet. You're the only one I can really talk about my business to, as sad as that is."

"Speaking of which. Where's your contract?" He held out a hand. Mia pulled a large manila envelope from her bag, handed it over, then watched him draw out the sheaf of papers inside. She had come to enjoy Carl's weekly challenges for her and she was learning a lot from him. This week the challenge had been to make a contract for her event planning services. She'd cobbled one together from contracts she'd seen online, but she wasn't sure it was what Carl had in mind.

"I found what I could on the Internet and changed a few things. I haven't shown it to a lawyer or anything."

"That's okay. I know what to look for."

The next few minutes were quiet as Carl read through the document she'd given to him. He pulled out a pen and made some alterations as he read, but in the end he nodded.

"Pretty solid. I added a few things." He pointed to some writing. "And I took out a clause or two that don't really pertain, but I think this will do until you're making enough money to want to pay for a lawyer's time."

"Thanks so much. I really appreciate it." Mia tucked the contract back into her bag, flashing Carl a grateful smile.

"I have another assignment for you, if you want it." Carl accepted the cup of coffee and slice of pie from Tracey. Mia waited for her milk and cobbler before she answered him.

"Sure."

"Can I get you anything else?" Tracey asked.

"We're all set for now." Mia winced when Tracey shot her another significant look as she walked away. Was Tracey the one spreading all the gossip that she and Carl were meeting? "What's the assignment?" she asked.

"I want you to hone the way you sell your services. Come up with an elevator pitch."

"What's that?"

"It's a description of what you do in a single sentence—or even a phrase. Imagine you step onto an elevator and spot a potential investor in your business. You've got about ten to fifteen seconds to make the sale. What do you say?"

"Ten to fifteen seconds? That's not very much."

"I hold patents for products that run everything from your wristwatch to the mechanical arm on the space station. Want to know more?"

Mia whistled. "That's a great elevator pitch."

"Let's hear yours."

"I create memorable weddings."

Carl made a face. "So does everyone in the business, right? That's okay—it takes time to come up with a good one. Think about it for a week and try to sell me next time we meet."

"Will do. How's the house hunting going?"

"Not great. The one I really want has already been taken."

Coming over again. Won't say a word.

Luke waited for Mia's reply to his text late that night when all his work—and Ned's—was done. It was later than he'd wanted it to be. He knew Mia needed lots of rest these days. The baby was growing bigger and bigger and so was her belly. Still, it was the earliest he could make it with all the ranch chores on his back. Ned was due to see a doctor again about his leg in a few days. Hopefully then they'd get a sense of when he'd be back to a hundred percent. Until then, Luke would keep on doing it all himself.

At least Amanda Stone wasn't as much of a burden as she used to be. Not that he minded helping her, but he was grateful he didn't have more expenses on his already overfull plate.

Hurry. Almost asleep.

He'd hurry. She didn't need to worry about that.

Ten minutes later he let himself inside the guesthouse and locked the door behind him. He turned off the living room lights and made his way upstairs, happy to see a glow from Mia's room when he reached the upper corridor. She was waiting for him under the covers, as naked as the day she was born, and Luke quickly joined her there, his body already humming with the need to bury himself inside of her. He'd come to anticipate each night they spent together. They still kept conversation to a minimum—their relationship was too tenuous to test with long discussions—but their love-making warmed his soul and kept him hopeful that they'd find a way to be together all the time in the future.

"How are you feeling?" he said as he climbed between the sheets.

"Shhh." Mia kissed him long and hard and his senses leaped. All the fatigue from his long day fell away, replaced by a driving desire to worship every inch of her luscious body. He started with her breasts, nipping and teasing them until they were peaked and rosy under his mouth. Then he worked his way lower, and lower still until she parted her legs for him and welcomed his touch in an even more intimate place. Luke couldn't get enough of her, and when she wrapped her fingers in his short hair and lifted her hips to his touch, he knew she couldn't get enough of him, either. Later, when he was poised above her, just pushing inside, he knew that soon something would have to change. He wasn't satisfied with slipping away to her room for silent lovemaking at night. He wanted all of Mia, all the time.

He wanted her to be his wife.

But they'd talk about that later. Right now he'd show

her his intentions with his body.

He held her gaze as he slid into her right up to the hilt. She gasped, and he took advantage of the moment to swoop down and capture her mouth with his, plunging his tongue into her warm, wet depths. He moved his body simultaneously, sliding out and back into her again and soon he set a rhythm that had her gasping with pleasure, and kissing him back with a need that equaled his own.

Luke slid a hand beneath her body, lifting her hips, the better to deepen his access. With the other, he cradled the nape of her neck. He kissed her until he was breathless, then kissed her more, the whole time moving in and out of her until he could barely hold back.

"Luke." That one word told him she was close, too. Luke redoubled his efforts, plunging in and out, revving her up to her own release, until she threw her head back and cried out with it, and he called out too, reaching his climax at the same time.

"Mia," he said when he had tumbled down next to her, still entwined. To hell with his vow to keep silent. He had to talk to her. Had to tell her how he felt.

"Luke, no." She pressed a finger to his mouth. He kissed it and moved it away.

"Yes. I want more than this. I want you. All of you."

She pulled back, but Luke captured her in his arms. Held her close to him. They were still joined and he wasn't willing to let that go yet.

"I need…" She gasped when he pulled out an inch and pressed in again, reminding her of what they'd just done.

"What do you need?" He kept his tone soft.

"I need you to be as good a friend as you are—at this." She sucked in a breath when he moved inside her again.

"Am I good at this?" His mouth curved into a smile.

"You know you are." She smiled, too. "You're the best."

"Glad to hear you say it. I thought we were good friends, though."

It took her a moment to focus as he played with her body, moving inside her, caressing her curves.

"A real friend listens. A real friend cheers you on. First you say you support me, next you tell me I should quit. That's not what I want from you."

He stopped his teasing. This was about her career again. "But doesn't a real friend say something if you're taking too much on? Not because he's trying to call the shots, but because he cares what happens to you?"

She searched his gaze with her own. "If that's the truth of it, then maybe. But you earn the right to do that by being a cheerleader first and foremost. You only doubt if doubt is really deserved."

"I do care about you." He brushed a kiss along her temple, his hand skimming her skin until it curled around her breast. He bent down to kiss its rosy tip. "I worry about you. I want to keep you safe."

"Then trust me. Trust that I know my own strength." Her eyes fluttered closed as he flicked her nipple with his tongue.

"Your strength, huh? I don't know. You don't look very strong," he teased.

Her eyes flew open again. Before he knew what hit him she'd pushed him on his back and climbed on top. He took in the view with appreciation. Her breasts had definitely grown in the last month or so, their areolas wide and dark. He cupped them both and enjoyed the heft of them, growing hard again inside of her.

Mia took hold of his wrists and pressed them back against the bed, a move that brought her delicious breasts well within range of his mouth. "I'm weak, am I?" she said.

"Baby, you know you've got the upper hand on me." But he took advantage of the situation to nuzzle first one and then the other of her beckoning nipples.

Mia rocked her hips, sliding up and down the length of him, making him harder still—something he'd thought was impossible. He didn't think he'd ever seen a prettier sight than his girl enjoying him like this. Every rock of her hips set her breasts in motion and every touch of her skin against his set him further alight. When she increased her tempo with obvious pleasure it was all he could do to hold back.

Soon he didn't need to. Mia came with a cry that rang in his ears and he quickly followed. Bucking against her, feeling her press down against him in equal measure, had his pleasure pulsing throughout his body until he was wrung out.

Mia collapsed in his arms with a passionate kiss.

"See what I mean?" Luke said. "We can't stay apart when we're this good together."

She pulled away from him and rolled to her side, reaching up to cup his jaw and hold his gaze. "Then learn how to be my friend. Trust me to make my own decisions. Support me in them. That's all I've ever wanted from you."

A million thoughts ran through his mind—that he loved her, that he wanted to protect her, that she was doing too much, working too hard. He pushed them all away, staring back into her beautiful blue eyes. "All I can promise is that I'll try."

Chapter Sixteen

"CAN I TAKE your order?" Mia asked the cowboy in line some days later, ignoring the buzz of her phone in her pocket. She kept it with her in case of emergencies, but tried not to use it on Fila's time. She took her job as the front woman for Fila's Familia seriously. Besides, the restaurant was always packed. Today, however, her phone had been ringing off the hook and she wondered who was trying to get a hold of her.

Fifteen minutes later, when there was a lull in the action, she escaped to the ladies' room and checked it, negotiating the tight space carefully now that her abdomen was taking up more space than it ever had before. Tracey had left a dozen messages. She tapped the first one with trepidation.

"Mia, it's Tracey. The florist called and she says she can't do the arrangements you sent me. She says some of the flowers aren't available. I told her to send me photos of what she can do and I hate all of them. I really hate them!"

Mia clicked Tracey's other messages to hear more

about the florist.

"I don't trust her, Mia. If she can't even copy a bouquet and get it right, she's bound to mess up on the day of the wedding. I don't want ugly flowers!"

Mia's heart was pounding by the time she heard all of the messages. She quickly called Tracey back, checking her watch to note that two minutes of her break had already elapsed.

"I know it's just flowers," Tracey burst out the second she picked up the call, "but I only get married once. I want it to look perfect."

"I know, I know," Mia soothed. "And it will. Trust me. I'll talk to the florist on my next day off and get it all sorted out."

"But—"

"Tracey, I'm at work. I can't talk right now. I'll call you tomorrow."

"Call me when you get off."

"That'll be practically midnight."

"I'll be awake."

But Mia would be exhausted. She was already. "I'll call tomorrow. First thing."

"But—"

She hung up and hurried back to the counter where a line now stretched nearly to the door. She took orders as fast as she could, relaying them to Camila and Fila in the kitchen. Camila eyed the crowd through the pass-through. "I know I should be grateful we've got so many customers, but I don't know how we can keep up."

"I don't think I can keep up," Mia said as the front door opened and more people filed in. She sent Camila a pleading look and Camila nodded in return.

"We need to find more help."

LUKE STOPPED IN surprise when he came home to find his mother seated at his kitchen table. He closed the door behind him, hung up his coat and flopped down in his seat, exhausted as usual. "Come for lunch?"

"No, I came to talk about this." She waved what looked like a children's book at him.

"What's that?"

"I think you know. And I have to say I'm disappointed in you. I know you and Ned have your difficulties sometimes, but resorting to teasing him about his dyslexia is really a low blow."

"I didn't—"

"Luke. Let me have my say. You're a grown man. I can't ground you or punish you anymore when you go astray. But this wasn't worthy of you. This... I don't like. I don't ever want to see this kind of behavior again. Make things right with your brother. Family should stick together, not tear each other down."

She got up, kissed him on the cheek as she walked by and left without another word. Luke didn't bother to contradict her, even if whatever she thought he'd done, he hadn't. He moved to the table and picked the book up.

See Spot run. Run, Spot, run.

Hell. Ned must have been ballistic when he saw this. He was a proud man and he hated that people knew about his difficulties with reading. He'd been working steadily with Camila, who volunteered at the local literacy center, and had been making good progress. Luke hoped this stupid joke didn't ruin it.

He threw the book in the trash and went to look for Ned, but his brother wasn't in the barn or stables, or even in the shed he used as a mechanic's shop. When he finally gave up the search, he was hungry and discouraged, so he returned to his cabin, rustled up a quick lunch and ran upstairs to change his shirt. The sight of the guest bedroom door—the nursery door—hanging wide open stopped him in his tracks.

He'd closed that door this morning.

Hadn't he?

A quick peek into the room confirmed his worst suspicions. Someone had been in there. Someone with a grudge.

Ned.

Luke stepped inside to take in the scene. Dozens of pairs of plastic eyes stared back at him out of baby dolls of every shape and size. There were tiny dolls and oversized dolls. Girl dolls with lots of hair. Boy dolls with plastic swirls to indicate hair. Lifelike baby dolls. And stuffed animals, too. Teddy bears, dinosaurs...

Ned must have raided the Salvation Army, Luke realized, remembering the bins of toys he always saw when he dropped things off for sale. Luke understood exactly what Ned meant to say, too; he might not read too well, but he had a wife and soon he'd have a family.

The only babies Luke could look forward to were the plastic ones staring back at him right now.

A slow burn of anger twisted with the pain the joke

had blossoming within him. Ned should have known Luke hadn't meant to tease him about his dyslexia and certainly wouldn't have compounded the insult by sending the book. He should have known someone else was yanking his chain. Instead, he'd rushed to play a trick he knew Luke would feel like a stab to the heart.

Well, Ned had better watch out. Forget making it right. Luke was determined to get revenge.

"I HOPE YOU'VE reserved the tents, dear. It can be quite hard to get a tent this time of year, you know," Lila White quavered into the phone. Mia checked the clock on her dresser again. She needed to leave for work in ten minutes. Would Lila stop talking by then?

"It's on my list to do today, Lila. Don't worry; I'll take care of everything. Your reunion will be a stunning success."

"There are seventy-five people coming."

"I know." Lila had told her a half a dozen times in this call alone.

"I might not live to see another reunion. I want it to be special."

"It will be. I promise. Lila, I have to run, but I'll check in tomorrow with an update, okay?"

"Okay, dear. Don't forget the chairs. Lots of chairs. Everyone needs to be able to sit down."

"Yes. I'll get plenty of chairs."

"And be sure to reserve the tent today, dear. You know how hard it is—"

"Lila? I'm sorry—I have to go right now. I'll call you tomorrow."

Mia ended the call feeling bad for cutting the elderly lady off, but if she didn't get her hair dried now she'd look a fright. There were never enough hours in the day now that she was working two jobs. She planned to meet Carl again during her break—a very quick half-hour break—this afternoon and she still hadn't perfected her pitch. She had a feeling *I deal well with cranky people* wasn't quite what Carl had in mind.

When she reached the restaurant, her cheeks stinging from the fresh April breeze that was sweeping away the last remnants of the winter snow, Fila took one look at her, pressed her lips together and retreated into the kitchen.

"What's wrong?" Mia looked at her watch. She was only a minute late—not bad considering what she'd accomplished already this morning.

"Luke played a really mean joke on Ned," Camila said as she, too, headed for the kitchen. "He made fun of Ned's dyslexia, which really isn't cool."

"Luke did?" Mia was surprised. "That's not like him at all. He gets furious if anyone says anything bad about Ned."

Camila shrugged. "Fila's upset. I'd keep my distance if I were you."

"She blames me because of what she thinks Luke did?"

"You're his girlfriend. She thinks you should have stopped him."

"I'm not his girlfriend." Not really—despite their interludes in bed.

Camila shrugged again and pushed through the

swinging doors into the kitchen. Mia took her place behind the counter and pulled on an apron, still wondering why Luke would act that way toward his brother. She reached for a cloth to buff the counter. Unless, he was so upset about them not being together all the time that he was taking it out on everyone else. She slowly moved the cloth back and forth across the already clean surface. She knew he wanted to marry her. Was he so frustrated that he was lashing out?

And was she being stupid to drag things out when she wanted him as badly as he wanted her?

No—she needed to establish her business and her identity as a self-sufficient, trustworthy adult before she entered into a relationship. He needed to prove he would respect her boundaries, too. But maybe she should go talk to Luke and tell him how she felt. She could clarify that she did love him and wanted to be with him, too. She just needed a little time.

And she'd tell him to behave himself while she was at it. Mia grinned. Then they could get it on to seal the deal. She looked forward to that.

She also hoped to send the letter she'd finally written for Inez later today, too. She wanted to look it over one last time, but she thought she'd done a fair job summarizing the events that had taken place six years ago. She'd copied Inez's style and kept things simple and to the point. That had made it a little easier.

She didn't know what would happen next. Every time she speculated about it, anxiety gripped her. What if Warner denied the allegations? What if he tried to get back at her?

No sense in getting overwrought, she told herself, but she found it hard not to expect the worst.

The rush started the minute the restaurant opened and continued until well past two, but by two-thirty there was enough of a lull that Mia was able to take her first half-hour break. She stashed her apron under the counter, grabbed her purse and rushed to Linda's Diner, savoring the fresh wind that lapped her cheeks on the blustery April morning. She'd noticed the last vestiges of snow in the shady spots were melting away. Soon the days would lengthen and the watery sunshine would strengthen into the strong hot heat of May and June.

Wedding weather. Her heart gave a little throb. She couldn't wait for her chance to show the world she could achieve what she set out to do. By the time she slid into the booth across from Carl, she felt invigorated.

"I ordered your glass of milk." Carl nodded at the full glass in front of her. "I wasn't sure what you'd want to eat though."

Mia was hungry. Her baby was really growing now and there was no doubt about her condition. Her baby bump pressed out against her clothing like a cantaloupe. When Tracey bustled over to take their order, Mia said, "I'll have a club sandwich and a side of French fries."

"I'll have some of that peach pie. And keep that coffee coming." Carl smiled at Tracey, who nodded absently and kept on going.

"Want to hear my pitch?" Mia said, folding her hands before her on the table. She'd actually come up with one while she was working.

"Sure. Lay it on me." Carl sat back and waited.

"Mia's Memorable Events—When You Want Perfection The First Time Around."

Carl drummed his fingers on the table. "That's an advertisement, not a pitch. It's a pretty good advertisement, but not what we're after."

"Darn." She'd thought she'd done a good job.

"Remember—you're trying to interest an investor, not a customer. Why would someone else want to give you money to grow your company?"

"Because in a year or two, I'm going to be the go-to girl for every event in this town. I've already got Ellie from Ellie's Bridals sending women my way. After these first few events, I bet the rental company will do the same. The restaurant I work for? Fila's Familia? They're already so busy they can't keep up and they'll be my first recommendation for catering. Chances are that will work both ways." As long as Fila got over her anger at Luke.

"Now you're getting somewhere. Sum that up in ten words or less."

"Invest in my event planning company because I own this town."

Carl laughed loudly and heads turned. "Okay, that's too succinct. But you're on your way. Next week I bet you'll have it nailed. You'd better eat up." They both sat back to allow Tracey to deposit their food on the table. "You've got to be back to work in fifteen minutes."

THREE BOOTHS DOWN the row, Luke hunched in the corner of his seat with a menu propped up as a shield. Across the table sat Jake, similarly arranged.

"Can you hear what they're saying?" Luke raised his

chin a fraction of an inch and peered over his menu. He could see a quarter of Mia's face as she chatted animatedly. All he could see of the man was the back of his head. But he knew all about Carl Whitfield—by reputation if not personally.

Carl Whitfield was the man who'd stolen Ethan Cruz's fiancée. Carl was the man who'd lowballed a family who could no longer afford to keep the ranch that had been in their family nearly a hundred years and bought it for a fraction of what it was worth. Carl was the man who'd hired Luke's brother, Rob, to build a fantastic walled garden for his bride-to-be and then got dumped by her at the unveiling in front of a dozen people. Carl was also the man who'd sold that ranch for twice what he bought it for to Evan and Bella Mortimer.

Like everyone else in town, Luke had privately sneered at the Californian when he first arrived dolled up like Hollywood's idea of a cowboy. A hack rider and useless at ranch chores, it was clear he wanted to play at running a spread and he didn't care who he hurt in the process. When he stole Ethan's girl, Luke had classified the man as a lowdown snake. When he took the ranch from an old Chance Creek family for a song, his estimation of Carl had sunk even lower, and when Lacey Taylor dumped him in front of everyone, Luke figured the man had gotten exactly what he deserved.

Now he was back—God knew why—and this time he'd set his sights on Mia. Would he steal her away, just like he'd done with Lacey? Carl looked different now— leaner, older. Wiser. Would he make sure this time the girl didn't get away?

Laughter rang out—first Carl's hearty laugh and then Mia's chiming one. Luke scowled. "What are they laughing about?"

"Your bank account?" Jake angled his head to get a better look.

Luke knew Jake meant it as a joke, but his barb hit home more sharply than his brother could know. Luke's bank account would have been pitiful compared to Carl's in any circumstances, but right now it was worse than ever. He'd bought all the baby furniture on a credit card already full to the brim. He was maxed out. He wouldn't ask to have his limit raised, either. It was time to sink or swim on the salary he earned—such as it was. He hoped to God no fresh disaster struck at the Stone place. He wouldn't be able to help Amanda if it did.

"What'll you have, boys?" Tracey's matter-of-fact tones startled him into awareness of his surroundings.

"Coffee, black. A cheese Danish," Jake said. "Luke will have coffee and pie."

"Peach or Apple?"

"Apple."

Tracey looked from Jake to Luke over to where Mia was laughing again. "Are you spying on your ex-fiancée? Because that's just lame."

"I'm having coffee with my brother. This is where I always get my coffee."

"Uh-huh. Be back with that coffee-you-always-get right away."

Luke worried that Tracey might point him out to Mia, but he was in luck. Mia was standing up and pulling on her coat. Carl Whitfield stood up, too, and said good-bye, but instead of leaving with her, he resumed his seat once she was gone.

"There's your chance." Jake nodded toward Carl.

"Yeah, I was thinking the same thing."

He got up and crossed over to Carl's booth, dropping down heavily onto the bench seat across from the man. "Hi, Carl. Long time, no see."

Carl squinted at him. "You've got to be a Matheson with that hair, but I don't know which one."

"Luke. Rob's older brother."

"Got it. Good to see you again." Carl held out his hand. When Luke didn't take it, Carl grimaced and pulled it back. "Maybe not so good, after all."

"No. Not so good, seeing as you're hitting on my fiancée."

"Aaah." Carl chuckled. "Where to start. First of all, I haven't hit on Mia. She's much too young for me—almost too young for you, too, buddy. Second of all, I didn't see a ring on her finger, which means you're either not her fiancé, or you're a lame son-of-a-bitch who can't afford a wife. Third, that girl is desperate to talk about her business with someone, and since she's coming to me that tells me that either you're not her fiancé and she doesn't want to talk to you about anything, or you are her fiancé but you have no business sense, which is probably the case because you haven't put a ring on her finger, or you're a complete fuck-up who doesn't care about the thing that's most important to his future wife. So which is it?"

Luke shook off the man's barrage of words, his anger unabated. "I'm her fiancé," he repeated. "And I'm telling you to leave her alone."

Carl leaned forward. "No."

Jake reached the table just in time to catch Luke's arm as he took a swing at Carl.

"Whoa! Easy now. Not here!" He half lifted, half dragged Luke up from the table. "Let's go. You two can reconvene this little meeting outside."

Luke allowed his brother to manhandle him up the aisle and out of the restaurant. A battle in Linda's Diner would bring wrath down on his head from every quarter. Outside, Jake let him go, but stood between him and Carl as Carl exited the restaurant, too.

"I've got no quarrel with you," Carl said, holding his hands out. "All I've got is advice. That's what Mia came to me for—advice on how to grow her business. Now I've got some advice for you: listen to her. Have you ever started one?"

"One what?" Luke couldn't see past the vision of Carl and Mia chatting, of Mia turning to the older man for help. Of Mia choosing Carl over him...

"A business." Carl's exasperation was plain to hear.

"No."

"I thought not. Otherwise you'd know how terrifying it is to find yourself solely responsible for every decision. She's young, Luke. She's feeling her way. She's pregnant, working two jobs....Why aren't you helping her?"

Luke blinked. Then lunged. Jake stopped him. Pushed him back.

Carl held up his hands again. "I'm going back to my motel room, but I'm not the man you have a problem with. Look in the mirror and you'll see who you should be angry at."

"Fuck you!"

Carl walked away, shaking his head. Jake kept his grip on Luke until the man had turned the corner.

"Shit, Luke. It's like being out with Ned."

"That's bullshit. Everything he said was goddamn bullshit."

"Really? Because it sounded like good sense to me."

Luke turned on him. "You're supposed to be on my side!"

"I am on your side, but Carl's right. If Mia is meeting with him because she wants someone to talk to, that means the two of you aren't talking enough."

"Maybe she isn't interested in just talking to him."

"What's that supposed to mean? You heard the guy. Mia's too young for him."

"When did that ever stop a man?" Luke thought about Warner. Shook it off. "Even if he isn't into her, which I doubt, she could be into him. Everyone knows he's rich as sin, right?"

Jake nodded slowly. "You think Mia would hit on Carl in order to get her hands on his money? Are you listening to yourself, asshole? Mia's the one who keeps refusing to let you pay her way because she wants to do it herself. She's the one who's set her heart on running her own business—an idea you keep trashing. If you're going to accuse her of whoring herself out for cash, maybe she should dump your sorry ass."

"Maybe I don't have enough money for her. Maybe that's what she's been trying to tell me all along."

"That she won't let you support her because you

don't have a million dollars? I don't think—"

"You know what? I don't need to know what you think. I need to figure this out on my own." Luke climbed into his truck, slammed the door shut and roared off down the street, not caring who saw him or what happened next.

Hours later he stood in the nursery watching the sea of dolls watch him back, still seething from his encounter with Carl. A long drive down country roads hadn't calmed him. Neither had slogging through the remainder of his chores. Ned was right. These were the only babies he'd ever see in this nursery, because there was no way he could compete with a millionaire. Maybe he could have once, back when Carl was the soft, pasty-white businessman he had been, but this new Carl was both rich and masculine enough to attract a woman like Mia. Had the asshole been working out?

Anger boiled up within him that it had ever come to this. That Mia had ever slept with Ellis. That she had held back from him when she moved in. That he'd blown his chance with her while she still lived here. That he couldn't have a simple conversation with her without turning it into an argument. Mia would sleep with him, but she wouldn't pledge her life to him. She'd have Ellis's baby, but she wouldn't let Luke become the father to her child.

His chest tightened until he could hardly breathe. His pulse pounded at his temples. The sea of dolls stared back at him unblinkingly until Luke couldn't stand it anymore. He charged downstairs, found the trash bags and grabbed a handful. Back in the nursery he opened one up and swooped armfuls of dolls and stuffed animals into it. When it was full to the brim he balanced it in front of him to tie off the ends. His fingers, shaking from rage, fumbled at the plastic ties and slipped, spilling half the dolls back to the floor. With a roar of anger, Luke kicked the nearest. It ricocheted off the crib and the dresser, and came to rest on the other side of the room. It felt so good to vent his fury he did it again, and again, sending the dolls and stuffed animals flying.

"Damn it! God-damn it!"

"Luke! What are you doing?"

Luke spun around to see Mia in the doorway, her coat still on and her mouth hanging open. He glanced around him and took in the room the way she'd see it—dolls scattered over the floor and furniture, most of them dented, scuffed and damaged from his kicks. The walls and furniture scarred. He noticed one curtain half torn from its rod.

Mia's face crumpled and tears filled her eyes. Luke went cold. "It's not what it looks like."

"What is it then? No!" She held up a hand, a tear spilling over her cheek. "No, I don't want to hear." She turned and ran down the stairs as fast as she could. Luke went after her, but halted halfway down when the front door slammed shut behind her. He sat down hard on the wooden steps. Kicked out at the railing once, twice—until it splintered and crashed to the floor.

What the hell had he done?

Chapter Seventeen

"**W**HAT DO YOU mean he was kicking babies?" Autumn asked, cradling Arianna closer.

"Baby dolls. Stuffed animals. Just kicking them all over the nursery!" Mia was still crying. She couldn't stop. She couldn't make sense of what she'd seen when she'd stopped by Luke's cabin on her way home. All she knew was that it felt like Luke had aimed all his anger at her.

"Had you bought them for your baby?"

"No!" Mia shook her head vehemently. Autumn sat on one of the guesthouse's sofas. Mia paced the room, unable to sit down. "I don't know where they came from. There were dozens of them everywhere. Do you think Luke bought them and then got mad when I wouldn't move back in?"

"I don't know." Autumn looked equally mystified. "I don't think you should be with a man who has a temper like that, either."

"He didn't used to have a temper. He was always sweet." Mia's tears ran faster. "Maybe I pushed him over the edge!"

"You are not to blame for this."

"Not to blame for what?" Claire came in, followed by Morgan, and Mia explained again what she'd seen.

"That seems awfully... strange." Morgan sat down on the couch and pulled her feet up under her. "But there's been some bizarre stuff going on. What's the deal with all the practical jokes?"

"Has there been more than one?" Autumn asked. "The Preparation H thing was pretty weird."

"Well, there was the topiary disaster," Morgan pointed out.

"And the Sexy Cowboy calendar. Jamie's been selected for August," Claire said. "Just what I need—a thousand horny women staring at his photo all month. As if he isn't vain enough already."

"So why the sudden rush of practical jokes?" Autumn shifted Arianna. "I mean, didn't all the men swear off of them after your marriage, Morgan?"

"I thought so. I'll ask Rob and see if he knows anything about the dolls, Mia. Maybe Luke wasn't mad at you at all. Maybe he was mad at the person who put them there."

"Maybe." Her voice was thick and uneven. She scraped at her tears with the back of her arm. "Maybe if someone put all those dolls there, Luke felt they were making fun of him, since I won't marry him."

Autumn brought her a box of tissues and Mia accepted them gratefully. She blotted her eyes but new tears fell as fast as she could dry them.

"That's the whole point of practical jokes, right?" Claire said. "To make the other person feel bad?"

"I guess." Mia dabbed at her face. "That's pretty

mean, though. Who would do that?"

The other women couldn't answer. "I think it's time to figure it out, though," Claire said. "I know I'm sick of this. Aren't you guys, too?"

"Definitely," Mia said. If the dolls were part of a joke, then maybe Luke hadn't lost his mind.

"Maybe you should talk to Luke, Mia. Give him a chance to explain," Autumn said gently.

"Maybe."

"Maybe tomorrow," Morgan said as Mia yawned so widely she swayed. "Look at her. She's exhausted. Mia— you go to bed."

Mia wanted to protest, but Morgan was right. She was too tired to even think straight. Too demoralized, too. No matter what the reason, seeing Luke destroying her nursery had devastated her. Another tear rolled down her cheek as she climbed the stairs and by the time she reached her room, she was sobbing again. This had to be the worst day of her life, and she didn't know how things would get better anytime soon.

Spotting the calendar on her desk, Mia realized she hadn't returned the phone calls she owed to Lila or Tracey. And she hadn't gotten everything organized for her meeting with Rose, either. But there was no way she could do it now.

Mia didn't bother to brush her teeth or change her clothes. She climbed into her bed, pulled the blankets around her and cried herself to sleep.

AT THREE IN the morning in April, the Double-Bar-K was cold, dark and as still as a graveyard. Luke let himself out of his cabin and walked carefully across the grounds until he reached the small outbuilding where Ned's tools were neatly stored around the workbenches where he fixed all the machinery that was needed for the ranch.

By flashlight he began to gather everything he could move—screwdrivers, rasps, a ratchet set, even the blades from the bandsaw. If it wasn't nailed down, Luke took it and loaded it into his truck. He held his breath when he started the engine, and let the truck roll down the dirt lane as far as possible in neutral with the headlights off until he felt it was safe to press on the gas and pull out onto the country highway. He drove south of town until he reached an old barn on the Hamm spread that was so ramshackle it was no longer used.

Ned would never, ever find his tools here. No one would. Luke might have lost Mia, but at least he'd have his—

Revenge?

Luke sat stock still in the seat of his truck, staring out at the black hulk of the Hamms' broken down barn. What good was revenge? It wouldn't bring Mia back. It wouldn't mend the gaping hole in his heart she'd left when she'd run out of his house.

It wouldn't fix anything.

Alone in the dark the only sound was the beating of his own heart. He drummed his fingers on the steering wheel, grappling for the anger that had sent him on this fool's errand. Somehow it had drained away, leaving only defeat behind.

What was he doing stealing Ned's tools instead of rebuilding Mia's nursery, fixing the stair railing, and doing whatever it took to win her back? Was he still a teenager, squabbling and bickering with his brothers until no one on the Double-Bar-K knew any peace or happiness?

No wonder Mia had run from him. He was a first class asshole.

He started up the truck again, revved the engine and turned around with a screech of tires. He drove back home quickly, but rolled into his driveway with the headlights off again. No sense letting his whole family know how low he'd sunk.

He put all the tools away except the ones he needed to repair the nursery. He couldn't stay up all night or he'd be worse than useless the next day, but in time he'd fix what he'd broken—in the nursery, yes, but also between him and Mia.

And tomorrow he'd get to work winning her back from Carl.

"I DON'T UNDERSTAND. You didn't reserve the tents?" Lila White said into the phone. "We talked about them just the other day. I thought I made it clear how important they were. I've got seventy-five guests coming, my dear."

"I know." It was a strain for Mia not to let her frustration show. "I got caught up in work and wasn't able to call the rental company, but I will do it today."

"That's what you said last time, dear. What about the silverware and plates? I don't have seventy-five settings, you know."

"Of course not, Lila. I'll reserve those the same time

I call about the tents."

"The tent company doesn't carry silverware. That's two different companies."

"Yes, two different companies and I'll call them both, just as soon as I—"

"I'm positive it's two different companies. Tents are very different from dinnerware. I'm sure they need two entirely different kinds of storage—"

"Yes, Lila. I know. Two different companies. How about we wrap this up so I can contact them?"

There was a long silence on the other end of the phone and Mia wanted to kick herself. Why had she snapped at poor Lila White? That wasn't kind, or good business.

"Well, if you have the time," Lila said finally. "I know how busy you are."

"Lila, I'm sorry. I shouldn't have said that. I'm worried about the tent rentals and dinnerware, too. I want your party to be the best party ever and I feel awful I haven't taken care of those details yet."

"You are taking a lot on, dear." Lila's voice softened. "I know you're working hard."

"It's important to me to do this right. It's important to me that you're happy, Lila."

"I'm sure I will be. I'll get off the phone right now and you call those rental places up."

"Thank you." As soon as Mia hung up with Lila, she searched for the tent rental company and dialed the number, shimmying into her work clothes at the same time. "Hello? I need to book three large tents on May fifteenth."

The woman who'd answered the phone hesitated only a second. "Sorry—we're all booked that day. Would you like to try another date?"

Mia froze, one foot into the pair of slacks she intended to wear to work. "What do you mean you're all booked?"

"Our large tents book up months in advance for the spring and summer. We have some weekdays left in May and June, but if you need a weekend it'll be the end of July before we have anything available."

"July?" Mia thought she might faint. "Are there any other rental companies you can recommend? I have to have three large tents for the fifteenth."

The receptionist made a doubtful sound. "Here's our competitor's number." She rattled off a number that Mia wrote down swiftly on a scrap of paper on her desk, one leg in her slacks, the other still out. "Good luck. Maybe you'll catch a break."

"Thanks."

But Lady Luck wasn't smiling on Mia; the other company's tents were booked as well. Mia didn't know what to do. Lila had been so nice to her, even after she'd slipped and been rude. How would the woman react when she found out Mia had botched her party?

"There have to be tents somewhere." Mia did an Internet search and called every rental company between Billings and Bozeman. None of them had tents available for the occasion that were large enough. Only when her phone rang again did she realize how much time had passed. She was going to be late for work at the restaurant.

She shuffled the rest of the way into her pants, grabbed a shirt and shrugged it on over her bra. "Hello?"

"Mia? It's Tracey. I've got a problem."

Of course she did. Everyone had problems these days. "What is it?" Mia pattered down the stairs, swept her purse off the counter in the kitchen and headed for the door, only stopping to pop into her coat and shoes.

"My sister hates her bridesmaid dress. She says it makes her look like a barn!"

Mia sighed. "Did you tell her the wedding is about you, not her?"

"If I said that, she wouldn't come. She has to come. She's my maid of honor!"

Mia bit back the words she wanted to say—that her sister had no concept of what being a maid of honor entailed. "Can she ask a local seamstress to alter the gown to flatter her better?"

"She says she doesn't have time!" Tracey's voice was rising to a hysterical pitch that had become all too familiar to Mia. She had to nip this in the bud before Tracey lost control.

"Tell her to mail it back, then. And to take a photograph of her favorite dress. One from her own closet she really loves. We'll figure out how to reproduce it in a color and fabric that works for the wedding."

"That's a terrific idea," Tracey said. "Thank you, Mia."

"You're welcome. I have to run. Let's chat later." She clicked off the phone and checked the time again. Damn, she was really late now.

Fifteen minutes later, she barged into Fila's Familia

at a run, circled around the few people already lined up at the counter and skidded to a stop behind the till.

"Sorry," she called to Camila, who had been running the till and was already hustling back into the kitchen. The silence in the back room seemed ominous. Usually the two cooks blared pop tunes and kept up a happy chatter as they worked. Today, Mia couldn't hear a word.

The tension in her stomach ratcheted up a notch. Fila was still acting distant. Mia understood why she'd be mad at what Luke had done—heck, she was mad at Luke, too—but she didn't understand why Fila was taking it out on her.

All she ever did was work, morning, noon and night. Mia couldn't remember the last time she had any fun—except her brief meetings with Carl, and those were about business, too. She hadn't had time to look at real estate, either. So much for finding a home before her baby was born. Time was running out.

As the morning progressed, Mia's spirits drooped. She was tired, her feet hurt and she'd managed to ruin Lila White's reunion before it even happened. During her break today she'd have to call other rental companies—ones farther away. If she had to drive to another state to secure those party tents, she'd do so.

"Mia? Are you okay?" Hannah faced her on the other side of the counter.

"Hi, Hannah. I haven't seen you in a while."

"Busy with school and work. You look a little pale."

"I'm really tired. And stressed. I made a pretty big mistake this week."

"Here at the restaurant?" Hannah stepped closer and

lowered her voice.

"No—with my event planning business. I was supposed to secure three party tents for Lila White's family reunion and I guess I waited too long. They're all booked up."

"But…" Hannah thought a moment. "Last year we had several weddings in town that happened pretty fast. Like Ethan and Autumn's wedding. And Jamie and Claire's. Those both happened outside. Didn't they have tents?"

Mia thought back. "I can't remember tents. Maybe they just didn't use them."

"I bet if you ask Autumn tonight, she'll have some ideas."

"Thanks. I will." Mia felt hopeful again.

Later that afternoon that hope drained right out of her when Camila took her break and Mia was forced to interact with a stony silent Fila each time she collected an order to give to a customer. After ten minutes, Mia couldn't stand it anymore.

"You know I wouldn't allow Luke to do anything mean to Ned," she hissed when she picked up an order of burritos. A few minutes later when she was back for some curry chicken she added, "Did you know Ned filled Luke's nursery room with dolls?"

Fila looked at her finally. "Dolls? Why would he do that?"

"Think about it." Anger filled Mia. "He knows Luke wants to marry me. He knows Luke fixed up that room as a nursery for me—for my baby. And he knows I've refused to move back in and marry him. He's rubbing it in Luke's face. And that's mean!" She whirled around and delivered the nachos, and for the rest of her shift kept the words she exchanged with Fila to a bare minimum.

Camila confronted her at the end of the evening. "Fila's really upset. What's going on between you two?"

"Ask Fila. Her husband's the one taunting Luke."

"Taunting him about what?"

"About—me." A wave of exhaustion overwhelmed Mia and tears pricked her eyelids at the thought Ned had used her to cause Luke pain. "I have to finish up and go home. I can't talk about this now."

"Neither can Fila." Camila's frustration was clear. "Go home. I'll finish up here. Just come back tomorrow in a better mood."

"I can't promise that. But thank you." She gave Camila a quick hug. "I really need some sleep."

Camila pulled back. "You do. You look a little green around the gills. Has your morning sickness come back?"

"What morning sickness?" Mia laughed. "No—I just feel… tired." Bad was what she meant to say. She felt *bad*. She ached all over and she'd lost her appetite these last few weeks. In fact… Mia hesitated. When was the last time she'd eaten?

Camila must have read her mind. "Hold on." She reappeared with a take-out container. "Go home, eat this and go to bed, okay?"

"Okay." Mia softened. "I will come back in a better mood tomorrow. I'm sorry you've been caught in the middle of all of this."

"I just wish I understood what *all of this* is."

"WHAT ARE ALL those people doing here?" Luke asked his mother when he popped in to update the ranch's accounts the next morning. He was referring to the unfamiliar trucks outside and the workmen milling around.

"They're here for that project of your father's. He's building something. Won't tell me what, though. He said for us to keep clear." Her tone held a warning. "They're working out near the highway."

"It looked like they were putting in a new water line out there when I drove by. Is Dad building a new house?"

His mother raised an eyebrow. "Think he's finally had enough of me?"

Luke gave her a quick hug. "Never. That man would be lost without you. See you later."

He drove to Amanda Stone's next, where he found the old woman rocking contentedly on her front porch. There was something different about her these days. She seemed more at ease.

"Mrs. Stone, do you have a boyfriend?" he asked. The question had been on his mind for some time.

Amanda laughed long and hard. "At my age? I should think not. No, no boyfriend. Just a good friend coming through for me. I'm glad I don't have to burden you anymore with taking care of me."

"It's no trouble," he assured her.

"You're a good boy, Luke," she said. "But it's time for you to marry that girlfriend of yours and take care of her. You don't have to worry about me anymore. I'll be okay."

"Who's helping you, then? Family?"

"No, not family. It's a secret." Her eyes twinkled. "It's a good secret, though. Be happy for me and rest easy."

He didn't know what to say to that. "Well, anytime you need me, just call. I'll come running."

He met up with Ned in the barn later that afternoon. They both drew up short when they saw each other. Ned turned away.

"Hey," Luke called after him. "That was you who filled my nursery with dolls, right?"

"What if it was?" He kept going.

"Look, I didn't send you that book." He swallowed hard and pressed on. "But I am sorry I spoke out of turn about your dyslexia. I was joking around and it popped out, but that doesn't excuse it. I'm proud of you for what you're doing. I know it ain't easy."

Ned slowed to a halt, his shoulders relaxed and he turned around. "Who do you figure sent the book, then?"

"I don't know. I don't care. And I don't care that it was you who put the dolls there, either. I don't even blame you. Let's just... put an end to it. Let's be a real family for once."

After a long moment, Ned nodded. "Need any help cleaning them up?"

"No. I got it." But even with the nursery fixed up, he wondered how he could lure Mia to come home.

Chapter Eighteen

"How about this one?" Ellie frowned as she compared the bridesmaid's dress in her hands to the party dress in the photograph Tracey's sister had sent for them to match.

Mia shook her head. "It's close, but not quite and I don't think you could alter it correctly. There isn't enough extra material."

"That's because no one wears a bridesmaid dress that looks like this." Ellie shook the photograph.

Mia agreed with her. The dress was as slinky as something you'd wear to a Hollywood nightclub, just skimming the tops of the thighs and leaving one shoulder bare. The fabric was gathered in a sunburst pattern near one hip and covered in sequins.

"We'll have to make one from scratch." Ellie hung up the dress she held.

"Can you do that?"

"It'll cost her."

"You were so good to give her a refund on the one she returned."

"The one I make will be triple the price. Will Tracey

want to pay it?"

"Will she want to stand next to the result?" Mia asked, gazing doubtfully at the photograph in Ellie's hand.

"I'll make sure she'll want to stand next to it, but I can't work for free."

"Of course not. I'll talk to Tracey. Can you give me a ballpark figure?"

Ellie named a sum and Mia whistled. "Give me twenty-four hours. I'll see what Tracey wants to do."

Mia drove home to the Cruz ranch next and found Autumn surrounded by cookbooks at the large dinner table in the guesthouse.

"Thank goodness you're here. You weren't up yet when I ran out to Ellie's this morning."

"Arianna let us sleep in." Autumn smiled at the baby who lay near her on the floor on a thick mat with play toys dangling overhead.

"I've got a problem I hope you can help me with. What company did you rent your tents for your wedding from?"

"What tents?" Autumn said. "Looking back I see how naïve we were. We just planned our wedding outside and figured it wouldn't rain. I don't know what we would have done if it did."

"What about Claire and Jamie?"

"Ditto. I take it you're looking for tents?"

"Desperately. I didn't realize you have to book them so far in advance."

"The big ones you do."

"I need big ones! Lila White has seventy-five guests

coming to her family reunion!"

Autumn thought a moment. "But you could use smaller ones and treat them like a number of rooms—one flowing into the next."

"I don't think so."

"Let's look and see. Bring me my laptop." She motioned toward the kitchen counter and Mia fetched the computer. A few minutes later Autumn turned the screen toward her. "Look at these. See? You could line them up next to each other. Or lay them out in a pattern, even."

"Do you think that would work?"

Autumn nodded. "I think so. There isn't going to be dancing at the reunion, is there?"

"No. Just a lot of eating and games—volleyball, badminton, lawn darts. That kind of thing."

"Then it'll work fine. Here." She handed Mia her phone. "Call them. See if they have enough of the small tents."

Mia did and bounced on her toes when the answer was yes. She reserved what they had, hung up and dialed the next closest rental company where she was able to secure enough more to get the job done.

Autumn, meanwhile, sketched out a plan for the tents' layout, and sketched fairy lights to decorate them.

"Can I take that with me to show Lila?" Mia asked. "I'd better get going so I can stop by her house before I get to work."

"Of course." Autumn tore the page off her pad of paper and handed it over. She cocked her head and looked at Mia. "Have you lost weight?"

Mia pulled back. "Of course not. Look how big my belly is." She ran a hand over her baby bump.

"I don't think it's big enough. When's your next appointment?"

"Shoot! I think it was yesterday." Mia scrambled for her phone and clicked to her appointment page. "Darn it—I missed it."

"Call them right now and reschedule." Autumn waited for her to do so.

Mia glanced at her watch. "I've got to go."

"Call. Right now."

Mia sighed but did what she was told. She quickly scheduled an appointment for the following week, thanked Autumn again and hurried out the door.

More than eight hours later, she stumbled back into the guesthouse and picked up her mail on the way to the room. In among two bills and a circular was another envelope with a poorly written address.

"Now what?" Mia asked aloud. She peeled it open as she climbed the stairs to her room.

Yu luk awfull.

"Well, that's nice." She tossed the note onto her desk. As she moved to discard her clothing and climb into bed, Mia caught sight of herself in the mirror and stopped short.

She did look awful.

Now she saw why Autumn had asked if she was losing weight. Her cheeks were gaunt. Her maternity clothes hung on her. Her hair, normally so thick and lustrous, fell in lanky threads. She crossed to the bed and sat down slowly, the ache that constantly nagged at her back making her movements tentative. She thought over the past few days and realized she really hadn't been eating enough for a pregnant woman in her second trimester. She would have to do better, and she would have to sit down more during the day. She'd ask Fila and Camila if she could buy a stool to keep behind the counter so that whenever the restaurant slowed down a little she could take a load off. And she'd ask them again to hire more help, since they hadn't managed to do so yet. If she could cut back her hours even a little, it would be much easier to take care of herself.

And to take care of her event planning clients. She wasn't giving any of them the kind of thought and attention she'd meant to. So far she'd managed to put out all the fires, but she had the feeling the worst was yet to come. Why, oh why had she agreed to do three events in one weekend?

And how were Fila and Camila going to cater all three events and still handle the normal weekend rush? They hadn't even talked about it yet.

Tomorrow she'd sit down with both of them and figure out a plan.

She checked her e-mail and found a message from Inez.

I heard from Montana Pageants today. There have been other allegations against Warner recently, and the police are involved. We'll need to make statements to the police and we could be called to testify in the case against him.

A statement to the police? Testify?

Mia didn't like the sound of that.

Her phone buzzed and she picked it up listlessly. Luke was calling.

"Hello?"

"Hey, Mia." He hesitated. "I know it's late. Were you sleeping?"

"Just going to bed." She missed the days when he'd sneak into the guesthouse and join her, back before she came upon him kicking the dolls around.

"I think we should talk. What you saw the other day. It really wasn't what you think."

"I know." And she found she *did* know. "The dolls were a practical joke, right?"

"Yeah."

"Why... why were you kicking them?"

"Because I thought the joker was right—that I'd lost you forever."

Mia bit her lip. She didn't know if he'd lost her or not. "Don't you think those so-called jokes are getting out of hand? Someone mailed Ned a *See Spot Run* book. Fila thinks you did it."

"It wasn't me. I promise you that. We talked today—Ned and me. I think we worked it out."

"Good. Because I'm sick of Fila being angry at me. Anyway, I better go. I need sleep."

"You sound tired." His voice softened. "Mia, take care of yourself, you hear?"

"Yeah. I'm trying to."

"Can we meet tomorrow?"

She thought about her schedule. She wanted badly to

see Luke. She wished she could rest her head against his shoulder and close her eyes for a minute. She missed him.

Unfortunately, tomorrow she was supposed to meet Carl on her half-hour break. "Not tomorrow. The day after? Two-thirty at Linda's Diner?"

Luke hesitated so long she thought he was going to say no.

"Sure," he said finally. "I'll see you then."

THE DAY AFTER tomorrow. Two-thirty at Linda's Diner.

Luke did the math. Mia must be meeting Carl again tomorrow, which was why she'd put him off until the following day. Did she want to hear what the millionaire might offer her before she made up with him? The thought made him clench his fists.

He slowly made himself unclench them. His temper hadn't helped him so far. First things first. He needed to finish cleaning up the nursery. He'd already done the bulk of the work, but there were still details to tend to. It didn't take long for him to touch up the scuffs and dings on the wall. He patched the one or two places where he'd put serious dents into the drywall. He'd sand the spots tomorrow and give them a coat of paint then.

He did his best to polish the furniture and get rid of the evidence of his temper tantrum. He'd have to take the torn curtain to his mother to fix. He hoped she wouldn't ask too many questions. By the time he went to bed, the nursery looked fit for habitation again. Too bad it didn't seem likely there'd be any babies to inhabit it any time soon.

The following day Luke was up before the sun doing his usual parade of chores. It was lunchtime before he could catch a break. He decided to bring the damaged curtain to the main house to see if his mother could repair it, but when he reached his cabin, an envelope with familiar shaky handwriting left on his doorstep brought him to a halt. He picked it up and after a moment's hesitation, opened it.

Share the load.

He snorted. Who with? That's what he'd like to know. He crumpled up the note and envelope and tossed them in the direction of the trash can in the kitchen. It missed by a mile, but he was already out the front door.

"Everything all right at your cabin?" Lisa asked when he handed the curtain over and sat down at the kitchen table.

"It's fine."

She fetched her sewing kit and joined him. "But you and Mia are still on the outs."

"So far."

She shot him a look. "You're letting it get to you."

"I want to marry her. And another man's trying to steal her away."

Lisa paused. "What other man?"

"Carl Whitfield."

"Carl's back in town? Where's he living now?"

Luke knew what she meant. Since Evan and Bella lived at Carl's old place there wasn't anything else nearly as big or expensive in town for the millionaire to buy.

"I think he's at the motel. Someone said he was looking for property."

"Hmph. I guess he'll build another log mansion." Her tone made it clear what she thought about that.

"A man that rich can do whatever he likes." Luke frowned. "Except with my girl."

"When do you have time to even see her these days? You're working your fingers to the bone. I saw you out until all hours tilling those pastures yesterday."

"She's working too hard, too." Luke sighed. "I don't get to see her. That's half the problem."

"What's the other half?"

"Me and my damned mouth." When his mother chuckled, he grudgingly smiled. "I say something wrong every time we get together. If I talk at all."

Lisa cocked her head at this last bit and considered it. "Maybe you should do less talking and more listening."

"That's what everyone says, but at some point I have to tell her what I think, right?"

"I guess."

"You and dad tell each other what you think."

Lisa laughed. "I guess we do—for better or for worse. I've been telling him what I think about him building that extra house."

"He's still at it?"

"There's a foundation in. Power. Gas. Water, you name it. But he won't tell me what it's for."

"You've been married a long time, though. You two have done something right."

"Well, now, I guess that's because most of the time we have a common vision. We're always heading in the same general direction. We might bicker a whole bunch on the way there, but that doesn't stop us from progressing toward our goal. Do you and Mia have a common goal?"

Luke wasn't able to answer that.

BY THE TIME Mia's break rolled around, her back ached so badly she found it hard to walk the two short blocks to Linda's Diner. She sat down in the booth across from Carl, leaned her head back against the wall and shut her eyes.

"Mia?" Carl's concerned voice made her open them again. "You okay? You don't look so good."

"That seems to be the consensus these days." She made herself lean forward and look at the menu that lay on the table in front of her, but all of a sudden she couldn't force her eyes to make any sense of the words. As they blurred in front of her she had the feeling she was falling. She dropped the menu and braced herself against the table.

"Tracey? Would you get us a glass of orange juice? Hurry, please," Carl called out.

Mia was dimly aware of Tracey rushing away and returning a moment later with a glass of juice.

"Drink it. All of it." Carl pushed the glass in front of Mia. Mia picked it up. Considered its contents. She wasn't sure she could.

"Just one sip, then." Carl leaned forward again. "Come on, Mia. You're scaring me."

She took a sip and the tart flavor woke her up a bit. She took another sip and soon found she could drink more of it than she expected.

"That's better." Carl sat back. "Your color is perking up."

"Thanks. I guess I'm dehydrated. It's so busy at the restaurant."

"You need to keep drinking. And eating." He waved Tracey back. "A club sandwich and fries for Mia. I'll have tomato soup and grilled cheese."

Tracey hurried away again. Mia kept drinking her juice. "I can't remember my assignment."

"Screw the assignment."

Mia blinked at his tone.

"Mia, you're pushing yourself too hard."

"Says the self-made millionaire." She pushed the empty juice glass away. "I have to push myself hard. I have to get my business running."

"I wasn't pregnant when I made my millions."

"It's not going to get any easier for me. When I'm done being pregnant, I'll have a newborn. I'll need to get a sitter all the time. Then what?" She hadn't meant to sound so angry.

"You're right. It's never going to be easy being a single mom."

A rush of tears filled Mia's eyes. "I didn't want to be a single mom. I never meant any of this to happen. I mean—I want my baby, but…"

"I know." Carl took her hand. "Look, you're tired. You're working too hard. You're not getting enough sleep. It will get better; I promise."

"You don't know that. What if it doesn't? What if I can't do it? What if I'm a lousy mom? What if I'm a lousy wedding planner?"

Carl handed her his napkin and patted her hand. He didn't say anything more, just let her cry, for which Mia was eternally grateful. She mopped up her face as best she could. "I'm sorry. I didn't mean…"

"You don't need to apologize. I'm the one who should say I'm sorry. I keep trying to slow down—to stop being a businessman all the time—and here I am teaching you to be just like I used to be." He played with his fork. "When I left Chance Creek, I spent months hiking the Sierra Nevadas. It was easy to be a different person there. Now that I'm back in civilization, my good habits are slipping away."

"Why do you want to change the way you do things? It's obviously worked for you." Mia wiped away the last of her tears and pushed the napkin aside.

"Because it hasn't worked for me—aside from the millions. I keep getting the rest of it wrong. Look at me—no wife, no children. I can't even find a house."

"I bet you could get a wife and kids like that if you wanted." Mia snapped her fingers.

"I don't want just any wife. I want a woman to love me. Me—not my millions."

Mia nodded. "I get that, but there are lots of single women in Chance Creek. I bet you'll find one."

"That's what I'm counting on." His sheepish grin made Mia smile for the first time that day.

THERE WAS CARL Whitfield, sitting with Mia. Holding her hand. Caressing it.

The slow burn in Luke's gut grew to a hot flame. This time he could only see the back of Mia's head from where he sat tucked into a corner booth at the front of the diner, but he could see every expression on Carl's face. His tender concern. His determination. The man was using every trick in the book to snare her.

A half-hour later, he ducked down and turned aside when Mia rushed from the restaurant, so when Carl dropped down in the seat across from him shortly afterward, Luke jerked with surprise.

"Buddy, you're a lousy spy." Carl rested his elbows on the table. "You suck as a boyfriend, too. Mia's got to slow down. She didn't look well at all when she came in."

"Why are you telling me? You're the one she wants to be with. You've gotten exactly what you wanted, didn't you? You laid the trap and she stepped right in."

Carl rolled his eyes. "How many times do I have to tell you; she doesn't want to be with me, she wants to *learn* from me—about running her business. Look, if I wanted to seduce Mia I wouldn't take her to a diner. I'd fly her to Paris or Rome. She'd never know what hit her. Like I said before—she's too young for me. And she's too in love with you, God knows why. Why don't you pull your act together and do something about it?"

"Like what?"

"Like *help* her, you fucking idiot. Like buy in to her dream. Like be her friend instead of spending all your time trying to get in her pants." Carl stood up. Threw a business card down on the table. "I'm not going to make a play for Mia, no matter what you think, but if you don't fix yourself up soon, someone else sure will. You want to have a real conversation about what you could do to help her make her business a success, you give me a call."

Chapter Nineteen

"YOU'VE DONE SUCH a fantastic job," Rose said happily two days later as Mia showed her the menu Fila and Camila had come up with for her wedding. Rose and Cab had chosen to hold their reception in the Cruz guesthouse and the meal would be served buffet style, as befitted a casual affair.

"Fila and Camila worked hard to pick entrees that wouldn't be too sloppy to eat." Not an easy trick with all the sauces they served.

"Good idea." Rose smiled. "I can't believe it's finally happening. And you know what? I've made up my mind. I'm going to exhibit my paintings after the wedding—just as soon as I can find a gallery or other space willing to show them."

"That's terrific! You must be so excited to see your art career take off."

"It hasn't taken off yet but I hope it will."

"I'm sure it will. Let's go over the flower arrangements one last time."

Mia felt better today. She'd made sure to eat a full dinner—sitting down—during one of the slow periods at the restaurant the night before. Camila had called everyone she knew and found a woman looking for a part-time job who would come in today to help work the counter. Fila had bought Mia a stool to sit on, too, although she rarely got the chance. Maybe that would change with an extra person up front.

Plus she had her meeting with Luke to look forward to this afternoon at Linda's Diner. She thought meeting in a public place was a good idea. Maybe it would force both of them to keep their tempers under control until they could talk their issues through.

By the time she arrived at Linda's Diner, however, her good mood had slipped away again. The new girl—Frieda Smith—had so much to learn that she slowed Mia down instead of speeding things up. Mia knew that would change with time, but right now her patience was worn to a thread.

"Sorry I'm late," Luke said, sitting down on the other side. "Got tied up at the ranch."

"That's okay. I only have a half-hour, though."

"The restaurant still doing good business?"

"Too good, if you ask me."

"And how's *your* business?"

Mia wasn't sure how to answer. "Do you really want to know?"

"Yeah. I really want to know." He took her hand. Squeezed it.

"It's good and bad," she said slowly, very aware of her hand in his. She felt alone a lot these days. She missed living with Luke—missed his presence beside her at night, too. She wished she knew which was the real

Luke—the man who cared enough about her to ask these questions, or the man who always thought he knew better than her what to do. "Rose loves what I've done for her wedding and it's all really coming together. Tracey has had more issues. So far I've managed to solve them, but it's been a rocky road, and Lila White...well, she's not as happy."

"What's wrong with Lila?"

She waited a beat to see if he really wanted to know the answer. When he didn't say anything, she pressed on. "I botched up her tents. I was supposed to reserve three large tents for her family reunion, but by the time I called the rental companies, all the really big ones were taken. Autumn helped me come up with a work-around, using a bunch of smaller ones in a creative way. Lila went for it, but she's not pleased and she lets me know about it every time we talk. No matter what else I do to make up for that, it's not good enough."

"That's too bad."

She waited for him to tell her what she'd done wrong, or to reiterate this was all too much for her, but he didn't.

Instead, he asked, "Is there anything I can do to help?"

Mia blinked back tears. Help? God, could she use help.

"No, I've got it," she said, but didn't pull away from him. Instead she found herself threading her fingers through his and holding on for dear life.

"Well, you just let me know if that changes. I've got two hands and a strong back, and I'd be glad to loan them to you."

She was definitely going to cry if he kept that up. "There are a few other parts of you I could use." She bit her lip at her lame attempt at a joke, but it worked to shift the conversation.

Luke squeezed her hand again. "Oh yeah? Which ones?"

"Why don't you come over tonight and see? Don't be too late, though. I'm exhausted these days," she confessed.

"I'll come over and rub your feet." He smiled at her. "If you're still awake afterward, we'll see what else happens."

LUKE WAS HAPPIER than he could say when Mia managed to stay awake through his foot massage that night and welcomed him into her bed afterward. He took things slow—really slow—because he worried about how tired she looked, but she seemed to enjoy his body moving within hers.

He enjoyed it, too. Going slow meant he could really concentrate on his movements and her reactions. He could learn exactly what she liked—and what she loved—and change things up to make the most of it. After he brought her to a first climax, he started over, going even more slowly, making love to her even more thoroughly. This time he came with her. The wave of sensation washed away any worry he had about what they were to each other.

Afterward, he cradled her in his arms until she fell asleep. As he lay awake watching her dream, the tension that had filled him for weeks slowly ebbed away. His focus had been on the wrong thing for a long time. Mia wasn't a prize to be won; she was a partner to be wooed and cared for and nurtured. He couldn't just put together a magic chain of actions that would result in them standing side-by-side at the altar, as if that was the final goal, because it wasn't. It was just the start. They had to create their goals together and figure out how to move toward them at the same time.

That meant he had to be a partner to her right now, before they were married.

Which meant he needed to get his priorities straight. Who was he to tell Mia what she could and couldn't do when his own business dealings were messed up? Why was he spending all his income paying off a fancy truck when Mia obviously didn't care a fig what he drove? Why was his credit card maxed out when he was working morning, noon and night? It was time to sit down and figure out where he'd gone wrong, and what he needed to do to get back on track. He might never be a millionaire, but he owed his future wife more security than his current debts could offer her.

He would set up an appointment with Matt Underwood, and lay everything out on the table. Matt would know what to do. He remembered Carl's business card sitting at home on his dresser. Carl might have some ideas as well, if he could swallow enough of his pride to ask the man. He heaved a sigh. He probably should do just that. Carl knew more about business than he did—that was for sure.

He settled closer to Mia, tucked a tendril of her hair

back behind her ear and kissed her neck softly. Wrapping an arm around her sleeping form, he basked in a peace he hadn't felt in months. He was right where he wanted to be.

"YOU REALIZE WHEN you ruin Lila White's reunion, everyone's going to blame me," Mia's mother said the afternoon before Tracey's wedding. Enid ran a finger along Mia's bureau in her room at the guesthouse and humphed, even though Mia was positive she hadn't found any dust. Autumn was a meticulous housekeeper and even though Mia had begged her not to consider it her job to clean her room, she refused to give up dusting and vacuuming it.

"It's good exercise for me," she'd said, when Mia told her not to bother. "I have all this pregnancy weight to lose, and you're so busy. It's a win-win situation for both of us."

Mia didn't believe that, but she accepted the help in the spirit it was given. It burned her that her mother would criticize Autumn's handiwork.

"I won't ruin Lila White's reunion."

"You already did. You forgot to order her tents. Yes, I know all about that. Everyone does." Enid's mouth was set in a hard line. Mia knew how much her mother hated to be judged and found wanting. Too bad Enid never considered how it felt to those around her when she passed those judgments on.

"I fixed that problem."

"I doubt your fix will meet her approval. If I were her, I would have broken my contract with you and found someone with more experience."

"Who would have charged her triple what I'm charging her," Mia snapped. "Lila White knows exactly what she's doing, Mom. And so do I. Her reunion will be beautiful." She hoped that was true.

"Well, it's a shame how you've triple-booked yourself this weekend. There's no way any of your clients are getting the service they expected."

"All of them are perfectly satisfied."

"We'll see about that."

"Yes, we'll see. Mom, is there a reason you're here?" It certainly wasn't to lend a helping hand, or to be a cheerleader.

"Rumor has it you and that Luke Matheson have been spending time together again. Is he going to marry you or just keep dangling the possibility in front of you so you keep putting out?"

"Mom!" Mia took in a shaky breath. She couldn't take this anymore. Wouldn't take it. "I need you to leave. Right now."

"But—"

"No buts. Don't come back, don't call, don't do anything until you're ready to be on my side for once." She strode to the door and held it open until Enid huffed and left the room. Out in the hall, she turned on Mia.

"You should be ashamed for talking to your mother like that."

"No, Mom. You're the one who should be ashamed." Mia herded her downstairs and out onto the front porch, then slammed the door.

The next morning Mia was still shaking with anger

over the incident, but she promised herself she wouldn't let her mother's remarks get under her skin. Still, when Morgan and Claire walked into the VFW hall where she and several of Tracey's friends were decorating for Tracey's wedding, Mia held her breath until Morgan exclaimed in surprised tones, "Oh, it's... beautiful!"

"Is it? I can't even be sure anymore, I'm so nervous," Mia said. Tracey's wedding started in six hours and she'd been up since dawn to get everything ready. She'd rented long, white drapes and white and fuchsia buntings from the party rental company that they had used to cover the plain hall's walls and make it more festive. The rented tables were set up, covered with tablecloths and surrounded by white rented chairs, all of which would be moved to the Cruz ranch tonight for Cab and Rose's wedding tomorrow. The floral arrangements were ready to go, but Mia wouldn't put those out until the last minute. Fila and Camila had hired extra help for the day, too, so the catering should be on track.

"I have to give you credit," Claire said. "I didn't think you could do it, Mia. Someone so young and inexperienced? I'm surprised how good it all looks."

Mia wasn't sure whether to feel complimented or insulted. "Thank you." She decided to feel complimented. "And thanks for stopping by."

"We wanted to know if you needed help, but it looks like you've got everything under control."

She did. Tracey's friends had been a world of help, and Mia had planned everything down to the last detail. She was sure she'd hit a snag or two during the course of the wedding, but she was determined she'd pull it off.

If only her feet didn't hurt so badly. And her back.

"I think I have a handle on it all. Thanks, though."

Twelve hours later, the wedding was over, the cleaning crew had the VFW Hall mostly restored to normal, and Buddy Hooks, a handyman who also ran a hauling business, was ready to truck the tables and chairs to the Cruz ranch.

"You'd better call it a night, Mia." Buddy frowned at her. "Don't you have to do this all over again in the morning?"

"And again the next day, too. I'm just about done here, though. I'll be in bed within the hour."

"Glad to hear it. You have to take care of yourself."

If only she had time to take care of herself. She wasn't finished with this batch of events and already she was ramping up for three more in June. She was grateful for the business, but it was taking its toll. Especially now. Buddy was right. It was time to go home and get to bed.

"Hi, Mia."

Mia jumped. "Luke—you scared me."

"Sorry about that. I wanted to make sure you got home okay."

"I'm fine." Just so tired she could barely keep her eyes open.

"You're going to be up first thing in the morning, right?"

"Yes." It sounded like a groan.

"Okay, how about this?" He swooped her up into his arms so fast she didn't have time to protest, then cradled her against his broad chest and smiled down at her. "I drive you home and spend the night. No funny stuff, unless you demand it." He waggled his eyebrows. "Tomorrow I get up with you and we swing back here to get your truck."

"That sounds really good."

"Okay. Let's go."

She rested her head against his shoulder with a sigh of contentment as he carried her out to his truck. She was home within twenty minutes, and in bed a scant five minutes later. True to his word, Luke didn't put the moves on her. Just snuggled up beside her. She found his presence more than comforting. Tonight's wedding had gone off without a hitch—even Tracey's sister's crazy bridesmaid gown had looked beautiful, thanks to Ellie's sewing skills—and she was grateful her first event had gone so well. Tracey, her new husband and both sets of parents had thanked her effusively. It felt good to know she'd helped a couple have the wedding of their dreams.

But tomorrow's event was much more important— to her, at least. Rose was one of her best friends and everyone she cared about would be at the wedding. They'd all be taking notes on the event—and they'd remember anything that went wrong. She prayed there would be no disasters.

Mia had thought she'd fall right to sleep when she got home, but now her mind buzzed with to-do lists and last-minute plans. Just when she thought she'd have to get up and get a notepad to write everything down, she felt Luke's hand smooth over her hair.

"Stop thinking and go to sleep."

"I can't."

"Worrying about tomorrow?"

"Yes. I want it to be perfect for Rose."

"It will be perfect, just like you. Close your eyes."

"But—"

"I'm serious. Close your eyes."

She did so, but opened them again when she heard him click on the small, dim bedside light. "What are you doing?"

"I'm going to read you a bedtime story."

She laughed. "Really?"

"Really." He bent down and shuffled through the paperbacks on the bottom shelf of her bedside table. "You read this one yet?"

"No." It was a mystery set in a small New England town.

"Good. Close your eyes and go to sleep."

At first she thought she'd never be able to fall asleep with Luke reading aloud to her, but she found she couldn't simultaneously think of to-do lists and follow the storyline, too. It wasn't long before her eyes drifted shut, and not much longer until she was dreaming.

IN THE MORNING, Luke was pleased to see that Mia looked much brighter than she had the night before. He knew she needed to get ready for another busy day, but his body wanted more alone time with her. He lay in bed considering his options as she got up, picked out her clothes and made her way to the bathroom. He waited until he heard the shower running before he got up, too, and knocked on the bathroom door. "Mia? Can I come in?"

"It's unlocked."

Luke slipped inside and shut the door behind him just as Mia pulled the shower's sliding glass door shut. She raised her eyebrows when he shucked off what little clothing he was wearing and made to join her.

"You don't mind, do you?" he asked, slipping under the warm water with her.

"I have to keep moving."

"I won't slow you down. Here, you wash your hair. I'll wash the rest of you."

"Luke."

"Get going—you don't want to be late."

"Fine." She took the shampoo from him and lathered up her hair, but as soon as he soaped up his hands and began to wash the rest of her, her movements slowed. Luke started with her shoulders and neck, moved down to her arms and chest, and when he skimmed his hands around to lather her breasts, Mia moaned and sank back against him.

"Is that good?" he asked as he circled her breasts and smoothed his palms over her nipples.

"That is so good," Mia murmured. Sensing her acquiescence, Luke took advantage of the situation. He did all the hard work, supporting her as she leaned forward to brace herself against the wall, spreading her legs with his thighs and then easing into her from behind.

He used one arm to keep her upright, but slipped the other hand between her legs to move in sensual circles as he moved inside her. Her lush, ripe, wet body turned him on until he found it difficult to keep Mia's pleasure foremost in mind. He wanted this to be a special experience for her, but his own need made itself known and soon he'd be hard pressed to hold back.

He needn't have worried. Mia came with a cry that echoed against the tiled walls and her obvious pleasure tugged him right there with her. His release shuddered through him until his whole body tingled with it. Afterward, he moved out of Mia and helped her clean up.

"I hope I didn't make you late," he said as he helped her out of the shower.

"I don't care if you did. I needed that more than anything," Mia said, standing on her tiptoes to give him a kiss.

"Don't ever be afraid to ask me for what you need—whatever it is. I'm yours—especially today."

"Well…" Mia considered this as she wrapped a towel around her body. "First, I have to eat. I refuse to collapse at Rose's wedding."

A grin spread across his face. "One pancake breakfast, coming right up."

Chapter Twenty

MIA THOUGHT SHE'D be exhausted after Tracey's wedding the night before, but her encounter with Luke in the bathroom energized her and she had a spring in her step as she went about the business of setting up for Rose's big day. The Cruz ranch's guesthouse made the perfect setting for a wedding, with its floor-to-ceiling windows in the great room and panoramic views. She should have guessed that all her friends would pitch in to help, too. The four couples who lived on the ranch were already hard at work by the time she and Luke arrived to set up, and pretty soon the other couples from the Double-Bar-K arrived to join in. Mia was afraid that she'd have a hard time making everyone listen to her, but when she showed up, clipboard in hand, with Luke standing guard behind her, her friends put themselves at her disposal and carried out her orders willingly.

"I could get used to this," she told Luke after she'd dispatched Ethan, Cab, Jamie and Rob to move into position the tables that had been dropped off the night before.

"You'll make the prettiest tyrant ever, princess."

With so many willing hands it was a cinch to get all the chairs set up in rows for the ceremony and all the decorations in place, too. Autumn was helping Fila and Camila with the catering, so Mia didn't have to worry about that. They finished setting up so early, Mia had plenty of time to help Rose dress for the wedding and soothe her friend's last minute wedding jitters.

Rose looked regal in her form-fitting white dress as she took her place at the top of the aisle. Mia thought all her hard work was worth it when she slid into her seat just as the wedding march started and she saw Cab's face as he caught sight of his bride. His love for her was so plain to see, and when she turned her head, Mia saw that Rose had eyes for no one but Cab, either.

"That's what I want," Mia whispered to herself.

"Me, too," Luke said in her ear and handed her a handkerchief. She took it gratefully and dabbed her eyes, her heart swelling at his words, and at the kind gesture. Luke put an arm around her shoulder as Rose joined Cab at the altar and Reverend Halpern began the service.

"You did great," Luke whispered in her ear.

"This is the easy part. Wait and see how the reception goes." But his praise touched her.

Was Luke finally on her side?

LUKE HAD TO hand it to Mia; she could really throw a party. He didn't think he'd been to a wedding where the guests had so much fun. The furniture that normally filled the guesthouse living room was gone, replaced by the same circular tables used at Tracey's wedding the night before. This time the color scheme was white and peach, and Mia had made the place a festive springtime oasis. Fila, Camila and Autumn had outdone themselves with the food and had hired several local teens as servers for the evening. A bartender kept drinks flowing, and when the meal was done the guests had pitched in to move tables and form a dance floor.

Through all of it, Mia's bulky form had moved more gracefully than he would have thought possible, as she solved problems, kept guests happy, made sure everyone had enough food and drink and kept the bride and groom circulating, dancing and performing every duty a bride and groom had at their wedding.

"Come on." Jake jolted him from his reverie with an elbow to the side. "Cab and Rose are leaving in a minute."

Luke followed the crowd to the front porch where Rose was just giving Mia a huge hug.

"Thank you. It was everything I've ever dreamed of," Rose said.

"Thank you for being my first and best fan," Mia said.

Luke felt a pang that he hadn't been Mia's first and best fan, and decided then and there that from now on he would be her most loyal one. He stood by her side as the crowd waved off Cab and Rose, who left in a limo for a quick drive to the airport, where they'd catch a flight to Italy and spend ten days on their honeymoon. Luke knew Rose was thrilled at the chance to see classical architecture and artwork—and that Cab was thrilled to get away with his new bride, no matter where they went. He had no doubt the couple would enjoy themselves immensely.

As the guests trailed back into the house, he sensed that more casual friends would soon leave, until only a core of those closest to the bride and groom remained. Before the music died down, he wanted one dance with Mia.

It took some persuasion, but some minutes later he was swaying to a slow song, Mia's belly pressing into him.

"This is awkward," Mia complained.

"It's terrific."

"Will you stay with me again tonight?"

"So I can read you to sleep again?"

"Yes." She buried her face against his chest. "And so you can be there. So I don't feel so alone."

Luke stopped. "Do you feel alone?"

She looked up at him. "Sometimes. A lot of the time, I guess."

"You're not, you know. I'm always here, even if we aren't together."

She didn't answer, just leaned against him as he began to sway to the music again. She didn't have to speak, though. He understood what she was saying. She might not like to ask for help. She might not be ready to accept his offer of marriage. But she needed him.

The baby kicked against his stomach and he chuckled, sliding a hand down to rest on her belly. "You can't get rid of me that easily, young'un."

"She's just saying hello."

"Hello, baby," Luke said back. "Can't wait to see your beautiful face." He heard Mia take a ragged breath.

"Hey, what's wrong?"

"I don't know why you stick around when I've been such a—"

"Shh. I've been hard-headed, too," he cut her off. "You know exactly why I stick around. I love you. I hope someday you'll let me stick around permanently."

She sighed. "Don't you think we ought to date before we decide something like that?"

Luke knew he'd have to tread carefully through this conversation. "Haven't we been dating?"

"Not really." She pulled back. "We've been sleeping together."

"I like sleeping with you."

She smiled. "Yeah, it's not bad. But that's not dating."

"So you want to be wined and dined, huh?"

"Something like that. I know one thing." She pulled away from him and rubbed her back. "I don't want to get engaged when I'm as big as a house."

He bit back his disappointment. He'd take her at her word. At least she was talking about getting engaged. That was progress. He could understand why she'd want to put off big decisions until after she had her baby, although he wished they'd be married before the birth.

As much as he wanted to plead his case and push for a wedding sooner rather than later, he decided this wasn't the time or the place. Mia was tired. She'd pulled off two major events in two days, with a third to come. He'd respect her wishes tonight, and think it over himself tomorrow.

"WELL, I WAS wrong," Lila said to Mia late in the day of the family reunion. "Everyone loves your tents. They're exotic and beautiful all at once."

As darkness fell, the fairy lights hanging around the tents made them seem like otherworldly halls. Children raced about playing tag and hide and go seek, slipping from shadow to light back to shadow again. Adults sat at tables and drank wine, laughing over shared remembrances and lingering over desserts. After sending Lila a set of questions, Mia had concocted a trivia game about the family and the questions and answers had set the whole crowd buzzing and laughing, and brought them all together.

"I'm glad you like them." Mia patted Lila's arm. "You have a wonderful family."

"And so will you. Your children will be lucky to have a mom like you. I bet they'll have birthday parties that will be the envy of all their friends."

Mia smiled. "I like that idea."

"I was just nervous—that's why I gave you so much trouble, dear," Lila confided. "But you kept me on the straight and narrow. You're good at your job."

"Does that mean you'll write me a glowing recommendation?" Mia grinned.

"You bet I will. Oh—Roger's just about to spill that juice all over Matthew."

Mia rushed over to the two boys just in time to prevent the accident Lila had spotted, smiling ear-to-ear. If she'd impressed Lila White, she had to be good at her job.

She'd done it. Three events in three days. Surely that

had to be a record.

"Another triumph." Luke slipped up to Mia and kissed her neck.

"Hey, you're still on the clock, you know." Mia had gladly accepted Luke's offer of an extra pair of hands today. Jake had taken over the chores at the Double-Bar-K, for which she was eternally grateful. Once again, Luke had proved willing to take orders and work hard during the set up process. Once the party was underway he'd been a godsend with some of the more troublesome kids. He'd invented games and races to keep them out of trouble while the parents socialized. Mia was so impressed she wished she could bring him to all her events.

"What do you think? Employee of the month?" He grinned at her.

"Damn straight, if you keep it up." She kissed him on the cheek.

"Is that all I get? I want a plaque."

"We'll see about the plaque. For now my only goal is living through the next few hours."

"YOU SURE ABOUT this?" Carl said as he made out a check to Luke.

Luke sighed. "Yeah, I'm sure. If you're going to be a real rancher this time, you've got to have a real truck, not one of your namby-pamby foreign excuses." They stood in front of Linda's Diner, where Luke had asked the other man to meet him for a cup of coffee. They'd talked business and finances, and then Luke had mentioned he wanted to sell his truck.

"I guess you're right." Carl scrawled his signature and

tore off the check. "For what it's worth, I think this is a good start. Cash in the bank is a solid foundation for any venture."

"I don't really need all the bells and whistles this baby has." Luke considered the vehicle. It stung a little to let it go, but not nearly as much as losing Mia would have. He could pick up a perfectly good used truck at half a dozen dealerships around town for a fraction of the price Carl had just paid for this one. Carl had been more than fair in the deal, paying nearly as much as Luke had when he bought it new, when everyone knew that when you drove a truck off the lot it immediately lost value.

"Guess I'll see you around," Carl said.

"Guess you will. You found the property you want yet?" At Carl's surprised expression, he added, "Mia said you two met in a realtor's office. She said you were looking to buy a house."

"I haven't found anything I like yet, so I've decided to rent for a bit. I'd hoped I could buy my old house back from the Mortimers, but they didn't even get back to me about my offer."

"The Mortimers? Wait a minute." Luke thought back to Ned's wedding. "Did you make them an offer face-to-face, or did you send it to them?"

"I dropped it off in their mailbox the first morning I was in town." Carl smiled deprecatingly. "I was a little on fire to get the deal done. Too on fire, I guess."

Luke rubbed a hand over his mouth, covering a laugh. "Well, that explains that."

"What do you mean?"

"You know what? It wouldn't make any sense if I tried to tell you now. Give me a day or two and I'll fill you in."

"Okay."

Luke tipped his hat and turned around. He was supposed to meet Jake at Fila's in fifteen minutes to go truck hunting. He wondered what Jake would think of what he'd just learned.

He wondered what everyone else would think when they knew, too.

"No spelling errors," Autumn exclaimed when she looked over Mia's shoulder at the latest handwritten note she'd received in the mail.

"You're right. Do you think the sender is taking lessons?"

"Maybe he's foreign." They'd long ago decided it was a man because of the strong, blocky handwriting.

"Maybe." Mia read it over again.

Enough already.

"Enough what?"

"Enough torturing Luke?" Autumn guessed. "Whoever it is seems to want you two together."

"I'm not torturing Luke."

Autumn shot her a look. "Really?"

"Not anymore. Not since he's decided my wedding planning business isn't such a harebrained scheme after all. Now I'm just waiting for the right time."

"To propose to him?" Autumn chuckled.

"To be proposed to. After the baby's born."

Autumn went to the kitchen, cut a slice of the quiche she'd recently taken from the oven and set it down in front of Mia. They were having lunch together since it was one of Mia's days off. "Why after?"

"Because I want to be pretty when he proposes. I don't want to look like this." She patted her belly, which felt like it had grown several inches in the last week.

"What...beautiful? Glowing? Goddess-like?"

"Hardly goddess-like. You know what I mean."

"I do," Autumn said gently, "but don't you think Luke would like to be engaged before the baby is born—maybe even married—so he feels he's a part of the family?"

Mia, about to take a bite of her quiche, lowered her fork. "You think so?"

Autumn nodded. "You have to see it from his point of view."

"I guess so. I guess I keep wanting a picture-perfect proposal. I want a picture-perfect wedding, too."

"Doesn't every bride? But you know what? Life keeps happening whether we're ready for it or not and sometimes you just have to grab hold of it and go on the ride, whether or not it's perfect. Think about it. I have a feeling it would mean a lot to Luke."

Of course it would, Mia realized, no longer hungry. He'd been consistent on that point since the first time he proposed. He wanted to marry her. He wanted to be her baby's father.

Wasn't it time to pledge to him that he could do just that? Maybe she'd been too hard on Luke. After all, he'd simply tried to be the best man he could be. With Holt as a father, it was a miracle that a little hardheadedness was his only vice. Maybe she could trust that he wasn't trying to undercut her when he tried to help. Maybe she could trust that he truly loved her. At his most aggravating, he'd always been trying to protect her.

Well, she needed a little protection now. She'd received another e-mail from Inez, letting her know they'd need to meet with the police in just a few days' time. She'd decided to go through with it, but she was nervous. She wondered what Warner would do.

For once she wouldn't mind if Luke took the lead and kept her safe. She pulled out her phone. She'd call him right now.

"I DON'T THINK I'm going to get my trip to Paris," Lisa said when Luke stopped by the main house that afternoon. He was having trouble keeping a smile off of his face. He'd just gotten a text from Mia asking for his help in a few days. She hadn't said what for—but she'd asked him to come by that evening to talk it over. Things were looking up.

"Dad hasn't screwed up yet, huh?"

"Well, has he?"

"No." And it was uncanny that his father had kept so much to himself, except for that conversation they'd had about the pageants. He'd have figured Holt would either be working to block the wedding, or working to promote it.

Instead, the old man was tied up in his building project. Luke hoped like hell he hadn't decided to break up the ranch and sell off a piece.

"Has Dad explained what he's doing yet?"

"No, but did you see the house? It's as cute as a bug. Going up fast, too. They'll have it done in no time."

"You don't know who it's for?"

"Not a clue. I guess he'll explain in his own sweet time. How about you and Mia? You two seem to be getting along now. Do you think there's a chance things will work out?"

Luke leaned against the kitchen counter. "Yeah, I do. But not until after the baby is born." He tried to keep his disappointment out of his voice, but didn't think he was successful.

His mother confirmed it when she said, "I'm sorry, honey. But I still think you'll make a good father for that baby girl."

"I wanted her to have my name." There. He'd said it aloud.

"She still can. You'll see. Mia can't be with a man as solid and steady as you and not grow to see how lucky she is."

Her praise made him uncomfortable. "I'd better get back to work."

"Okay. Just remember—you're a fine catch for any girl."

He escaped while he could.

Chapter Twenty-One

"OF COURSE I'LL go with you," Luke said when Mia explained the situation with Fred Warner that night.

"You don't sound surprised."

"I heard a little about what happened," he admitted. "Rose told me a little. Dad told me more."

"Your dad knew about Warner?" Mia was surprised.

"Turns out he helped run him out of town six years ago."

"Really?" Holt always surprised her. "Good for him."

"He didn't run him far enough away." Luke took her hand. "I hope you won't have to see him again."

"I might at the trial if I'm called to testify, but someone has to stop him. Who knows how many other girls he's molested."

"I wish I could put him out of business for good."

"But you can't." Mia was firm. "Not like that. We have to live within the law."

"I'll do what you want me to do." He pulled her close and kissed her head. "And I'll be there every moment. You will never be alone with him, I promise."

She nodded and snuggled into his arms. She could get used to this kind of support.

"HOW'S MORGAN DOING?" Mia called out several days later, as she rushed into the waiting room at the Chance Creek Hospital. She'd gotten the call from Rose that Morgan had gone into labor and come as fast as she could. She had to work in a couple of hours, but she'd stay as long as possible to offer support.

"She's doing great," Rose said. "Her contractions are really close now—barely a minute apart. Rob says the doctor thinks she'll be pushing any minute."

"When did her labor start?"

"Just after midnight," Hannah said. "No crazy thirty minute deliveries for her." She grinned at Autumn, who was nursing Arianna in one of the fabric-covered waiting room chairs.

Autumn smiled back. "Arianna can't help it that she was excited to see me."

Mia settled into the chair next to her, her toe tapping with excitement. In just four weeks it would be her in one of these rooms, getting ready to meet her own little one. She couldn't wait.

They conversed in fits and starts, all of them too anxious about Morgan to be distracted for too long from the reason they were there. A bustle in the hallway had them all on their feet, as Rob burst into the room.

"It's a boy! We have a boy! Seven pounds, six ounces!"

"How's Morgan?" Rose cried.

"She's doing great. Just great. She was amazing!"

Mia sent up a prayer of thanks that Morgan and her baby were both fine. The pride in Rob's voice made her heart squeeze with love for both her friends. She wanted Luke to be proud of her like that.

She wanted Luke, period.

As the women rushed to hug Rob and offer their congratulations, Mia hung back knowing clearly for the first time she didn't want to face her baby's birth alone. She didn't want to go another day without telling Luke how much she loved him—and needed him, too.

And she knew what she had to do. Let Luke know she was ready to throw all in with him.

To let him know she was ready to say yes.

SIX HOURS LATER, Mia pushed the door open and entered the diner, spotting Carl immediately. She slowed down when she saw the cupcake with a lit birthday candle sticking out of it at her place.

As she slid awkwardly into her seat, she asked, "What's this for?"

"Graduation day."

"Graduation from what?"

"Business school. You've learned all you need to know."

"I'm no millionaire," she grumbled as she began to peel the paper away from the bottom of the cupcake.

"No, but you have a successful business with customers clamoring for your service. Everyone's talking about your events. You have a unique set of skills that you've put to use to create your brand. You've made connections all over town that will help build your business for you. You've set goals and you achieved them." He put out his hand and shook hers. "Congratulations."

"Thank you." Mia beamed back at him. She straightened her shoulders. "I feel good about what I've done."

"You should. Next, you'll have to figure out how to balance your work with raising that baby."

"I'm beginning to feel good about that too," she said. "I've made my mind up about something."

"What's that?" Carl signaled for more coffee. A new waitress brought it over for him—a young woman Mia didn't recognize.

"No more Tracey," Mia said. "And I'm going to follow her example. I'm going to get married, too."

"Does Luke know?"

"Not yet. I'm trying to give him subtle hints. I told him a while ago I didn't want to marry until after the baby's born, but I've changed my mind."

"Hmm. I said I was done teaching you things, but would you mind one more lesson?" Carl lifted his coffee cup. Took a sip. "Don't ever try to give a man a subtle hint. Not if you want it to work. Just do the poor schmuck a favor and whack him over the head with it, whatever it is."

"Really?" Mia nibbled the cupcake.

"Really."

"Okay." She decided she'd think that over when she was alone. "So, what about you? Any luck yet with buying a house?"

"No. But I decided that's a good thing. When I got

here I was in a rush to buy a place and start feeling like I belong, but I think that's backwards. I think I'll figure out how to belong here first—then find the right property."

"So you'll be looking for a long-term rental? I could put out the word for you."

"I've found a situation, actually. There's another family moving back to town—the Coopers. Apparently they pulled stakes and moved to Wyoming for some years to be part of a venture there, but now they're coming home and getting back into the ranching business. I'll get their house in order for them, supervise some repair work, that kind of thing, and I'll move into one of the other houses standing empty on the property. I figure it won't hurt me to get some hands-on ranching experience before I buy my own spread, and living with the Coopers should give me an in with the community I never had before."

"Sounds like things are looking up for you, too," Mia said.

"Here's to progress." He raised his cup of coffee and Mia raised her cup of milk in return.

Marry her now.

If only he could, Luke thought as he crumpled up the latest mystery message and tossed it in the trash. He'd marry Mia any day of the week, in his best suit or fresh from a day of work in his jeans and a sweaty T-shirt. All he wanted was to know they'd spend the rest of their lives together, come what may. But Mia had been perfectly clear—no proposal and no marriage until after the birth.

At least he'd get to see her tonight. They were eating with his family—the whole gang from the Double-Bar-K and the Cruz ranch, plus the Mortimers and a surprise guest he'd invited without the knowledge of anyone but his mother. Lisa was cooking her signature baked chicken and he was sure there would be all his other favorite fixings. The meal would taste great, even if the company got ornery.

He and Ned were back on speaking terms at least, although things weren't entirely smooth between them. He knew Fila and Mia had patched things up much more thoroughly than he'd managed to do with his brother.

A half-hour later, he was sitting around the large oak dining room table in his parents' house, laughing at Jake's rendition of Ned's first time mounting a horse since he broke his leg back in January.

"It wasn't that bad," Ned protested.

"It was that bad," Jake returned. "But you'll loosen up again in time. I'm just glad Fila was there to get your leg back on straight when you broke it. Otherwise who knows if you'd be riding today at all."

"That's right," Lisa said, passing a platter of chicken to Jake. "Fila, we'll always be grateful to you."

"Thank you."

"And Morgan, that son of yours is as cute as a bug. Are you getting any sleep?"

"A little." Morgan smiled at Rob. "Not much."

"No, not much," Rob agreed.

"Who's the empty seat for?" Evan Mortimer spoke up.

"A friend's joining us for dessert," Luke put in quickly.

"Mia, how are you holding up?" Lisa asked. She caught Luke's eye and winked. He smiled to show he appreciated her help in diverting the question. He meant to bring up the practical jokes soon and Carl's unwitting part in starting them off.

"I'm okay. Tired. Achy. Sleep-deprived."

"The last few weeks of a pregnancy are the hardest. I was like that with all four of my boys."

At the far end of the table, Holt shifted. Luke wasn't sure if his father was uncomfortable with the topic of conversation, or if he had something to say. But his father remained uncharacteristically quiet, as he had for weeks now.

"This time next month you'll have your little one, too," Morgan said to Mia. She was holding baby Jack in her arms and trying to eat one-handed.

"I can't wait."

Holt shifted again.

"Are you all set? Do you have a bag packed for the hospital?" Hannah asked.

"I'm going to do that tomorrow. I didn't want to jump the gun." Mia smiled. "I'm off work now, so all I have to do is lounge around and wait for this baby to arrive."

"What about a crib?"

"I've got a bassinet for now." It was Mia's turn to shift in her seat and Luke figured she didn't want the question of her living arrangements to be the topic of conversation. They hadn't said as much, but he felt pretty sure that soon after the baby was born, Mia would move back into his cabin. With the nursery all set up there, it didn't make sense for her to buy a crib.

"Luke's got a crib," Ned said, echoing his thoughts.

Luke frowned.

"I know," Mia said. "It'll come in handy if I ever visit."

Holt dropped his silverware on his plate. "When the hell are you two getting married?"

Everyone froze in shock at his sudden outburst, then Lisa's laughter pealed out. "Paris! You owe me a trip to Paris, my dear!"

"Don't Paris me, woman! No one here is talking about Paris."

"You're right. We don't have to talk about it. We just have to pack our bags." Lisa beamed.

Holt turned on Luke with a growl. "What are you waiting for? That girl's as big as a barn. Marry her already!"

"We're waiting until—"

"You're waiting too long! Get on with it! What do you want—Christ to descend from heaven to do the ceremony himself?"

"Holt!" Lisa's smile vanished. "No need for blasphemy."

"I'll blaspheme all I want if that's what it takes to light a fire under their asses. Look at you two! What a pair you make!"

"Dad—"

"I thought for once one of my sons wouldn't need my interference to get himself wed, but I was wrong, wasn't I? Every last one of you needed me to hold your hand all the way up to the altar. I raised a pack of fools!"

"I want to marry her!" Luke couldn't restrain himself any longer. "I've been trying to marry her. I proposed twice! Maybe you should have meddled a long time ago. I'll take any help I can get!"

"Wait a minute," Mia said. She'd been staring at Holt ever since he started talking. "You've been interfering all along, haven't you? The notes—those were yours!"

Luke's jaw dropped. He turned to Mia. "You got notes, too?"

She nodded.

"Notes!" Lisa shook her head. "Holt didn't write any notes, that's for sure."

"I think he did." Mia leaned forward. "Am I right?"

Holt didn't answer, but his struggle to hold back was plain for anyone to see.

"Did you butt in with *notes*, you old goat?" Lisa said. "Then you owe me a trip to Paris twice over." She slapped her palm on the table. "Although I want to know how you managed it."

"I don't have to take you anywhere," he burst out. "You said I couldn't *say* a word about marriage. You didn't say I couldn't write about it."

"How could you? You don't even know how to write!" Ned said.

"I guess I do, after all," Holt said, and folded his arms across his chest. "You aren't the only one who can hire a tutor."

"Well, I'll be damned." Rob leaned forward. "Next thing you know, pigs'll fly. Dad getting some schooling—that's unexpected."

"I know what I want for my next wedding anniversary." Lisa smiled at Holt.

"A trip to the moon?" Holt eyed her back.

"A love letter."

Luke fought to regain his footing in the conversation. The last person he'd suspected of writing those notes was his father, but while revelations were being spilled, he might as well tell everyone what else had happened.

"Looks like you fooled us all, Dad. You're a real joker."

"Not the only one around here from what I've heard." Holt turned serious. "Seems like the jokes have gotten out of control, too."

"I didn't start it," Ned said, as if he suspected he'd get blamed.

"I didn't start it, either," Rob said, holding up his hands.

"Sure you did! You stole my dress boots on Ned's wedding day!" Jake pointed a finger at him.

"I had nothing to do with that and I have no clue why Cab here felt like he had to butcher my topiary."

The sheriff looked indignant. "I didn't butcher anyone's topiary! I'm the victim here. Jamie's the one who put that damn *Honk if I'm Sexy* sign on my cruiser. I still get crap about it from my deputies."

"I didn't do anything to your cruiser. I'm the one who's half-naked on a Cowboy calendar because of Ethan here."

"Are you serious?" Ethan exploded. "I don't have

the time or energy to enroll cowboys in calendar contests. I'm too busy taking hemorrhoid medication deliveries from Ned!"

"Let me guess." Holt's voice cut across the table and the hubbub subsided. He jabbed a finger at Ethan. "It was you who sent Ned the children's book, not Luke. You just made it look like Luke."

Ethan sat back. He ducked his head. "I guess that wasn't cool. But like I said, the hemorrhoid joke wasn't cool, either."

"I had nothing to do with that." Ned looked like thunder.

"I was the one who sent the hemorrhoid cream." Jamie spoke up. "Because of the calendar."

"And I was the one who signed you up for the calendar." Cab nodded at Jamie. "Because of the sign."

"I'm the one who put the sign on," Rob said. "Because of that damn bush."

"Which I turned into a bulldog," Jake said, chuckling a little. "Because I thought you stole my boots on Ned's wedding day."

"Sorry, that was me," Evan confessed. "When I got that envelope with the offer to trade my ranch for The Breakers, I thought you were making fun of me—especially with that note that said The Breakers was worth so much more."

"That wasn't Jake," a new voice said. "I'm afraid that was me." Carl rounded the corner and hesitated in the doorway to the room. "When I got to town I was so excited about getting my ranch back, I drove straight to your place and left the envelope in your mailbox. When you never answered me—not even to say no—I figured you had no intention to sell, so I moved on. It wasn't until Luke here told me you thought it was a joke that I went back and looked through my things. I found the letter I was supposed to include explaining my offer—which meant all you got were the photos and that scrawled note. No wonder you didn't take it seriously." He shoved his hands in his pockets. "The offer still stands, by the way. I thought I didn't want the ranch anymore back when Lacey—my fiancée," he explained to Evan, "broke things off with me, but I've realized since then that I didn't move to Chance Creek for her. I moved here to be the person I've always wanted to be. So now I'm back."

All around the table Luke saw stunned faces. Evan spoke first. "I don't think we're planning to sell. Sorry to disappoint you."

"We really love the ranch, too," Bella added, "and we're already building my animal shelter and clinic there. I hope that won't be a problem for you."

"Not at all," Carl said, although a flicker of disappointment crossed his face. "I have temporary lodgings, and I'll keep looking." He looked from face to face. "I guess I'll be on my way."

"Oh, no you don't," Lisa said, standing up. "Luke, where are your manners? Show your guest to his seat. It's time for dessert. Ladies, will you help me clear?"

In the general bustle, Luke led Carl to his seat. Mia leaned forward to smile and say hello. Others around the table called out greetings, and those close by moved to shake his hand. Carl looked pleased by the friendly welcome he was receiving.

Mia whispered in Luke's ear, "That was nice of you to invite him."

"Carl's okay." He kissed her neck. "Just don't get any ideas."

"You're the man for me, Luke Matheson." She kissed him back.

Luke stilled. Did she mean that?

He sure as hell hoped she did.

"I WOULDN'T HAVE believed it if I wasn't there," Mia said to Luke as they walked back to his cabin. "Who knew your dad would learn to write?"

"I hate to admit it, but those notes nudged me along a couple of times."

"Me too—shocking as that is. Holt the matchmaker. That's a dangerous proposition. You need to put that man back to work full-time on the ranch."

"Actually, I think I do—whenever he's done with that building project. But I also think he's right—I think we've waited too long to get engaged."

"I think so, too," Mia said softly. "I wish I'd said yes a long time ago."

He turned to face her. "Really?"

She nodded.

"So if I proposed to you right now, you'd say yes?"

"Only if you had a ring with you." She chuckled.

He dropped down onto one knee. "I do happen to have a ring with me." He fished in his pocket and pulled out a small velvet case. "And you'd make me the happiest man in the world if you'd do me the honor of becoming my wife, Mia Start." He opened the case to show her the delicate ring she'd first chosen from Thayer's.

"Luke! You were carrying that around?" Love for him welled up within her. This was the man she'd fallen in love with. This was the man she wanted to spend her life with.

"Answer the question."

"Yes. Yes, I'll marry you." She blinked back tears as Luke stood up, slid the ring on her finger and pulled her in for a kiss. She'd never forget where she stood the moment she became engaged to the man she loved above all others, halfway between the main house and Luke's cabin, on a soft May evening with a canopy of stars shining overhead. "I love you," she whispered into his neck.

He tilted her head back and kissed her soundly. "I love you, too."

"ALL I'M SAYING is, you were right. I could use some more help around the place, Pops—even when Ned's leg is healed. It used to take all four of us plus you to run the show. Now with Jake and Rob busy with their own businesses, we're shorthanded." Luke sat in the passenger seat in his father's truck the next day, still buzzing with the knowledge that Mia had consented to be his wife. They hadn't been able to celebrate with quite the rambunctious round of lovemaking that he'd have liked, but they'd come together in a gentle, sensuous way that was just as good. He'd lain awake long after Mia dropped off, planning for the future. He was determined to make a good life for his wife and child and that meant having the time to spend with them.

"Last year it was all the lot of you could do to shove me aside so you could run the show." Holt turned the vehicle onto the highway. He'd told Luke he had something to show him. Luke figured it was the new house he'd built. Maybe he'd finally learn the mystery of who would live there.

"I'm not asking you to take charge."

"So you want to give me orders?"

"How about we work together—you, me and Ned, with Jake and Rob lending a hand when they can. That oughta work."

"I suppose. Since you can't handle things on your own."

Luke knew that was as close to gratitude as Holt came.

His father pulled up in front of the brand-new house that bordered the highway. It had a little yard of its own, and pansies planted along the walkway. A front porch sported a rocking chair. The whole thing was as spotless as anything. In fact, it reminded him of…

"Luke! Hello!" Amanda Stone walked out onto the porch and waved as they got out. "Isn't this a wonderful surprise?"

"You built this house for Amanda Stone?" Luke turned to his father in surprise.

"She called me up a while back. Let me know what my son had been doing for her all these years—what I should have been doing for the widow of one of my hired hands all along." He lowered his voice. "I'm proud of you." He squeezed Luke's shoulder and moved past him to greet Amanda.

Luke rocked on his feet, so stunned he couldn't move. His father was proud of him?

"Come on, don't keep the lady waiting," Holt called.

Luke snapped back to life and took the steps two at a time.

"We'll be able to keep an eye on things for you now, Amanda," his father said, accepting the glass of lemonade she handed him.

"And now that the house is built you can start helping me out with the ranch chores," Luke said to him, accepting a glass as well.

"Of course you'll have to make do while your mother and I are off gallivanting around Europe."

"We can hold it together for a week or two."

Holt snorted. "You'll have to do more than that. We'll be gone nearly two months."

Luke cocked his hat back, the better to see Holt's face. "You joking again?"

"No joke about it. They pack a lot of countries into that one little continent. No wonder those Europeans are all so scrawny."

Luke narrowed his eyes. "A lot of countries, huh? Just how long have you been planning this trip, Dad?"

"Ask me no questions and I'll tell you no lies. Sit down and drink your lemonade."

"You got it, old man." Luke lowered himself into one of the wicker chairs.

"And show some respect."

"Sure thing, Pops."

Chapter Twenty-Two

"I CAN'T GET comfortable," Mia complained as she helped Autumn wash up the lunch dishes. It was the first week in July and she hadn't worked for a week now. She thought she'd enjoy the rest, but the truth was she didn't know what to do with herself. At least her ordeal with Warner was over. She, Inez and Luke had gone to meet the police who were working on the case, and given their statements. They had met another young woman there who had also come up against Warner. She was seventeen, and she was the one who had reported him to the police. Mia was in awe of the bravery it had taken for her to speak up and told her so.

The detective she and Inez spoke to said that it was unlikely they'd have to testify, after all, since there were several girls willing to do so whose assaults had happened so much more recently. Warner wasn't behind bars yet, but Mia was confident he would never judge another pageant again.

"You did a good thing here," Luke had said on their way home. "A brave thing."

"Inez is the one who was brave," Mia responded.

"I'm glad she gave me the chance to speak up."

Now that she didn't have Warner to worry about, and she didn't have any work to do either, she found herself trailing Autumn and Arianna around the guesthouse as Autumn prepped for her next set of clients.

"Is it your back?"

"Yes. Down here." She patted the base of her spine awkwardly. "It aches all the time."

"Why don't you sit down and put your feet up?"

"I'm sick of sitting. I'm sick of waiting for this baby. How am I going to last another two weeks?"

"You'll manage," Autumn said, eyeing her. "Maybe it won't be two weeks. That baby looks like she's sitting awfully low."

"Everything's uncomfortable. I just feel… ow." She pressed her hand to her back again. "Oh… ow!"

"Mia? Are you okay?"

"Yes. Oh—oh—I don't know. Ow!"

"Are you having a contraction?"

Mia couldn't catch her breath. She couldn't talk. A band of steel tightened around her midsection and squeezed until she gripped the counter in pain. "Oh my God! Autumn!" Something gave within her and wetness drenched the lightweight pajama pants she wore. "Autumn—my water just broke!"

"All right, we're going to get you to the hospital. Let me grab my keys!"

But Mia was already in the grips of another contraction and this one nearly brought her to her knees. She didn't recognize her voice in the sound that she was making—guttural and fierce. The vise that gripped her body seemed determined to push the life out of her.

"Mia! What are you doing? You can't bear down. You just started your contractions!" Autumn's voice rose as she juggled Arianna into her carrier car seat, strapped her in, then grabbed her phone.

"Nine-one-one? It's Autumn Cruz." She gave her address and a brief rundown of the situation. "Do I put her in my truck and drive? Or do I wait for an ambulance?"

Mia cried out again, sinking to her knees, still gripping the kitchen counter and arching her back with the pain. "Autumn!" She panted when the contraction was finally over and looked up to see Autumn staring back at her helplessly. "Call Luke!"

Autumn straightened. Ended the call with the emergency worker and made a new call. "Luke? It's Autumn. Mia's having her baby. We're at the ranch. In the guesthouse. No—it's happening too fast!" She turned back to Mia. "We've got to move you, honey. Can you walk?"

"I don't think so." Mia cried out with renewed force as a new contraction—an even stronger one—squeezed her so hard she could barely breathe.

As soon as it ended, Autumn moved to her side and got her shoulder under Mia's arm. "Come on, we're going to get you to your room." Mia didn't say anything, just moved in the direction Autumn pulled her. The stairs were the worst. A new contraction brought her to her knees halfway up and they knelt there together through the long round of pain. Afterward, Autumn half-hauled her the rest of the way to her bedroom. "I don't think that ambulance is going to make it. Come on, climb onto the bed."

"I can't believe it's happening like this. I thought it was supposed to take hours."

"So did I." Autumn faced her. "I think in both our cases, it actually took days. You've been complaining about pain for a long time now, just like I did. Neither of us put two and two together. I'll be right back."

Mia was barely aware of Autumn's movements as her friend brought towels, a glass of water and other supplies. Mia groaned with the pain and tried to find a comfortable position, finally ending up on all fours.

"I'm never… doing… this… again," she panted after a contraction ended.

Autumn laughed. "I remember that feeling. Luckily it passes. You're doing great, honey."

"Mia!"

Both women started at the sound of Luke's voice downstairs. They heard his footsteps as he climbed the staircase, two steps at a time, by the sound of it. "Mia!"

"In here," Autumn called.

A second later, Luke burst into the room. "Are you okay? Let's get you to the hospital."

A contraction overtook her before she could answer and Mia's momentary embarrassment about Luke seeing her in such an extreme moment disappeared as she felt the baby move lower within her. The contraction seemed to go on and on, and the interval between it and the next one was so brief she could only say, "No time. She's coming!"

Mia lost track of everything after that except her own body, her straining muscles, the band of steel that was the contraction itself. She gave in to the pain and cried out, the sound ending with a moan that tore itself from her lungs.

"You're crowning. I can see her!" Autumn cried. "You're doing great, Mia!"

"Honey, she's coming. Our baby's coming—I can see the top of her head. She's got pretty black hair, just like you!"

Luke's voice gave her the strength to push again, and this time Mia felt her baby being born.

"That's it! That's it!"

"Mia, I can see her face—just one more push, baby!"

Mia gasped for breath, waited for the contraction to start again and pushed with all her might.

"I've got her! I've got her, Mia!" Luke's voice broke. "Darling, she's beautiful! She's as beautiful as her mother."

Mia collapsed as she heard the high-pitched wail of a newborn ring out. Almost simultaneously, another voice called out from downstairs.

"Hello? It's Emergency Services!"

Autumn rushed to go meet them, and in the moment of calm, Luke bent down to guide the baby up to Mia and laid her on her chest.

"Meet your daughter, Mia. Look at her."

Mia did look at her, from the dark cap of hair on her head to her blue eyes to the tip of her button nose, to her little round belly and tiny feet. In an instant Mia fell in love with what she saw. "Luke—"

"I know, sweetheart. I know." He sat down next to her and kissed the top of her head. "You were amazing, you know that? If we weren't already engaged, I'd have to ask you to marry me right now."

Mia laughed, but it came out half a sob from exhaustion and her high emotions. She couldn't believe how fast it had all happened. She couldn't believe how the process of giving birth had overtaken her body.

The emergency team swept into her bedroom and the moment was gone, but Mia knew that she'd always remember her first sight of her baby—in Luke's hands.

WHEN THE AMBULANCE crew swept in and took over, Luke staggered out into the hallway.

He'd seen births. He'd seen dozens of births. Just like when Autumn was in labor, he recalled his experiences with the farm animals he'd tended all his life.

This was different though. This was the woman he loved. This was her baby—their baby—being born. This was a true miracle.

And he'd gotten to be there for it. According to Autumn, he was the one Mia called for. He was the one she wanted.

And he wanted her—more now than ever before. He remembered how calm he'd been standing outside Autumn's door four months ago, guarding her birth. He hadn't been calm at all with Mia. He'd been overcome with emotion. Overcome with love. Overcome with fear—just for a moment—that something might go wrong. But it all was so evidently right he couldn't stay scared, and he'd been back to love and awe in just an instant.

"You okay, Dad?" Autumn asked, appearing by his

side with a glass of juice. He took it, uncomprehending, until she gestured to it. "Drink up. I think you're in shock."

He did so. "Yeah, I'm okay."

"It's a hell of a thing, isn't it?" She waved a hand at Mia.

"Yeah. A hell of a thing." He focused on Autumn. "You must have wanted Ethan there with you when you had Arianna—not me."

"You were a good substitute, but yes—I hope next time Ethan's there." In answer to his unspoken question, she said, "No, there isn't a next time on the horizon yet, but I hope there will be in a few months. I've always wanted a house full of kids."

"I guess that's what I want, too."

And for the first time, he had a feeling he would get to have them.

"SO WHAT'S IT like to plan your own wedding?" Rose asked a month later. Mia was sitting with her at the dining room table of Luke's cabin—their cabin, now— studying bridal magazines.

"It's fun. Especially now I've had some practice." She grinned at Rose, snuggling baby Pamela, who she cradled in her arms.

"If it's even half the wedding you threw for Rose, it will be fabulous," Hannah put in.

"Exactly," Rose said.

"I'll say one thing. Luke is going to have to build me an addition to hold all my wedding planning stuff. I don't have anywhere to put it."

Rose looked around the small kitchen at the stacks of magazines, clipboards, fabric swatches and more. "I see what you mean. You need an office. Somewhere clients can come to meet with you."

"You're right. Linda's Diner doesn't exactly cut it. Even if the coffee is good."

"And I need a gallery space," Rose said. "I feel like I could sell some of my paintings—especially to tourists—if people could see them. Waiting for one of the local venues to show my work is really frustrating."

"Do you think you'd earn enough from sales to make a dedicated gallery worthwhile?" Mia asked, then smiled privately. Carl's business sense was definitely rubbing off.

"I've been thinking I need a sideline, too. Something that always sells, that draws people in to see my art."

"Like jewelry?" Hannah said. "I still think you should buy Thayer's. You'd be a natural."

Rose made a face. "That's a going concern. I wouldn't have time to paint."

"Sure you would," Mia said. "You'd hire help, just like Emory always did."

Hannah looked from one to the other. "You two don't even see the possibilities, do you? Mia, you could pair up with Rose and open your event planning business there, too. Thayer's has a lot of odds and ends that I don't think sell very well. Distill the jewelry part of the business down to the important things, use the walls for Rose's art, and enclose a corner for your office, Mia. People will come in to buy a ring and end up booking a wedding!"

Mia stared at Rose. "That's not a bad idea at all.

What do you think, Rose?"

"I think I don't have the money to buy Thayer's."

"I do."

"YOU'RE GOING TO buy Thayer's? How?" Luke stared across the kitchen table at Mia, who was nursing Pamela. He didn't want to raise his voice and scare the baby, but Mia wasn't making any sense.

"Remember how I said Ellis gave me some money before he walked out?"

Luke still hated the man's name on Mia's lips. "What about it?"

"You jumped to the conclusion it was a few hundred dollars and I didn't correct you. At the time I didn't feel like it was your business."

"Now you do?"

"Now I do. It was a few hundred thousand dollars. Two hundred thousand, to be exact. I've barely spent any of it yet. I'd like to use it as a down payment on Thayer's."

Two hundred thousand dollars? Luke sat back, stunned. His bank account never contained more than a couple of thousand at most. Ellis had given Mia a present that he could never hope to match.

"I gotta go." He stumbled to his feet. "I for-got…something."

As he strode to the door, Mia called after him, "Luke? What is it? I thought we were going to have lunch."

"Be back… soon."

Outside he kept walking, his long strides eating up

the ground until he'd passed the main house and all the outbuildings and was heading toward the far pastures.

"Luke? You forgot your horse!" Ten minutes later, Ned caught up to him easily on Silver and reined her in to walk beside Luke. "Where are you going?"

"I don't know."

"Did something happen? Is Mia all right?"

"She's fine. She's more than fine. She's rich."

Ned swung out of the saddle to the ground and began to lead Silver at a walk beside Luke. "Mia's rich? Did someone die?"

"I wish." Luke got himself under control. "Ellis bought her off with two hundred grand. Now she wants to buy Thayer's with Rose and run her wedding planning business out of it."

"That's an interesting idea. Rose would go back to selling rings?"

"And her paintings, I guess."

"Seems like that could work."

"That's not the point. The point is Ellis gave Mia two hundred grand."

Ned shot him a look. "Let me guess. You think that makes him the better man?"

"In her eyes, yes."

"Luke." Ned stopped and Luke stopped, too, although he didn't want to. "She isn't marrying Ellis Scranton. She's marrying you—because you're the kind of man who sticks with a woman, who offers her his home. His heart. Ellis is the kind of man who fools around with a woman, throws money at her and heads for the hills."

Luke shook his head. Those were just words. Money was money.

"Don't be an idiot," Ned went on. "You're part of this ranch and it's worth a lot. It might not be cash in the bank, but it's still something. Mia knows that."

"That's not all of it." Luke adjusted his hat, looking at the mountains in the distance, the cattle in the pastures—anywhere but at his brother. "I'm still in debt, even though I sold my truck."

Ned nodded slowly. "I think we all were until we started to get paid some. How bad is it?"

Luke named a sum.

Ned made a face. "That's not too bad. You can pay that off in a couple of months if you put your mind to it."

"I'm marrying Mia next month. I want to take her on a honeymoon. I want to help build her an office for a business."

"You don't need to build her an office anymore, do you?" Ned was practical. "Put off the honeymoon until you can afford it. And tell her exactly what you just told me."

"About the debt? Hell, no!"

Ned leaned closer. "About everything, if you're smart. Starting with the debt."

By the time Luke got back to his cabin, Mia had already eaten her lunch and was packing up the remains.

"There you are. Is everything okay?" she asked when he walked in.

"Yeah, it is." He fiddled with the doorknob, noticed what he was doing and moved farther into the house.

"Actually, it isn't. But it will be."

"Is this about money?"

Luke stopped. "How'd you know?"

"Because we were talking about it when you high-tailed it out of here." She sighed. "I knew you wouldn't like it that Ellis gave me all that cash."

"This isn't about Ellis. It's about me."

"I love you. You know that."

She looked so worried, Luke moved to her and pressed a kiss on her mouth. "I do know that. Just give me a few minutes to say what I have to say."

"All right." Mia sat at the table. "Go ahead."

He sat down across from her. "You know Dad kept us all on a short leash for a long, long time. We all pitched in and worked the ranch, but he didn't pay us a lot for that. Since we'd been doing chores here all our lives, we didn't think much about it until recently."

"Until Rob decided to marry Morgan?"

"That's about the size of it. It's easy to be single with a little cash when your house and food are paid for. But when you take on a wife and start a family, things change. Now we all take a salary based on the amount of work we do. The thing is, I still have some debts from those days. Credit cards. That kind of thing."

Mia expelled a breath. Was that relief he wasn't mad at her? Luke wasn't sure. He went on before she could say anything, wanting to get it all out at once.

"I want to give you things. I want to take you on a honeymoon, and help you buy Thayer's, if that's what you want. I want to support you, Mia. I've always wanted that. I need time, though." He braced himself. He knew what would happen next. Mia would offer to pay his debts with Ellis's money. He didn't think he could stomach hearing that offer.

Mia surprised him, though. "I can give you time. We'll go when you're ready. Between us, Rose and I have enough to buy Thayer's and get a start. Since the jewelry business is already established, we'll have enough income to pay our mortgage. We're working out the details."

"I wish I could just buy it for you."

"I know that, but here's the thing." She gathered her thoughts. "I like business. I like thinking about it, planning for it, figuring out how to make it grow. I like talking about it, too—that's why I kept meeting with Carl. I'm not afraid of money anymore. And you and I— we're a partnership. You don't have to buy me things. You don't have to do everything all on your own. Look what you've already given me." She gestured to the cabin. "More importantly, you've given me your heart. That's what I want from you. The rest we'll do together."

Luke didn't bother with words. He pulled her close and showed his appreciation in other ways. Ways that soon had them naked and tangled together on the living room couch.

"You sure Pam's sleeping?" Luke said when things got to a critical juncture.

"Positive. Just keep the noise level down."

"You're the one who makes all the noise. You keep it down." He gathered her close.

"I can't help it if you make me scream." Mia arched back as Luke entered her. "Oh, that feels good," she gasped.

"I can't help what your body makes my body do."

The time for words was over, though. Luke kissed Mia whenever her cries rose in volume and Mia kissed him back when his release came hard and fast and had him calling out, too.

Afterward, they snuggled together as best they could on the couch.

"I can't wait to marry you," Mia said.

"No, *I* can't wait to marry you."

Chapter Twenty-Three

MIA HAD DREAMED about her wedding day ever since she was a little girl, and now she was about to walk down the aisle on her father's arm to meet the man she loved at the altar and join her life to his forever.

Her mother held Pamela, dressed in a soft yellow daisy dress for the occasion, in the front row of the Chance Creek Reformed Church. Reverend Halpern stood waiting to perform the ceremony. Once Mia's mother had held her granddaughter for the first time, all her need to control the wedding seemed to disappear like so much dust before the wind. Mia felt closer to her than she had in years, which healed a part of her heart she hadn't realized was so broken.

When the music swelled, Mia took her father's arm and began a slow, stately walk down the aisle.

"I'm proud of you, honey. You've really made something of your life," he said.

"Thanks, Daddy." She was proud of herself, too. For having the strength to see her pregnancy through. For having the guts to start her own business. And for her wisdom in choosing a man like Luke to spend her life with.

Standing tall and proud at the altar, Luke looked so handsome that her breath caught. He would be hers forever. He would support her in times of trouble, be a friend to her during their rounds of everyday life, and love her—at every opportunity. Her lips curved into a smile.

When her father passed her hand to Luke, a shiver of anticipation traveled through her. From this day forward they would always be together. There would be no question of if she'd end up in his arms—the only question would be how often. And that was exactly the way she wanted it.

Pamela cooed and a ripple of laughter ran through the congregation.

"She says, hurry up already!" Jake called out.

This time the laughter was louder.

"I'm ready," Luke said, looking into her eyes. "How about you?"

"I'm ready, too."

The **Cowboys of Chance Creek** series continues with
The Cowboy's Christmas Bride.

Be the first to know about Cora Seton's new releases!
Sign up for her newsletter here!

Other books in the Cowboys of Chance Creek Series:

The Cowboy Inherits a Bride (Volume 0)
The Cowboy's E-Mail Order Bride (Volume 1)
The Cowboy Wins a Bride (Volume 2)
The Cowboy Imports a Bride (Volume 3)
The Cowgirl Ropes a Billionaire (Volume 4)
The Sheriff Catches a Bride (Volume 5)
The Cowboy Lassos a Bride (Volume 6)
The Cowboy Rescues a Bride (Volume 7)
The Cowboy's Christmas Bride (Volume 9)

Sign up for my newsletter HERE.
www.coraseton.com/sign-up-for-my-newsletter

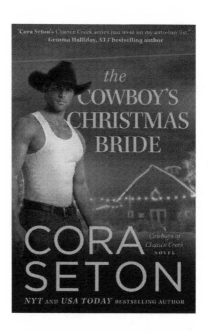

the
COWBOY'S
CHRISTMAS
BRIDE

A Cowboys of
Chance Creek
NOVEL

CORA
SETON

NYT AND *USA TODAY* BESTSELLING AUTHOR

Read on for an excerpt of
The Cowboy's Christmas Bride.

"READY TO GO home?" Cole Linden reached out to stroke his fiancée's cheek.

She smiled back at him. "I think so."

Going on four hours in between flights at Heathrow Airport, she was just as bright and cheerful as ever. That was just one of the things Cole loved about Sunshine. Her disposition resembled her name: upbeat, easygoing, happy to be alive. Sitting on a hard plastic seat, her winter coat undone, a scarf hanging every which way over her shoulders and her beautiful blonde hair spilling out of a felted wool hat, she still took his breath away. After traveling around the world together for nearly three years they probably should have been at each other's throats, but they'd hardly exchanged a cross word in all that time, which Cole counted as a miracle. The real miracle, of course, was that they'd met at all. Cole was a country boy through and through. He loved everything to do with small town living from riding horses to hunting, and he'd been running an indoor rifle range when they'd met. Sunshine was a city girl—and a vegan—and a chef who'd never set foot in a range before that fateful day.

"It'll be good to spend the holidays in Chance Creek." He couldn't wait for Christmas morning. He had a surprise for Sunshine—a real doozy. One that would guarantee she'd never want to leave town again. After their extended trip, he was more than ready to settle down.

"What was it you got me for Christmas again?"

Cole smiled at her none-too-subtle question. They'd been joking about presents for the past few weeks. Sunshine claimed she had a surprise that would knock his socks off, but Cole had warned her that nothing could beat what he'd gotten for her.

"Weren't you the one who said Christmas wasn't a competition? I'm sure whatever paltry gift you bought for me will be just fine. Even if it is overshadowed by my incredible present for you."

"Paltry gift? You're going to eat your words, mister." She elbowed him companionably. He kissed her on the tip of her nose. In truth, he was worried he couldn't carry off his Christmas surprise for Sunshine. It was going to take a lot of work, and he'd have to slip away almost every day during the next few weeks in order to accomplish everything. That might be difficult when they were staying in a motel room and would need to share a rental car. It would have been easier if they'd been able to return to the apartment they'd once shared next to his rifle range and her café. Scott Preston inhabited it now, however. He'd been acting as their caretaker while they'd been gone, and since they were returning on such short notice, they didn't want to evict him.

Besides, it was time to hunt for a real house as soon as the holidays were over. They'd long outgrown the apartment and when they finally married, they'd want a more permanent arrangement.

Three years was an eternity to be away from the town where he'd grown up. He was sure it was different for Sunshine. She'd only lived there for about eight months in all. She'd only come to town because her aunt Cecily left her the building that housed Cole's rifle range, a tiny restaurant space and an apartment. Unfortunately, Cecily had left them to Cole too. She'd pitted them against each other in a contest to see who would ultimately win sole ownership, and at first they'd regarded each other as enemies. That didn't last once they began to share close quarters. The attraction between them was instant and electrifying. It wasn't long before they figured out a way to share everything. Cole continued to run the rifle range and manage the apartment building he owned. Sunshine ran her café from the restaurant space. They lived together in the attached rooms.

But several months later, when they became engaged, they'd received another message from their attorney. It seemed that Cecily's will had a secret codicil to be read only if Sunshine and Cole stayed together for six months. The old woman had left them each a large sum of money. As soon as Cole found out about it, he knew what they needed to do. Sunshine had always talked about traveling the world. Here was their chance. He'd paid off the mortgage on the rental complex, which freed up funds to pay Scott a salary to run the range and apartment house while they were away. Scott had moved into their rooms beside the restaurant to keep an eye on things, and Cole and Sunshine had embarked on an epic journey, the likes of which Cole had never imagined taking.

He'd determined at the start to let Sunshine call the shots about the itinerary and duration of the trip. This was her chance to study cooking in the field, so to speak, and learn from experts in all kinds of situations. He found it easy to be patient. For one thing, he was head over heels in love with Sunshine, for all their talk about a long engagement. For another, Sunshine had assured him that when they were done they'd return to the town he dearly loved. That was a huge concession from a city girl and he wanted to honor the spirit in which she made it by throwing himself into the adventure whole-heartedly.

He'd never guessed she'd make the trip so long, though. He'd begun to think they'd never get home.

Still, he was proud of Sunshine and the way she'd negotiated through the rigors of so much travel. They hadn't stuck to tourist destinations; far from it. Sunshine was fascinated by indigenous recipes, and in every country they visited, she took them off the beaten track into villages and hamlets and somehow convinced women—and men—to teach her everything they knew about cooking. Cole had done his best to photograph the locales, people, ingredients and food preparation steps. They'd taken copious notes in order to correlate recipes, photographs and information about people and locations. When they got home, Sunshine hoped to combine them into a cookbook and get a publishing deal.

Cole had watched people all around the world take to Sunshine. He wasn't sure if it was her smile, her laugh, or the shimmer of her blond hair that caught their attention and made them go out of their way for her, but he couldn't count the number of kindnesses complete strangers had performed for them during the past three years.

He'd worried that such an intense journey might cause trouble between them, but the more they traveled the more he loved Sunshine. With Christmas looming and their return home at hand, he'd decided to give her the one other thing he knew she wanted: a restaurant. He'd purchased one already, sight unseen, from a realtor he knew and trusted back in Chance Creek. Located in the heart of town, he figured Sunshine could make it a success.

"That snow doesn't look promising," Sunshine said, glancing out of the airport window where a cold afternoon was fading into a premature dusk. "I think it's coming down even harder."

"I'm sure it'll be fine."

She nodded. "I hope so." Fidgeting in her seat, she

added, "We're not due to board for another half hour. Want to go for a little walk?"

"If we stand up now, we'll lose our seats." The waiting room was packed with travelers. Cole was thankful they'd gotten tickets at all since they'd left it until the last minute.

"You're right," she admitted with a sigh. "I hope I can sleep on the plane. It's a long flight."

He doubted he would. He was too wired thinking about all he needed to do in the next ten days. Sign the paperwork on the restaurant, hire contractors, rip out anything that needed repairs. He knew it was unlikely he'd get everything done before Christmas, but he wanted to make the restaurant look its best before he presented it to Sunshine. He took her hand. "It's going to be busy when we get home. I'll probably have to spend a lot of time at the rentals." Best to lay the groundwork for his disappearances now.

"You don't think Scott's doing a good job?"

"I'm sure he is, but he's not the owner."

"Of course. I have a lot of shopping to do anyway. I need to throw packages together fast for my family and get them in the mail."

"I guess we'll both be busy, then." Cole was relieved. It was crucial his present remained a surprise: that's what made it so much fun. If Sunshine was busy, she wouldn't ask difficult questions—or have time to pry. Last year she'd found his gift three days before he was supposed to give it to her. Refusing to concede defeat, he'd had to rush out and find a replacement gift. "You feeling all right?" She looked a little pale.

"All the travel is catching up to me, I think."

"It'll be good to be home."

"You've got that right."

PREGNANT. SHE WAS pregnant. For the last four weeks Sunshine hadn't been able to think of anything else. She was thrilled and terrified and so confused she didn't know which way she was heading most of the time. When Cole announced he'd be busy with the rental complex once they got home, she breathed a sigh of relief. Her pregnancy wasn't her only secret; the ranch she'd bought for Cole was the big surprise.

She'd bought it on an impulse only days after she'd realized she'd missed her period. First she'd had to confirm her pregnancy, without letting Cole know. She'd gone out of her mind with impatience until Cole had wandered off one afternoon to visit an agricultural museum outside of Prague. Then she'd rushed to the closest pharmacy, bought an over-the-counter pregnancy test, taken it in a public restroom... and tossed the evidence in the trash as soon as she'd snapped a photograph of the results.

Pregnant.

Sunshine hadn't known whether to laugh or cry. She'd been struggling for months to decide what to do about her future. Now the question had been answered for her. She'd called a realtor she knew in Chance Creek, told her what she wanted and was thrilled to find a listing had crossed the realtor's desk that fit the bill. "I'll take it," she'd said; she knew ranches were hard to come by and she didn't want to risk losing the place and the chance to give Cole a fabulous Christmas present. In the rush to sew up the deal she had no time for second thoughts.

Now—after she'd put her money down on the ranch—she'd succumbed to doubts again. On the one hand, she couldn't wait to be a mother and she adored Cole. She'd enjoyed living in Chance Creek far more than she'd expected to during the months she'd stayed there.

On the other hand, she had ambitions it would be difficult to pursue in a small Montana town. She was a vegan chef, for heaven's sake. How could she take the world by storm in cowboy country?

It made far more sense to return to Chicago where she'd once helped to run a highly successful restaurant. If she sold the ranch she'd just bought she could put a hefty down payment on a restaurant and build a real business.

Unfortunately, she couldn't picture Cole happy in Chicago. He was a country boy through and through. He had definite thoughts about the kind of home he wanted to raise their children in, too. He wanted them to have lots of space to run and play and he wanted them to grow up on a property that could one day be theirs.

In other words, he wanted a ranch.

And thanks to the help of a realtor, she'd found him one. Everything was signed, sealed and delivered.

She couldn't change course now.

Sunshine pushed her worries away and thought

about Cole's face on Christmas morning when she took him out to show it to him. Of course, between now and then it needed a lot of spiffing up. She hoped she could get at least some of that done before Christmas.

And if she had to put her dream of one day owning a real restaurant—not just a hole in the wall café like the one attached to the rifle range—well, she was sure it would happen someday. Until then she'd make do.

Her train of thought took her back to her first days in Chance Creek and Sunshine shook her head over the memories. When she'd first arrived in town to collect her inheritance, she'd been aghast to find the building already inhabited by an uncouth cowboy with a penchant for firearms.

Soon she'd fallen for Cole hook, line and sinker, however, and they'd had so much fun during those first months when they'd buried the hatchet and worked together. Cole had ruled the roost at his indoor rifle range and she'd cooked for his clients and anyone else who'd ventured into the neighborhood. When customers were scarce, they'd fooled around. She found it hard to keep her hands off of the man.

Three years abroad hadn't changed that. Cole could set her nerves alight with a single touch. Every night when they slid into bed she felt like she had the first time they'd been together. His body gave her endless pleasure. What more could she ask for?

She pressed her hand to her belly, tingling with the knowledge that her baby was growing inside of her.

Their baby.

It was such a precious secret. A secret it had been killing her to keep. Every time Cole made love to her she'd wanted to scream it out loud.

But she had to wait just a little longer.

End of Excerpt

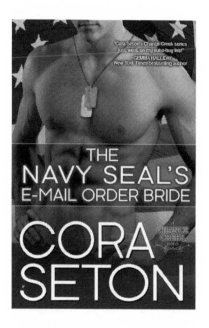

Read on for an excerpt of Volume 1 of
The Heroes of Chance Creek series –
The Navy SEAL's E-Mail Order Bride.

"BOYS," LIEUTENANT COMMANDER Mason Hall said, "we're going home."

He sat back in his folding chair and waited for a reaction from his brothers. The recreation hall at Bagram Airfield was as busy as always with men hunched over laptops, watching the widescreen television, or lounging in groups of three or four shooting the breeze. His brothers—three tall, broad shouldered men in uniform—stared back at him from his computer screen, the feeds from their four-way video conversation all relaying a similar reaction to his words.

Utter confusion.

"Home?" Austin was the first to speak. A Special Forces officer just a year younger than Mason, he was currently in Kabul.

"Home," Mason confirmed. "I got a letter from Great Aunt Heloise. Uncle Zeke passed away over the weekend without designating an heir. That means the ranch reverts back to her. She thinks we'll do a better job running it than Darren will." Darren, their first cousin, wasn't known for his responsible behavior and he hated ranching. Mason, on the other hand, loved it. He had missed the ranch, the cattle, the Montana sky and his family's home ever since they'd left it twelve years ago.

"She's giving Crescent Hall to us?" That was Zane, Austin's twin, a Marine currently in Kandahar. The excitement in his tone told Mason all he needed to know—Zane stilled loved the old place as much as he did. When Mason had gotten Heloise's letter, he'd had to read it more than once before he believed it. The Hall would belong to them once more—when he'd thought they'd lost it for good. Suddenly he'd felt like he could breathe fully again after so many years of holding in his anger and frustration over his uncle's behavior. The timing was perfect, too. He was due to ship stateside any day now. By April he'd be a civilian again.

Except it wasn't as easy as all that. Mason took a deep breath. "There are a few conditions."

Colt, his youngest brother, snorted. "Of course— we're talking about Heloise, aren't we? What's she up to this time?" He was an Air Force combat controller who had served both in Afghanistan and as part of the relief effort a few years back after the massive earthquake which devastated Haiti. He was currently back on United States soil in Florida, training with his unit.

Mason knew what he meant. Calling Heloise eccentric would be an understatement. In her eighties, she had definite opinions and brooked no opposition to her plans and schemes. She meant well, but as his father had always said, she was capable of leaving a swath of destruction in family affairs that rivaled Sherman's march to Atlanta.

"The first condition is that we have to stock the ranch with one hundred pair of cattle within twelve months of taking possession."

"We should be able to do that," Austin said.

"It's going to take some doing to get that ranch up and running again," Zane countered. "Zeke was already letting the place go years ago."

"You have something better to do than fix the place up when you get out?" Mason asked him. He hoped Zane understood the real question: was he in or out?

"I'm in; I'm just saying," Zane said.

Mason suppressed a smile. Zane always knew what he was thinking.

"Good luck with all that," Colt said.

"Thanks," Mason told him. He'd anticipated that inheriting the Hall wouldn't change Colt's mind about staying in the Air Force. He focused on the other two who were both already in the process of winding down their military careers. "If we're going to do this, it'll take a commitment. We're going to have to pool our funds and put our shoulders to the wheel for as long as it takes.

Are you up for that?"

"I'll join you there as soon as I'm able to in June," Austin said. "It'll just be like another year in the service. I can handle that."

"I already said I'm in," Zane said. "I'll have boots on the ground in September."

Here's where it got tricky. "There's just one other thing," Mason said. "Aunt Heloise has one more requirement of each of us."

"What's that?" Austin asked when he didn't go on.

"She's worried about the lack of heirs on our side of the family. Darren has children. We don't."

"Plenty of time for that," Zane said. "We're still young, right?"

"Not according to Heloise." Mason decided to get it over and done with. "She's decided that in order for us to inherit the Hall free and clear, we each have to be married within the year. One of us has to have a child."

Stunned silence met this announcement until Colt started to laugh. "Staying in the Air Force doesn't look so bad now, does it?"

"That means you, too," Mason said.

"What? Hold up, now." Colt was startled into soberness. "I won't even live on the ranch. Why do I have to get hitched?"

"Because Heloise says it's time to stop screwing around. And she controls the land. And you know Heloise."

"How are we going to get around that?" Austin asked.

"We're not." Mason got right to the point. "We're

going to find ourselves some women and we're going to marry them."

"In Afghanistan?" Zane's tone made it clear what he thought about that idea.

Tension tightened Mason's jaw. He'd known this was going to be a messy conversation. "Online. I created an online personal ad for all of us. Each of us has a photo, a description and a reply address. A woman can get in touch with whichever of us she chooses and start a conversation. Just weed through your replies until you find the one you want."

"Are you out of your mind?" Zane peered at him through the video screen.

"I don't see what you're upset about. I'm the one who has to have a child. None of you will be out of the service in time."

"Wait a minute—I thought you just got the letter from Heloise." As usual, Austin zeroed in on the inconsistency.

"The letter came about a week ago. I didn't want to get anyone's hopes up until I checked a few things out." Mason shifted in his seat. "Heloise said the place is in rougher shape than we thought. Sounds like Zeke sold off the last of his cattle last year. We're going to have to start from scratch, and we're going to have to move fast to meet her deadline—on both counts. I did all the leg work on the online ad. All you need to do is read some e-mails, look at some photos and pick one. How hard can that be?"

"I'm beginning to think there's a reason you've been single all these years, Straightshot," Austin said. Mason winced at the use of his nickname. The men in his unit had christened him with it during his early days in the service, but as Colt said when his brothers had first heard about it, it made perfect sense. The name had little to do with his accuracy with a rifle, and everything to do with his tendency to find the shortest route from here to done on any mission he was tasked with. Regardless of what obstacles stood in his way.

Colt snickered. "Told you two it was safer to stay in the military. Mason's Matchmaking Service. It has a ring to it. I guess you've found yourself a new career, Mase."

"Stow it." Mason tapped a finger on the table. "Just because I've put the ad up doesn't mean that any of you have to make contact with the women who write you. If it doesn't work, it doesn't work. But you need to marry within the year. If you don't find a wife for yourself, I'll find one for you."

"He would, too," Austin said to the others. "You know he would."

"When does the ad go live?" Zane asked.

"It went live five days ago. You've each got several hundred responses so far. I'll forward them to you as soon as we break the call."

Austin must have leaned toward his webcam because suddenly he filled the screen. "Several hundred?"

"That's right."

Colt's laughter rang out over the line.

"Don't know what you're finding so funny, Colton," Mason said in his best imitation of their late father's voice. "You've got several hundred responses, too."

"What? I told you I was staying…"

"Read through them and answer all the likely ones. I'll be in touch in a few days to check your progress." Mason cut the call.

REGAN ANDERSON WANTED a baby. Right now. Not five years from now. Not even next year.

Right now.

And since she'd just quit her stuffy loan officer job, moved out of her overpriced one bedroom New York City apartment, and completed all her preliminary appointments, she was going to get one via the modern technology of artificial insemination.

As she raced up the three flights of steps to her tiny new studio, she took the pins out of her severe updo and let her thick, auburn hair swirl around her shoulders. By the time she reached the door, she was breathing hard. Inside, she shut and locked it behind her, tossed her briefcase and blazer on the bed which took up the lion's share of the living space, and kicked off her high heels. Her blouse and pencil skirt came next, and thirty seconds later she was down to her skivvies.

Thank God.

She was done with Town and Country Bank. Done with originating loans for people who would scrape and slave away for the next thirty years just to cling to a lousy flat near a subway stop. She was done, done, done being a cog in the wheel of a financial system she couldn't stand to be a part of anymore.

She was starting a new business. Starting a new life.

And she was starting a family, too.

Alone.

After years of looking for Mr. Right, she'd decided he simply didn't exist in New York City. So after several medical exams and consultations, she had scheduled her first round of artificial insemination for the end of April. She couldn't wait.

Meanwhile, she'd throw herself into the task of building her consulting business. She would make it her job to help non-profits assist regular people start new stores and services, buy homes that made sense, and manage their money so that they could get ahead. It might not be as lucrative as being a loan officer, but at least she'd be able to sleep at night.

She wasn't going to think about any of that right now, though. She'd survived her last day at work, survived her exit interview, survived her boss, Jack Richey, pretending to care that she was leaving. Now she was giving herself the weekend off. No work, no nothing—just forty-eight hours of rest and relaxation.

Having grabbed takeout from her favorite Thai restaurant on the way home, Regan spooned it out onto a plate and carried it to her bed. Lined with pillows, it doubled as her couch during waking hours. She sat cross-legged on top of the duvet and savored her food and her freedom. She had bought herself a nice bottle of wine to drink this weekend, figuring it might be her last for an awfully long time. She was all too aware her Chardonnay-sipping days were coming to an end. As soon as her weekend break from reality was over, she planned to spend the next ten months starting her business, while scrimping and saving every penny she could. She would have to move to a bigger apartment right before the baby was born, but given the cost of renting in the city, the temporary downgrade was worth it. She pushed all thoughts of business and the future out of her mind. Rest and relax—that was her job for now.

Two hours and two glasses of wine later, however, rest and relaxation was beginning to feel a lot like loneliness and boredom. In truth, she'd been fighting loneliness for months. She'd broken up with her last boyfriend before Christmas. Here it was March and she was still single. Two of her closest friends had gotten married and moved away in the past twelve months, Laurel to New Hampshire and Rita to New Jersey. They rarely saw each other now and when she'd jokingly mentioned the idea of going ahead and having a child without a husband the last time they'd gotten together, both women had scoffed.

"No way could I have gotten through this pregnancy without Ryan." Laurel ran a hand over her large belly. "I've felt awful the whole time."

"No way I'm going back to work." Rita's baby was six weeks old. "Thank God Alan brings in enough cash to see us through."

Regan decided not to tell them about her plans until the pregnancy was a done deal. She knew what she was getting into—she didn't need them to tell her how hard it might be. If there'd been any way for her to have a baby normally—with a man she loved—she'd have chosen that path in a heartbeat. But there didn't seem to be a man for her to love in New York. Unfortunately, keeping her secret meant it was hard to call either Rita or Laurel just to chat, and she needed someone to chat with tonight. As dusk descended on the city, Regan felt fear for the first time since making her decision to go ahead with having a child.

What if she'd made a mistake? What if her consultancy business failed? What if she became a welfare mother? What if she had to move back home?

When the thoughts and worries circling her mind grew overwhelming, she topped up her wine, opened up her laptop and clicked on a YouTube video of a cat stuck headfirst in a cereal box. Thank goodness she'd hooked up wi-fi the minute she secured the studio. Simultaneously scanning her Facebook feed, she read an update from an acquaintance named Susan who was exhibiting her art in one of the local galleries. She'd have to stop by this weekend.

She watched a couple more videos—the latest installment in a travel series she loved, and one about over-the-top weddings that made her sad. Determined to cheer up, she hopped onto Pinterest and added more images to her nursery pinboard. Sipping her wine, she checked the news, posted a question on the single parents' forum she frequented, checked her e-mail again, and then tapped a finger on the keys, wondering what to do next. The evening stretched out before her, vacant even of the work she normally took home to do over the weekend. She hadn't felt at such loose ends in years.

Pacing her tiny apartment didn't help. Nor did an attempt at unpacking more of her things. She had finished moving in just last night and boxes still lined one wall. She opened one to reveal books, took a look at her limited shelf space and packed them up again. A second box revealed her collection of vintage fans. No room for them here, either.

She stuck her iTouch into a docking station and turned up some tunes, then drained her glass, poured herself another, and flopped onto her bed. The wine was beginning to take effect—giving her a nice, soft, fuzzy feeling. It hadn't done away with her loneliness, but when she turned back to Facebook on her laptop, the images and YouTube links seemed funnier this time.

Heartened, she scrolled further down her feed until she spotted another post one of her friends had shared. It was an image of a handsome man standing ramrod straight in combat fatigues. *Hello*. He was cute. In fact, he looked like exactly the kind of man she'd always hoped she'd meet. He wasn't thin and arrogant like the up-and-coming Wall Street crowd, or paunchy and cynical like the upper-management men who hung around the bars near work. Instead he looked healthy, muscle-bound, clear-sighted, and vital. What was the post about? She clicked the link underneath it. Maybe there'd be more fantasy-fodder like this man wherever it took her.

There *was* more fantasy fodder. Regan wriggled happily. She had landed on a page that showcased four men. Brothers, she saw, looking more closely—two of them identical twins. Each one seemed to represent a different branch of the United States military. Were they models? Was this some kind of recruitment ploy?

Practical Wives Wanted read the heading at the top. Regan nearly spit out a sip of her wine. Wives Wanted?

Practical ones? She considered the men again, then read more.

Looking for a change? the text went on. *Ready for a real challenge? Join four hardworking, clean living men and help bring our family's ranch back to life.*

Skills required—any or all of the following: Riding, roping, construction, animal care, roofing, farming, market gardening, cooking, cleaning, metalworking, small motor repair…

The list went on and on. Regan bit back at a laugh which quickly dissolved into giggles. Small engine repair? How very romantic. Was this supposed to be satire or was it real? It was certainly one of the most intriguing things she'd seen online in a long, long time.

Must be willing to commit to a man and the project. No weekends/no holidays/no sick days. Weaklings need not apply.

Regan snorted. It was beginning to sound like an employment ad. Good luck finding a woman to fill those conditions. She'd tried to find a suitable man for years and came up with Erik—the perennial mooch who'd finally admitted just before Christmas that he liked her old Village apartment more than he liked her. That's why she planned to get pregnant all by herself. There wasn't anyone worth marrying in the whole city. Probably the whole state. And if the men were all worthless, the women probably were, too. She reached for her wine without turning from the screen, missed, and nearly knocked over her glass. She tried again, secured the wine, drained the glass a third time and set it down again.

What she would give to find a real partner. Someone strong, both physically and emotionally. An equal in intelligence and heart. A real man.

But those didn't exist.

If you're sick of wasting your time in a dead-end job, tired of tearing things down instead of building something up, or just ready to get your hands dirty with clean, honest work, write and tell us why you'd make a worthy wife for a man who has spent the last decade in uniform.

There wasn't much to laugh at in this paragraph. Regan read it again, then got up and wandered to the kitchen to top up her glass. She'd never seen a singles ad like this one. She could see why it was going viral. If it was real, these men were something special. Who wanted to do clean, honest work these days? What kind of man was selfless enough to serve in the military instead of sponging off their girlfriends? If she'd known there were guys like this in the world, she might not have been so quick to schedule the artificial insemination appointment.

She wouldn't cancel it, though, because these guys couldn't be for real, and she wasn't waiting another minute to start her family. She had dreamed of having children ever since she was a child herself and organized pretend schools in her backyard for the neighborhood little ones. Babies loved her. Toddlers thought she was the next best thing to teddy bears. Her co-workers at the bank had never appreciated her as much as the average five-year-old did.

Further down the page there were photographs of the ranch the brothers meant to bring back to life. The land was beautiful, if overgrown, but its toppled fences and sagging buildings were a testament to its neglect. The photograph of the main house caught her eye and kept her riveted, though. A large gothic structure, it could be beautiful with the proper care. She could see why these men would dedicate themselves to returning it to its former glory. She tried to imagine what it would be like to live on the ranch with one of them, and immediately her body craved an open sunny sky—the kind you were hard pressed to see in the city. She sunk into the daydream, picturing herself sitting on a back porch sipping lemonade while her cowboy worked and the baby napped. Her husband would have his shirt off while he chopped wood, or mended a fence or whatever it was ranchers did. At the end of the day they'd fall into bed and make love until morning.

Regan sighed. It was a wonderful daydream, but it had no bearing on her life. Disgruntled, she switched over to Netflix and set up a foreign film. She fetched the bottle of wine back to bed with her and leaned against her many pillows. She'd managed to hang her small flatscreen on the opposite wall. In an apartment this tiny, every piece of furniture needed to serve double-duty.

As the movie started, Regan found herself composing messages to the military men in the Wife Wanted ad, in which she described herself as trim and petite, or lithe and strong, or horny and good-enough-looking to do the trick.

An hour later, when the film failed to hold her attention, she grabbed her laptop again. She pulled up the Wife Wanted page and reread it, keeping an eye on the foreign couple on the television screen who alternately argued and kissed.

Crazy what some people did. What was wrong with

these men that they needed to advertise for wives instead of going out and meeting them like normal people?

She thought of the online dating sites she'd tried in the past. She'd had some awkward experiences, some horrible first dates, and finally one relationship that lasted for a couple of months before the man was transferred to Tucson and it fizzled out. It hadn't worked for her, but she supposed lots of people found love online these days. They might not advertise directly for spouses, but that was their ultimate intention, right? So maybe this ad wasn't all that unusual.

Most men who posted singles ads weren't as hot as these men were, though. Definitely not the ones she'd met. She poured herself another glass. A small twinge of her conscience told her she'd already had far too much wine for a single night.

To hell with that, Regan thought. As soon as she got pregnant she'd have to stay sober and sane for the next eighteen years. She wouldn't have a husband to trade off with—she'd always be the designated driver, the adult in charge, the sober, wise mother who made sure nothing bad ever happened to her child. Just this one last time she was allowed to blow off steam.

But even as she thought it, a twinge of fear wormed through her belly.

What if she wasn't good enough?

She stood up, strode the two steps to the kitchenette and made herself a bowl of popcorn. She drowned it in butter and salt, returned to the bed in time for the ending credits of the movie, and lined up *Pride and Prejudice* with Colin Firth. Time for comfort food and a comfort movie. *Pride and Prejudice* always did the trick when she felt blue. She checked the Wife Wanted page again on her laptop. If she was going to pick one of the men—which she wasn't—who would she choose?

Mason, the oldest, due to leave the Navy in a matter of weeks, drew her eye first. With his dark crew cut, hard jaw and uncompromising blue eyes he looked like the epitome of a military man. He stated his interests as ranching—of course—history, natural sciences and tactical operations, whatever the hell that was. That left her little more informed than before she'd read it, and she wondered what the man was really like. Did he read the newspaper in bed on Sunday mornings? Did he prefer lasagna or spaghetti? Would he listen to country music in his truck or talk radio? She stared at his photo, willing him to answer.

The next two brothers, Austin and Zane, were less fierce, but looked no less intelligent and determined. Still, they didn't draw her eye the way the way Mason did. Colt, the youngest, was blond with a grin she bet drew women like flies. That one was trouble, and she didn't need trouble.

She read Mason's description again and decided he was the leader of this endeavor. If she was going to pick one, it would be him.

But she wasn't going to pick one. She had given up all that. She'd made a promise to her imaginary child that she would not allow any chaos into its life. No dating until her baby wore a graduation gown, at the very least. She felt another twinge. Was she ready to give up men for nearly two decades? That was a long time.

It's worth it, she told herself. She had no doubt about her desire to be a mother. She had no doubt she'd be a great mom. She was smart, capable and had a good head on her shoulders. She was funny, silly and patient, too. She loved children.

She was just lousy with men.

But that didn't matter anymore. She pushed the laptop aside and returned her attention to *Pride and Prejudice,* quickly falling into an old drinking game she and Laurel had devised one night that required taking a swig of wine each time one of the actresses lifted her eyebrows in polite surprise. When she finished the bottle, she headed to the tiny kitchenette to track down another one, trilling, "Jane! Elizabeth!" at the top of her voice along with Mrs. Bennett in the film. There was no more wine, so she switched to tequila.

By the time Elizabeth Bennett discovered the miracle of Mr. Darcy's palace-sized mansion, and decided she'd been too hasty in turning down his offer of marriage, Regan had decided she too needed to cast off her prejudices and find herself a man. A hot hunk of a military man. She grabbed the laptop, fumbled with the link that would let her leave Mason Hall a message and drafted a brilliant missive worthy of Jane Austen herself.

Dear Lt. Cmdr. Hall,

In her mind she pronounced lieutenant with an "f" like the Brits in the movie onscreen.

It is a truth universally acknowledged, that a single man in possession of a good ranch, must be in want of a wife.

Furthermore, it must be self-evident that the wife in question should possess certain qualities numbering amongst them riding, roping, construction, roofing, farming, market gardening, cooking, cleaning, metalworking, animal care, and—most importantly, by Heaven—small motor repair.

Seeing as I am in possession of all these qualities, not to mention many others you can only have left out through unavoidable oversight or sheer obtuseness—such as glassblowing, cheesemaking, towel origami, heraldry, hovercraft piloting, and an uncanny sense of what cats are thinking—I feel almost forced to catapult myself into your purview.

You will see from my photograph that I am most eminently and majestically suitable for your wife.

She inserted a digital photo of her foot.

In fact, one might wonder why such a paragon of virtue such as I should deign to answer such a peculiar advertisement. The truth is, sir, that I long for adventure. To get my hands dirty with clean, hard work. To build something up instead of tearing it down.

In short, you are really hot. I'd like to lick you.

Yours,
Regan Anderson

On screen, Elizabeth Bennett lifted an eyebrow. Regan knocked back another shot of Jose Cuervo and passed out.

End of Excerpt

The Cowboys of Chance Creek Series:

The Cowboy Inherits a Bride (Volume 0)
The Cowboy's E-Mail Order Bride (Volume 1)
The Cowboy Wins a Bride (Volume 2)
The Cowboy Imports a Bride (Volume 3)
The Cowgirl Ropes a Billionaire (Volume 4)
The Sheriff Catches a Bride (Volume 5)
The Cowboy Lassos a Bride (Volume 6)
The Cowboy Rescues a Bride (Volume 7)
The Cowboy Earns a Bride (Volume 8)
The Cowboy's Christmas Bride (Volume 9)

The Heroes of Chance Creek Series:

The Navy SEAL's E-Mail Order Bride (Volume 1)
The Soldier's E-Mail Order Bride (Volume 2)
The Marine's E-Mail Order Bride (Volume 3)
The Navy SEAL's Christmas Bride (Volume 4)
The Airman's E-Mail Order Bride (Volume 5)

The SEALs of Chance Creek Series:

A SEAL's Oath
A SEAL's Vow
A SEAL's Pledge
A SEAL's Consent
A SEAL's Purpose
A SEAL's Resolve
A SEAL's Devotion
A SEAL's Desire
A SEAL's Struggle
A SEAL's Triumph

The Brides of Chance Creek Series:

Issued to the Bride One Navy SEAL
Issued to the Bride One Airman
Issued to the Bride One Sniper
Issued to the Bride One Marine
Issued to the Bride One Soldier

The Turners v. Coopers Series:

The Cowboy's Secret Bride (Volume 1)
The Cowboy's Outlaw Bride (Volume 2)
The Cowboy's Hidden Bride (Volume 3)
The Cowboy's Stolen Bride (Volume 4)
The Cowboy's Forbidden Bride (Volume 5)

About the Author

With over one million books sold, NYT and USA Today bestselling author Cora Seton has created a world readers love in Chance Creek, Montana. She has twenty-eight novels and novellas currently set in her fictional town, with many more in the works. Like her characters, Cora loves cowboys, military heroes, country life, gardening, bike-riding, binge-watching Jane Austen movies, keeping up with the latest technology and indulging in old-fashioned pursuits. Visit **www.coraseton.com** to read about new releases, contests and other cool events!

Blog:

www.coraseton.com

Facebook:

www.facebook.com/coraseton

Twitter:

www.twitter.com/coraseton

Newsletter:

www.coraseton.com/sign-up-for-my-newsletter

Made in the USA
Las Vegas, NV
13 May 2021